ZION

A NOVEL

Dayne Sherman

PREVIOUS BOOKS

Welcome to the Fallen Paradise: A Novel
Published by MacAdam Cage in 2004
Reprinted by Accendo Books in 2014

ZION

A NOVEL

Dayne Sherman

Accendo Books

Hammond, Louisiana
AccendoBooks.com

Accendo Books, L.L.C.
1905 W. Thomas St., Ste. D, 137
Hammond, LA 70401, U.S.A.
www.accendobooks.com
Email: accendobooks@gmail.com

Publisher's Note: This is a work of fiction. Names, characters, places, and incidents are a product of the author's imagination. Locales and public names are sometimes used for atmospheric purposes. Any resemblance to actual people, living or dead, or to businesses, companies, events, institutions, or locales is completely coincidental.

Author's Note: No rednecks were harmed in the making of this novel.

Book Layout © 2014 BookDesignTemplates.com

Author Photo: Kristy Williams

Cover artwork: Dayne Sherman: Acrylic on Burned Southern Pine.

Zion: A Novel / Dayne Sherman. -- 1st ed.
ISBN 978-0-9906303-0-2

Library of Congress Cataloging-in-Publication Data

Sherman, Dayne
   Zion: a novel / by Dayne Sherman.
     p. cm.
   ISBN-10: 0-990630-30-7 (pbk. : acid-free paper)
   1.   Violence—Fiction. 2. Fathers and sons—Fiction. 3. Carpenters—Fiction.
4. Librarians—Fiction. 5. Louisiana—Fiction. 5. Methodist Church—Fiction.
I. Title
PS3619 .H4645 Z9 2014
813' .6—dc22

Printed in U.S.A.
10 9 8 7 6 5 4 3 2 1
First Edition/First Printing

Paperback Edition: October 2014
ISBN-10: 0-990630-30-7 (paperback)
ISBN-13: 978-0-9906303-0-2 (paperback)

For my son

To set the state of perfection too high is the surest way to drive it out of the world.

--The Works of John Wesley, May 13, 1772

By the rivers of Babylon we sat and wept when we remembered Zion.

--Psalm 137:1

CHAPTER ONE

Tom Hardin sat on the small back stoop of the old farm house with a cotton rag and an unloaded rifle in his hands. A half-dozen bullets were lined up on the top step like tacks in a row beside a small tin of Western Field gun oil. He was a meticulous man as precise as a surgeon, and he took good care of his guns and tools. He'd never put away the rifle after hunting without wiping it down with oil, thoroughly cleaning the barrel and action. He heard a vehicle cross his iron cattle guard near the blacktop road, the thump-thump noise of tires. Then his dog barked. Jubal was a large stud dog, half Catahoula and half bulldog, weighing over eighty pounds. The dog was chained in the yard under a live oak tree not far from the house. The vehicle was pulling into the gravel driveway. Tom picked up the Winchester and six bullets, stood, and walked around to the back corner of the house. The horn honked twice, a rapid beep-beep, and Jubal barked even more. Tom could not see the car, so he slid the six rimfire cartridges into the rifle tube and worked the pump action once.

He held the rifle in the crook of his left arm as he passed the front corner of the house and saw the Ninth Ward Marshal standing at the door of his white Plymouth. Both Tom and Marshal Donald Brownlow were lifelong members of Little Zion Methodist Church in the community of Zion in Baxter Parish. They sat on opposite sides of the center aisle of the church on Sundays with their families. Though never close friends, they were always cordial.

The lawman grimaced and said, "You aim to fire on me with that peashooter?"

"It's not a peashooter. It's a .22 magnum," Tom said. "And I wouldn't shoot a man unless he truly deserved it." He pointed the barrel toward the ground.

Tom walked over to the patrol car. The men shook hands.

"You don't deserve shooting, do you, Marshal?" Tom asked, smiling.

"Well, if I did, I'd never tell you." He laughed a strange-sounding snort and fished in his shirt pocket for a pack of Winstons.

Tom was compact and thin, built wiry, the kind of man who could climb a tall tree by scooting up the trunk without any help beyond the strength of his legs and arms and will. Barely five-seven, he had good posture and muscled biceps and a natural discipline that caused him to appear taller than he really was. He was a contrast to the dough-faced Marshal Brownlow, a flabby man of six feet. In a fair fight, Tom would beat Brownlow to a ripe pulp.

"It sure is getting cool out in the evenings and mornings. I guess it's getting to be a good enough Saturday to kill a few squirrels," the marshal said.

"It is. I bagged three this morning," Tom said.

"Any of them have wolf worms in the neck? I've seen them before in barn cats this time of year. That's the bad thing about squirrel hunting early in the season."

"No, we've had a frost. They were all fine."

"Where'd you kill 'em?"

"Over on Turnpike Road. But you didn't drive over here to talk about the weather and squirrels."

"No."

"Then what can I help you with, Donald?"

"Why don't you put that rifle on the hood of my car? You make me a little uneasy holding a gun." The marshal struck a match on the car mirror and lit his cigarette. He took a drag.

"I kind of like holding the rifle," Tom said. "It keeps me from feeling uneasy myself."

Brownlow let out a lungful of smoke. He gazed at Tom for a few moments.

"Say what you came here to say. Or do you plan to arrest me for something I know nothing about?" Tom asked.

"I didn't come over to arrest you," Brownlow said.

"Donald, you're kind of making me nervous. Please get to the point."

"Okay. Last night more than a hundred acres of young pines burned. Land owned by Fitz-Blackwell over on Traylor Branch. It was torched to the point of ruin, at least two-thirds'll have to be replanted, they say."

"That's a shame. Probably just heat lightning, an act of God." Tom scratched his chin with his thumb and forefinger. "It did seem a bit smoky last night and this morning."

"Look, I've heard that men are repeating a slogan, 'For every oak a pine.' It's just plumb crazy talk. Folks can't go around playing arsonist in the whole damned parish. Burning one pine for every oak killed, or a hundred pines for every oak killed. It's just plain loopy. The fires are getting out of control. This is 1964. It ain't 1864."

"I don't know what you're talking about."

"Well, a week ago, Fitz-Blackwell brought in some arson investigators from Salem, Oregon, plus Louisiana state forestry men, and the Lord only knows who or what else they've sent down here. That was on account of the Rogers Road fire, and more fires are ablaze all over God's creation. They say somebody started the fire by horseback and on foot and maybe by automobile. Seems like it was more than one person, a true conspiracy. You wouldn't happen to know anything about it, would you?" The marshal released a trail of smoke out of the side of his mouth.

Tom frowned. "No, I don't know anything about it. Not about Traylor Branch or Rogers Road. Like I asked, what brings you to my door?" His forehead wrinkled with the question. He had wondered if his friend

James Luke Cate and some others were behind the fires, but he'd never say a word to the marshal.

"Tom, I seem to recollect that you've got a riding horse?" The marshal took a pull from the Winston.

"Yeah, a horse that I use to plow a garden and ride, work my stock with, but having a horse is something I've got in common with about half the men in Zion."

"Is your horse shod?"

"No, I don't shoe horses. I don't have the extra money to pay for somebody to come do it." His horse, Sam, was not shod, but he could indeed pay the six dollars for a farrier to nail a set on the horse if necessary. The gelding was mostly Appaloosa, and his hooves were as hard as stone. Unless he rode the horse on asphalt, Sam didn't need iron shoes.

"Tom, I'm here because one of the Fitz-Blackwell men said you was watching them whilst you was riding horseback off Kinchen Road. They was killing some hardwood trees to plant pines a week or so ago. Said you more or less tried to stalk them. They felt threatened. Said you had a high-powered deer rifle with you. And the investigators told me that the arsonist had him a horse that wore steel shoes. I'm just trying to look into this thing from all possible directions."

"My horse doesn't have shoes. He's never had a set of shoes since I bought him four years ago. Now I did see them out yonder killing oaks with some kind of poison, jabbing the base of the trees with long hollow spikes full of herbicide. I was looking for my hogs, which had wandered behind the old Gibson place on the Big Natalbany. As you well know, I've been forced by the new law to catch up all my stock by the New Year. That said, it's a free country, and watching somebody do their work isn't illegal. Not yet. Watching them doesn't mean I was the one that started the fires either. I tell you, I did not start any fires. The fires were probably from lightning anyhow. You're welcome to go inspect my horse's hooves." He motioned to back lot with his hand and shifted the rifle to the crook of his right arm.

Tom hadn't burned any woods, though he'd pondered doing it himself after watching the men kill healthy hardwood trees, grown trees, for no better reason than they were less valuable than the pines, and the pines needed space to grow, more daylight and less shade.

"It means something, you watching them out yonder," Brownlow said.

"No, sir. It means nothing at all. I don't know the men. They don't know me. I was out there and saw them. I'm not denying it. But that doesn't mean I was threatening them or burning pines. How would they know I was the one watching them anyway?"

"Sloan Parnell, Judge Parnell's grandson, says you were out there last week riding a sorrel horse with a white snip or blaze on his face, a horse with a few black and white spots on his hips."

"Hum. There's your answer, Donald. Sloan would be my number one candidate for lighting the fires. That's if you're asking me. I had trouble with him once before when I was hunting in the woods near his place. I said near his place, not on his place. He's no good. It's like folks thinking the CIA had a hand in assassinating President Kennedy. Most unnatural wickedness is an inside job. Sloan is real sorry, just like his daddy and Judge Parnell, too. The Parnells and the timber companies have robbed the public coffers as empty as a dry well. All the land they stole from widows and poor people back in the Depression. But I never saw Parnell in the woods that day."

The marshal stared past Tom. He smoked the Winston in silence. "I'm not accusing you, but you need to stay far away from the workers doing their jobs and—"

Tom cut him off. "It ought not to be any man's job to kill perfectly good hardwood trees and let them rot in the forest. The hogs and what few deer we have live off the acorns. Squirrels like them, too. Besides, the trees are pretty to look at. Can you believe that they are leaving the trees in the woods? They won't even let folks cut firewood off the dead timber anymore. It's a true disgrace and a crime."

"The men are required to kill the oaks because the pines are what keeps the lumber business going, and the timber companies pay a whole lot of taxes, and them tax dollars pay my salary."

"That's where you're wrong. They don't pay a mere tithe of their rightful taxes on what they ought to be paying. Fitz-Blackwell alone has more than thirty thousand acres in this parish, and the crooked tax assessor lets them pay nearly nothing. Pennies on the dollar. He assesses their land for fifty dollars an acre when everybody knows it's worth two hundred, and some land's worth more. Fact of business, a lot of it is worth close to four hundred dollars an acre. You ought to go today and lock up the assessor and every one of the Fitz-Blackwell men up at their Ruthberry office. But that would mean trouble, wouldn't it? I hear the tax assessor has a daughter studying up at Louisiana College in Pineville on a full scholarship, as people tell it, paid for by Fitz-Blackwell. Don't you reckon that's more of a coincidence than me watching some men work while I was riding horseback and then a stand of pine trees catches fire? Doesn't it all sound a little peculiar to you, Marshal Brownlow?"

"Be careful is all I'm telling you, Tom," he said. "You're a decent, God-fearing man, and you ought to keep it that way." He got into his car and shut the door. "I'll be calling on you again," the marshal said out of the open window.

CHAPTER TWO

A t the kitchen table, the Hardin family gathered for supper. After Tom said grace, the family ate the squirrels that had been cut into quarters and cooked in brown flour gravy with black pepper and milk. Sara, Tom's wife, baked buttermilk biscuits that were light brown on top, passed from hand to hand in a small cloth-covered wicker basket. On the oak table sat a jar of mayhaw jelly along with fresh butter. Ten-year-old Wesley placed a dollop of jelly on his biscuit. Sara dished herself some boiled okra from a blue and white ceramic bowl. She had picked a mess of fresh okra from the garden while Tom was hunting earlier in the day.

A radio played in the background. The station was in nearby Pickleyville, Baxter Parish Radio, 1410 AM. Bill Evans was on the piano. He was a jazz musician who'd graduated from the local junior college and gone on to become famous. Tom knew Evans from his short stint as a student at Baxter State Junior College during the late 1940s. The Hardins liked listening to the radio every evening, though some neighbors said the jazz music was a backdoor attempt at integration, liberal claptrap pushed by the meddling station owner. Because of the nightly jazz, many of the folks out in the country had quit listening to the radio at night. However, few of them dared to miss "Swap-n-Shopper," a live classified show that sold everything from rebuilt carburetors to plow mules. It aired three times daily and had a fanatical following.

When the station wasn't playing jazz late in the evening, the disc jockeys spun old-time country records such as Maybelle Carter, Flatt and Scruggs, and Bill Monroe. The Hardins liked both the jazz and the bluegrass music.

They had no television despite Sara and Wesley's wishes. The Hardins were frugal, prudent out of necessity and habit. Though they had enough money saved for a new GE, which cost two hundred dollars at the Goodyear store in downtown Pickleyville, they were delaying the purchase until an after-Christmas sale. If Tom had his way, they'd probably never purchase a television set at all. Tom put aside money for hard times, and he believed hard times loomed just around the corner. He planned accordingly, predicting the struggles were apt to start as soon as he sold the hogs and cows on a flooded local market for half their value.

"Tommy, what did the marshal want this morning?" Sara asked.

"Not much. He stopped by to shoot the breeze," Tom said, knowing she suspected more. He thought perhaps she had watched them from the window, and he'd already been evasive earlier when she asked about the visit. They'd been married for thirteen years.

"The marshal is one to talk a lot," Wesley said, eating a long, slimy piece of boiled okra, his fork stabbed through the center.

"That's right. He talks plenty," Tom said.

The land along the Baxter-Louisburg Parish border was Tom's native country. He had lived in the area all of his forty years, except for three years spent in the U.S. Navy Seabees. He was the only child of an old jackleg carpenter and farmer. He did not have to go to war but enlisted anyway during World War II. After naval service, he returned to his home in Zion, where he'd lived ever since. The community was founded in the 1880s as a logging camp during the time when the virgin timber was clear cut. The area had water access to Lake Tickfaw through the Big Natalbany River. The village earned its name from Little Zion Methodist Church, a congregation founded during a brush arbor revival in 1883. The Hardins were among the first members of the Methodist congregation. Tom's grandparents were charter members and builders of the first sanctuary. They were distantly related to the son of a Methodist circuit rider, John Wesley Hardin, the Texas outlaw.

Tom owned nearly one hundred head of hogs and two dozen cattle. They foraged the unfenced rangeland, most of which was owned by Fitz-Blackwell, a multinational timber company. But a month earlier, the Baxter Parish Police Jury passed a binding ordinance in the dark of night, which would make the grazing of livestock on the open rangeland illegal on January 1, 1965. Tom hunted wildlife and ran his animals on the timber company land, property soon to be posted. This already caused him to feel somewhat like an outlaw. He realized that in a measure of two months this way of life would end forever. Unlike the relative calm of a late October day, the fires of change were already stirring. Tom was not ready to make adjustments, but he knew he would have to make changes soon enough.

Livestock was a major stake in the Hardin family's livelihood, and the money earned through the stock meant that Sara could stay at home and not work outside the home. But now Tom was bracing for economic hardship, including more work laboring as a carpenter and general roustabout at the brickyard over on Highway 190 to make ends meet, more overtime if the foreman would grant him the extra hours.

Most people in Zion and southwest Baxter Parish, as well as southeast Louisburg Parish were of Scotch-Irish extraction. The exceptions were small enclaves of French and Germans in Milltown, the Hungarians in Kilgore, the Sicilians up in Liberty City, and the sections of blacks scattered across the region in their settlements. But these were all minority populations. The Scotch-Irish residents were predominantly Protestant, typically Baptists or Methodists, and their frontier religion was keenly anti-intellectual and clannish, often bigoted, and fearful of those outside their kith and kin.

Tom, however, saw little truth in the common notions of white supremacy or other obsessions taken up by the racists in the newly formed White Citizens' Council in Pickleyville. He had been influenced early in his life by Methodism's key doctrines of sanctification and Christian perfection, the teachings of John Wesley from the 1700s. Tom worked hard to live an upright and pious life, and he spent no time looking down on other races of people. Yet he, too, could be cautious around outsiders and somewhat distrustful. This was practiced in general and not necessarily along racial lines. The pine tree war was causing him more than casual concern, especially after being accused of arson by the marshal, and there were times when he was somewhat paranoid about the conflict in his community.

But Tom was a different sort of man because he was one of Pickleyville Public Library's best patrons. He had been the salutatorian of Milltown High in 1941. As a boy, he'd read the works of Zane Grey and Sir Arthur Conan Doyle, as well as *The Iliad* and *The Odyssey*. In recent years, he'd read Harper Lee's *To Kill a Mockingbird* twice. Each week, he would pick up a few books from the library and read them during the late evenings when he wasn't hunting or doing small carpentry projects. Tom planned to vote for Lyndon Johnson on November 3rd when many of his neighbors were voting for Barry Goldwater, most casting a Republican ballot for the first time in their lives.

Over the years, men had made snide comments about Tom's peculiar ways, his reading habits, and his weekly forays into the public library collection. Some called him "Little Einstein" behind his back because of his regular library patronage, but he never worried much about what people thought.

Sara also read widely and regularly. Wesley, too, was an early and voracious reader. In the years prior to meeting Tom, Sara had studied at Newcomb College, the women's college at Tulane University in New Orleans, where she earned a liberal arts degree. Tom had met her soon after she'd started working as a clerk at the public library in downtown Pickleyville following her graduation from Newcomb.

When World War II ended, Tom studied at the junior college in Pickleyville, enduring several part-time semesters on the GI Bill of Rights, and he considered becoming a history teacher. However, the parish public schools were run by a semi-literate mob of fraternity boys, Delta Tau Deltas and Kappa Alphas, local men he did not care for, the likes of which also ran the timber companies. The idea of teaching school for these stooges gave him pause about furthering his formal education.

Dealing with naturally corrupt folks discouraged him, so he left the college without earning a two-year degree. Instead of becoming a high school history teacher, he lived as a subsistence farmer on a patch of family land and raised hogs and cattle in the open range, working jobs locally—at the brickyard, over at the creosote plant for a time, and at the bag factory during different periods. For several years, he milked cows at a friend's dairy until the farm finally went under. Sometimes he remodeled houses and undertook small carpentry jobs for neighbors, but the earnings were paltry at best. Tom was the peculiar embodiment of a man with a strong work ethic but very little ambition. He believed that the parable in Luke chapter 12 cautioned the faithful against building bigger and bigger barns. He worked hard but never had dreams beyond Zion.

Tom harbored few regrets until recently when he was forced to begin removing his cattle and hogs from the land. People believed Fitz-Blackwell had paid bribes to pass the ordinance that banned the livestock from the woods, the unfenced open range owned by big landholders and timber companies throughout Baxter Parish, and this corruption made the loss of range rights all the more grievous. The stock ban was not what enraged Tom the most. It was the utter waste of killing the oaks and other hardwoods, poisoning them with dimethylamine salt and other chemical herbicides. Some large trees were killed by ringing them through the bark with a gas-powered "beaver machine." The timber companies would employ any means necessary to kill hardwood trees, even cutting them down with chainsaws just so they'd die in the forest and make room for young pines. To Tom's way of thinking, killing a hundred-year-old live oak tree and letting it rot in the forest was a form of fratricide and poor stewardship of God's resources, a testament to man's greed.

* * *

A few days after the marshal's visit, Tom drove to the feed store in Milltown to buy a sack of grain for his horse. It was half past four o'clock, and he was dog-tired from stacking green bricks most of the day in the kiln when he wasn't driving the Gravely tractor that pulled the brick cart on a narrow railroad track through the place. The Gravely and cart hauled bricks to and from the kiln, and then Tom and a black laborer stacked pallets of fired bricks onto larger pallets that were loaded by a diesel forklift.

Beam's Feed and Farm fronted the railroad tracks on Main Street. Tom parked down from the store entrance. As he got out of his Ford pickup truck, he heard a catcall. Tom saw Sloan Parnell, a well-connected timber company hack, sitting on the tailgate of a brand new International Scout, a red four-wheel drive vehicle with a white top and a short box for a bed. He was smoking a little cigar, talking to a tall black-haired woman with a blouse that showed plenty of cleavage. Tom recognized her as Charity LeBlanc, a local preacher's daughter, nothing more than a child in a woman's body. She often ran with upper crust men.

He looked at Sloan and made eye contact with him. He headed toward the store entrance, offering no gesture of friendship or acknowledgement. Several months earlier, while making his rounds checking on his hogs not far from Parnell family land, Tom almost had to draw his rifle on Sloan after he made a verbal threat, claiming he had a loaded pistol in his truck and calling Tom a criminal trespasser. He still wondered how he had avoided bloodshed, but Sloan finally backed off before he had to pull out the Savage deer rifle from the saddle scabbard.

Tom's father was a pious Methodist layman, but his father's two brothers were lapsed, backslid and wayward, often bad to drink. Some nights during Tom's childhood in the 1930s, his two uncles would come to the house in Zion and want to fight his father, and he would have to oblige them to protect the family. Occasionally, his father got bloodied fighting the pair of drunkards, and they'd come back the next day when they were sober with a new shirt or other items to replace what they'd destroyed the night before. As a result, Tom never drank, not even while in the navy, and he was always one to avoid violence whenever he could despite the region's notoriety for hotheadedness and blood feuds.

"I'm a Fitz-Blackwell man now," Sloan hollered to Tom. He stood up from the tailgate and made a flanking jog toward the feed store entryway.

Tom knew he'd have to pass Sloan to buy the sack of grain. "Is that so?" he said and kept walking.

"Damn straight it is, and I've got a thousand-dollar reward out on the arsonist that burned the pines over on Rogers Road, you silly son of a bitch," Sloan said, closing in.

"Great. Maybe I ought to go claim it by bringing you in," Tom said. He took a quick glance at the man as he approached, but he kept walking.

Tom had not set fire to the patch of woods, not the patch on Rogers Road, not any forest at all. There were dozens of men who hated Fitz-Blackwell, hated the killing of the oaks. They despised the removal of the livestock and the end of open range in the Zion community and elsewhere. Almost any man in the rural area could be guilty. He understood Sloan had no evidence against him. He was free of guilt, but he often wondered what good this was in such a crooked and fallen world.

When Tom placed his hand on the brass doorknob, he felt a shove to his shoulder, then a second push to his back almost simultaneously. He was nearly knocked off balance, his chest hitting the door, but he was able to spin around, and Sloan was the perfect distance from Tom's right fist. He hit the man square in the nose with a solid blow, one sure and effective punch to the face, which made his nose butterfly into a crimson spectacle of smashed flesh.

"Don't put your hands nowhere on me," Tom said.

Sloan was stunned. He was as large as Marshal Brownlow, even a little taller, and stouter. Now he was holding his nose with his hat knocked off his head. He started backing up, crawfishing like a coward down the sidewalk.

Tom pursued him with his fists in front of his chest like a welterweight boxer. He slammed him with a right jab to the torso and then a left fist to the temple. Sloan went down, his knees buckling, and he looked to the sky as if watching a long line of shooting stars in the broad daylight.

So Tom stood his ground and saw Sloan pull to his knees and spit out a line of bloody phlegm. He watched the man almost a minute, trying to ascertain if there was any fight left in him. Sloan started staggering back to his Scout.

Thinking the threat was over, Tom went inside the store.

"Howdy, Hardin," Jack Beam said.

"I'd like a hundred pound sack of heavy grain," Tom said to the storekeeper. The place smelled of mothballs and fertilizer. His hands trembled.

Beam stood behind the counter. He wore a striped railroad engineer's cap, overalls, and a starched long sleeve shirt. "All right," he said, writing on a gray receipt pad. "You been doing okay, Hardin? I say, you look a bit flustered."

"I was fine until recently."

"Yeah. Why's that?"

"I had to knock the fire out of Sloan Parnell on your front steps."

"No kidding? I saw Parnell and some half-dressed girl out yonder earlier." Beam looked up from his receipt pad.

"I don't know what the hell's wrong with him," Tom said.

"He's got that bad Parnell blood in him is all. They're rich and inbred as a coop of speckled chickens. All of 'em is so damned scared somebody outside the family might steal their money. He's just like his old daddy, P.T. 'The Drunk' Parnell, a trifling cur of a man, if you were to solicit my honest opinion. I hate like hell to see a Parnell come in here on account they're always trying to beat me out of something I've got."

"Well, that's according to their nature."

"That's the Lord's own truth. You think you're going to have trouble with him when you go back to your truck?" Beam asked. He turned around and picked up a worn Fox double barrel shotgun from where it was leaned against the wall. He popped open the breech and checked the two sixteen gauge shells, the brass showing.

"I don't think I'll have any trouble. He's probably long gone by now. I rattled him pretty good. Might have broken his nose."

"I'd be pleased to run him off or call the law or something, but the law won't do nothing."

"No, not much around here."

He leaned the shotgun against the wall again. "It'll come to two and a quarter."

Tom paid him in cash.

Beam called his helper. "Go get Mr. Hardin a sack of heavy grain and load it on his truck."

When the feed store man carried the sack to Tom's truck a minute later, there was no sign of Sloan Parnell and his International Scout or the LeBlanc woman.

Tom stood on the street looking around. Cars passed. A Mercury honked, and the driver waved. Staring down the street, Tom wondered how he'd found himself in such a strange period in parish history.

CHAPTER THREE

Tom tried to avoid trouble. He stayed away from Milltown for a few days. He wanted to keep the peace, but the pines kept burning in and around Zion. Among the locals, there were debates about how far the fires were heading, whether or not the killing of the pines was escalating to an outright war and if the casual blows would turn deadly. Tom began to worry about it himself, not knowing if he would face a risk greater than a tussle with a spoiled rich man.

He never went into the woods unarmed out of general fear, and he worked with his neighbor, James Luke Cate, as they attempted to catch the rest of their missing hogs and cows. James Luke was the husband of Tom's first cousin once removed, Nelda, and he was Tom's primary hunting partner. James Luke was originally from Slaughter, Louisiana, a dying little hamlet north of Baton Rouge. He and Nelda lived a mile south of the Hardins on Lower Louth Road. For all practical purposes, he was Tom's best friend.

James Luke swore to Tom that he wanted blood vengeance against the Parnells and the men killing the hardwoods and banning the livestock. He had a number of hogs and cows in the woods himself, and he was dead set against giving them away at the auction. Tom also knew that James Luke constantly passed along the rumor that Fitz-Blackwell had bought off the Louisiana Wildlife Commission, and he claimed this was the reason they'd sent game wardens to hassle the hunters and farmers. He told Tom that he'd placed Sloan Parnell in the crosshairs of the telescopic sight on his deer rifle one day, and he regretted not shooting him in the woods. Tom downplayed the declaration, thinking that perhaps James Luke was just talking trash after too much beer one evening.

But Tom wasn't an outlaw, and the harassment by the authorities was only a mild inconvenience. Until recently, he had never even seen a game warden north of the landing at Lizard Bayou. Now, however, the pine forests of Zion, Kilgore, Milltown, Packwood Corners, and Watermelon were teeming with wardens from all over the state. It reminded him of the FBI during the summer when they searched for the three missing civil rights workers in Neshoba County, Mississippi. It seemed like there were authorities behind every bush.

Financially, the parish stock law served a hard blow to Tom and the other small farmers. Because Tom owned a mere twenty acres, more than half of which was thick forest, he couldn't graze two dozen cows and one hundred head of hogs on such a small tract. The new ordinance showed that the open range farmers were no match for the money doled out under the table by a multinational timber company. And everyone knew that Louisiana police jurors, the governing council for the parish, weren't champions of virtue. They usually followed whatever pot was sweetest. The number of farmers was already diminishing. Men were leaving the woods and farms to work in the oil industry along the Mississippi River. But the stock law was the death knell, Tom thought, the end of local men being sustained from the land.

He knew things were off kilter. It seemed to be getting harder and harder to make ends meet. His father had homesteaded the land and rarely held down a public job outside of the farm and forest, except for taking intermittent odd jobs as a carpenter. Now Tom needed to hold down a full-time job, as well as working the little farm and livestock operation. He believed the day might come when his own son would have to work two jobs off the home place, and his wife would need to leave the house for public work. Afterwards, ends still wouldn't meet, and he couldn't imagine what might happen to his grandchildren in this economic paradise.

Tom decided to do the only thing he knew to do: try to catch the animals and take them to the auction in Ruthberry. Selling them to the highest bidder in a flooded livestock market would barely cover his expenses. Tom was more than a little tempted to leave the hogs in the woods.

It bothered him to know that Sloan was in line to be named to the plant superintendent post at Fitz-Blackwell's big lumber mill in the center of neighboring Louisburg Parish. A plant manager was a white hat job, one where he'd dress in a coat and tie for work, a position of power and privilege in the region. Sloan was nothing more than a political appointee for the mill, a man with adequate connections to make things go smoothly in the parish.

After Brownlow's visit and the latest altercation with Sloan, Tom grew angrier by the day. To be accused of setting fires by the marshal was an affront to his integrity. In a manner of speaking, it was a slap in the face, an insult that was a violation of goodwill between local men. There was a certain amount of dignity afforded by years of relations and established character, and this had been thrown by the wayside.

One morning while eating his wife's cooking, a fried egg and some grits, Tom listened to the Swap-n-Shopper on the radio. The caller said that he was selling his cattle and would take almost any offer for them, no price beyond consideration. He recognized the cracking voice and the phone number. It was Mr. Leo Mullins, an elderly World War I veteran whose cattle were his livelihood. The ungodly thieves, Tom thought. If they treat us like a bunch of criminals, maybe we should start acting like criminals. At the table, he stiffened and pushed the half-eaten plate away from his chest.

Earlier in the week Tom had driven over to the old Weathersby farm to see if some of the hogs a neighbor had penned up were some of his stock. It was nearing dusk when he left, and he drove through a patch of land owned by Fitz-Blackwell. Smoldering fires burned on both sides of the road, smoke everywhere like a bad haze. He came to a checkpoint where two game wardens and a state forestry investigator stood, and they made him get out of his truck. They searched the inside, under the seat, behind the seat, in the glove box and the bed for anything connected to arson. They found nothing but held him up for twenty minutes asking him questions. The lack of respect enraged Tom. By the time they were done, it was too dark to deal with the penned hogs, and he had to turn around and go back home.

So he began to entertain ways to get even with the timber companies. And though James Luke had never come out and said he was one of the arsonists, Tom figured he'd done some of the burning in the woods. His whereabouts were often questionable, and Tom suspected that James Luke was seeing a woman at the state highway barn where he worked as a safety supervisor. Perhaps he was both burning pines and running around on Nelda. Tom couldn't say for sure.

Sara walked into the room and asked, "Tom, what's the matter?"

"Nothing," he said, leaving the kitchen table for the barn. If he'd been inclined to drink like his long passed away uncles, he would have gotten a bottle of whiskey, and if he'd been a violent man, he would have done more than just contemplate ways to seek revenge.

James Luke had asked Tom to go raccoon hunting later that evening. At dark, Tom saddled old Sam, slipping his Winchester .22 magnum rifle into his large leather scabbard, which swallowed the small rifle. The horse stood tied to one of the posts on the front porch of the house, both of his eyes closed and one back hoof propped up to rest.

Tom sat in the kitchen doing the crossword puzzle in Friday's *States-Item* newspaper. He listened to the radio playing The North Carolina Ramblers, Uncle Dave Macon, Jimmie Rodgers, and The Stanley Brothers. The station played Earl Scruggs and his "Foggy Mountain Breakdown," one of Tom's favorites. It grew later and later as he waited for James Luke to arrive on horseback to go hunting. Sara and Wesley had gone to bed, and after he'd finished the puzzle, he sat reading a history book and listening to old-time music for what seemed like the longest time.

Finally, James Luke knocked on the back door.

Tom could see him in the window as he stood on the steps. He opened the door.

His buddy was dressed in his work clothes. "Let's go find us a coon," James Luke said.

"It's ten o'clock," Tom said. "I was about to unsaddle Sam. I've been a little concerned about you, and I almost called your house, but I was afraid I'd wake up Nelda. What happened?"

"I had some things to do tonight, a few errands to run."

Tom looked into the darkness. "It sure is smoky out."

"Uh-huh."

"I don't suspect I ought to ask." Tom shrugged his shoulders.

"Don't. Let's go turn the hounds loose a little ways to the east of Boss Gibson's place, and we'll make it a short hunt if we can."

"Good. That'll work."

Out in the yard, Tom and James Luke climbed on their horses. Tom rode Sam, and James Luke straddled Diablo. The two men hunted in the woods north of Tom's house for a while. James Luke's black and tan coonhounds treed once, and Tom shot a big sow raccoon out of the top of a gum tree. Then the two men called it a night, heading home.

Back at Tom's barn, they skinned the animal, James Luke saving the hide to sell. Tom said he'd put the carcass in his freezer, one foot left attached to prove that it wasn't a common housecat. He planned to offer it to the Widow Ruby Lazarus who lived just down the road. She was an elderly woman without any pension who survived on the charity of neighbors and family members. She had a great love for any wild game folks brought her, and she'd trade preserves or pies for raccoons. In the late winter, Tom would bring her half of a hog to help her sustain herself through the winter months. That is, if he had any hogs left on the place.

It was a quarter to one. After turning his horse out to pasture, Tom went inside to go to bed. James Luke returned home on horseback, riding in the darkness, his two hounds trailing.

CHAPTER FOUR

On Saturday morning, Tom, Wesley, and James Luke rode the horses through the Big Natalbany River swamp with six dogs, five of them baying curs. James Luke rode with a bullwhip in his hand, which he would pop occasionally, making the sharp sound of a rifle as the cotton popper at the end of the leather plait broke the sound barrier. Wesley rode one of James Luke's horses, a thinly built Welsh pony not quite as large as a mature horse. The boy weighed eighty-five pounds and the horse fit him well. In fact, he was the only person who ever rode the little horse. James Luke had offered to let Wesley have the horse as a Christmas present the year before, but Tom declined, not wanting to accept such an expensive gift from James Luke.

The curs were loose, but Jubal trailed Tom's horse tethered to a rope. Tom usually kept him on a rope leash because he would catch animals at inopportune times, sometimes the wrong animal, perhaps even a human, friend or foe. Tom was thankful that it was dry out, because otherwise the horses were apt to bog down in the muddy flats that followed alongside the river.

They'd caught a half-dozen hogs where they foraged in some bait corn on the ground near a livestock pen in the woods, the swine now loaded into a pipe stock trailer hitched to the bumper of Tom's truck. The pigs' ears were already notched with Tom's mark, a flat tip cut off of the right ear and three notches on the left.

"At this rate, hell will stop taking sinners by the time we catch all our damned hogs," James Luke said. He inspected the pigs in the back of the stock trailer, his hands gripping the pipe walls.

"Yeah, it doesn't look real promising," Tom said, scraping a briar from a boot heel with a stick.

"The hogs are getting real wary of the sound of a pickup truck," James Luke said.

"They hear us and start running the other way. I guess we'll need to get the jump on them somehow or another, start doing more than just baiting and chasing them with the dogs. Maybe set up some kind of trapdoor pens or something." Tom slapped the side of the trailer and a hog squealed as if hit by an electric jolt. "I just don't know. There are so many folks in the woods gathering hogs that they're really stirred-up. Wouldn't it be something if we missed the deadline and ended up in jail for trespassing on posted land?"

James Luke shook his head, lit an unfiltered Camel with a white-tipped kitchen match. "That'll be the end of it all. If they don't like the fire in the woods now, somebody's house'll get torched. They keep pushing me, and somebody pays in blood."

"At least we have these few to carry to the sale. That's enough for today," Tom said.

Wesley walked over to them. "Pops, you care if I load the horses into the trailer?" he asked.

"No, but don't let the red hog out. Push him into the front compartment with a stick and latch the gate," Tom said. "If you need help, holler."

There was a good-sized red boar locked up alone in James Luke's stock trailer. The trailer was hooked to the back of his 1958 Chevrolet pickup.

Tom and James Luke stood beside the trailer attached to Tom's truck. They were talking, trying to figure out how to catch the remaining hogs, and how Tom was going to make a living once the hogs were out of the woods and sold. The dogs were tied in the bed of Tom's truck that was parked in the shade of a live oak tree where the men stood.

A few minutes later, Wesley screamed. When Tom turned and looked toward the bumper-hitch trailer, he could see that Wesley had a two hundred pound boar by a leg and it was dragging him out of the trailer, pulling him like a mad bull.

"Damn it," James Luke hollered.

But the hog had not gotten away. Instead, it turned on Wesley, knocking him down, making a skillful attack. The hog had no tusks, but his jaws were razor sharp and as hard as cast iron.

In the seconds before the men ran over to help him, Tom had the presence of mind to release his hog dog from the bed of his truck, the place where he was tethered to a rope leash. "Get 'em, Jubal. Catch 'em," Tom yelled.

The dog made a beeline toward the boy in the back of the open trailer, never barking. Jubal passed James Luke who was already running. In a flying leap, the Catahoula bulldog lunged into the back of the trailer as silent as a sniper, and it appeared at first that he was mauling Wesley. As fast as the strike of a poisonous snake, the dog grabbed the boar by the ear in a snarling jump. The red hog began to squeal like he was being skinned alive, and he shook the dog that was locked on his ear. Jubal was thrown from side to side, and both the dog and hog fell out of the back of the trailer and onto the ground, but the dog never let go.

James Luke picked the boy up by the arms while Jubal stayed clamped to the wayward pig, the squeals ear-piercing. The two men checked on Wesley. His clothes were covered with rank hog and cattle feces. "Son, you all right?" James Luke asked.

"I think so, Uncle Jimmy," said the boy.

Tom tried to brush off Wesley's shirt and could see that he was scraped but otherwise in good shape.

Then James Luke fought to hobble the hog's legs with leather straps while the dog kept his teeth locked onto a bloody ear, the animal squealing even more, but unable to get away. Once the men got the animal's legs secured, Tom called the dog off and snapped a rope leash to Jubal's collar, praising him for the faithful work, rubbing his ears and head.

"Can I kick the hog?" Wesley said, as he stared at the tied up boar on the ground, his legs in fetters.

"I think you'd better not," Tom said.

"Just once, Pops?"

"Not even once."

The immobile boar was laid out like a sack of feed in the compartment in the front of James Luke's steel stock trailer. They loaded the horses into the trailer behind where the hog lay bound.

Jubal rode in the back of Tom's truck with the other curs, all of them fastened on lines near the cab so they wouldn't fight each other.

After pulling out a fresh shirt from behind the truck seat and giving it to Wesley, Tom let the boy drive his truck. Tom rode beside him. Wesley sat atop a two by twelve pine board and a worn copy of the 1960 Sears and Roebuck catalog. Tom cautioned him to drive slowly on the gravel road, being careful not to jostle the pigs, which squealed as the truck traveled the rutted roadway.

"Am I driving okay, Pops?" Wesley asked, a smile on his face that seemed as wide as the windshield.

"You're doing fine, son," Tom said.

CHAPTER FIVE

It was almost winter, cool during the day and downright chilly at
night. Tom kept working forty-hour weeks at the brickyard, and on
top of this, he tried to catch and sell as many hogs and cattle as
possible. Now and then, a local farmer would pen some of Tom's stock,
and he'd go pick up the cows or hogs, and thank his neighbor, remembering the goodwill and mutual help for the future.

The forest fires weren't slowing. New fires were being set most
nights. Tom realized there wasn't much he could do about the changing
times, and he was without hope that the politicians would stop the ordinance ending open range. He had not seen Sloan Parnell since the fight
at the feed store, and he only saw Marshal Brownlow at church on Sundays. When he did see the marshal, relations were cordial.

On Monday afternoon, November 9th, Corrine Travis, Tom's closest cousin, came over to the Hardin home to pick up some fresh yard
eggs from the family's chicken coop and saw the front door ajar. Jubal
was loose, a short piece of broken chain dangling from his thick neck.
Tom's truck was parked beside the house in its normal spot. Tom had
caught a ride to work with a neighbor so that Sara would have transportation to go to the grocery and run some errands. Corrine beat on the
doorjamb and then called out, but no one answered. Fearful that something was wrong, she went into the house and looked in the rooms. The
interior doors were open. Corrine found Sara in the bedroom. At first,
she thought the woman was dead, but she found a faint pulse at her
wrist, showing life left in the battered body.

While Tom was working at the brickyard and Wesley was at the school in Milltown, Sara had been attacked. She was raped, beaten unconscious, naked and tied to an iron bed with stiff ropes.

There was no sign of a break-in, but the doors of the house were never locked anyway. The only signs of trouble were the dog's broken chain and Sara's crippled body.

Marshal Brownlow found Tom at work. He was sitting atop the little Gravely tractor, pulling a cart of green bricks, hauling them to the kiln, a thirty-foot tall dome-shaped oven heated by coal.

Tom looked up from his tractor and saw the marshal and his foreman walking toward him. The foreman waved a hand and Tom shut the tractor engine. He sensed death in the air. Hours later, he could still recall the peculiar smell. Something was stuck in his nose as he stood up from the tractor seat.

Brownlow said, "We need you to come with us to the office. Something's happened to Sara, and we need to talk to you about it right now."

"What happened, Donald? What in the hell happened?" Tom asked. "Did she get into a wreck or something?"

"It would be better if we talked at the office. Let's go over yonder," the marshal said, motioning for Tom to follow.

As they walked quickly toward the building where the business was run, Tom asked, "What's going on? Is she alive?"

"Barely," the marshal said.

Once inside the foreman's office, which was nothing more than a glorified shack, the marshal told him what had happened. He described the bedroom scene as Corrine had found it.

Tom cried out in anger, pounding his right fist in his left palm. The marshal drove him over to the hospital in his patrol car, and Tom fought back tears the whole way. How did his well-ordered life and family fall into such a tragedy? He wondered what they'd done to bring on such a curse as he prayed for his wife.

The Pickleyville hospital room was humid, almost water-damp. When Tom saw his wife, she was not dead but narrowly hanging on to life. Her face was drawn to one side as if stricken by a palsy. Sara was in a semi-coma, but she wasn't placid or still. Instead, she was restless, appearing as though she was being assaulted in her sleep, often wide-eyed but focusing on nothing, constantly kicking off her sheets. She had to be restrained with leather straps at the wrists and feet.

She was blinded by the darkness of her own mind, a war taking place in her soul that manifested itself in the current struggles. And the doctor had little conclusive information to tell the family, a prognosis as mysterious as the attack.

Tom sat at her bedside for a few moments before the nurses made him leave. In the hallway outside of the ward, he offered his simple prayers, the same petitions of men through all time, the prayers of anyone traveling a dark wood, those who faced senseless damage and gratuitous evil. He tried to make sense of his broken world but the heavens were brass, and nothing came back from his petitions but the echo of his own voice.

Sara, thirty-six years old, was a pretty woman. She was slim and strong with long auburn hair, and not one white strand in it. Now her hair was matted and stringy, her face swollen almost twice its normal size.

The new preacher at Little Zion Methodist arrived at the hospital. Reverend Charlie Poole stood in the hallway, put his hand on Tom's shoulder and hung his head, saying few words.

Tom's cousin's wife, Martina, picked up Wesley from school. The boy did not know what happened other than his mother was in the hospital and that he could not go back home.

James Luke had been off work on Monday from his job at the highway department, but nobody could find him, and Nelda was at the bank in Pickleyville where she worked as a teller. She'd heard the news within a half an hour of Sara's admission to the hospital ER. Her boss allowed her to leave work early, and she went directly to the hospital.

During the time Sara suffered at the Ninth Ward Hospital, Wesley worked with a handsaw and hammer, building a birdhouse out of scrap lumber in Martina and Sid Hardin's backyard. He was always building something with wood, drawing sketches of things around the farm and forest, oftentimes helping his father with projects on the home place. He'd won a blue ribbon at the parish fair in Ruthberry for an oil painting of their barn. Now he sat beneath a Chinaberry tree and cut boards while holding them steady on the wooden table. After he was done sawing, he concentrated on keeping the boards secure while nailing together the sides of the little birdhouse with a rusty claw hammer. Boyhood was its own balm, its own natural protection against the blows and hardness of the surrounding adult world. When he looked at the finished birdhouse, he couldn't wait to show his mother and father.

At the hospital in Pickleyville, Tom longed for his wife's healing. The only consolation to her injuries was that she was still alive and breathing on her own, which offered him some hope. She lay there broken, her body crippled by the attack. Tom sat outside the ward in the hallway. The smell of ammonia was in the air. Though he appreciated Nelda and the preacher's presence, he could find little comfort in it.

His thoughts raged. He needed to find the man who'd left his wife for dead. But his heart was at odds, torn between health and vengeance, an ungracious emotion that left him in anguish. He knew if he could get his hands around the neck of the man who did this to his wife, he'd offer no quarter. And in his mind he had only one possible suspect: Sloan Parnell.

"You want any coffee?" Reverend Poole asked.

"Yes," Tom said, waking from the nightmare ever so briefly.

"Let's go get us some. The coffee's down the hall."

So the two men walked the corridor to the hospital cafeteria and drank for a half an hour. After they finished the coffee, the pastor prayed with Tom for his wife's restoration and strength to weather this calamity through the mercy of God.

Four days later, Sara was out of the coma but still in the hospital. The doctors said in time she would recuperate, though her shoulder was broken and there were other injuries to her face and genitalia. She could barely speak. Several of her teeth had been knocked out during the attack, and she was struck with an inexplicable palsy on one side of her face.

She claimed to have no memory of the attack. No images. Nothing. Her speech was staccato. "I can't—uh—uh—re—mem—ber—any—thing," she told Tom.

"That's okay, honey, rest," he said. For some reason he could not pin down, Tom doubted her complete memory lapse. But he was not a cruel man, and he did not want to press her for details. He wished he didn't have to work at the brickyard. Had he been at home when the predator arrived, he could have defended her. Tom asked for a second week off from work, which was granted with pay, something he didn't expect.

Corrine came to the hospital to sit with Sara, even though Tom was available to stay. Tom went to town and bought a new GE television set, and he got James Luke to help him put it in the living room where it awaited Sara's return home. Tom climbed a sweet gum tree in the backyard, thirty feet up, and installed an antenna to get decent reception.

Marshal Brownlow stopped by the Hardin home that evening. He brought a casserole wrapped in tinfoil that his wife had sent over. Despite the friction over the forest fires, Brownlow seemed to be genuinely concerned about the fate of this family in his jurisdiction. By contrast, the Baxter Parish Sheriff's Office hadn't shown any interest in the case whatsoever. Rarely did the sheriff do anything south of Liberty City unless there was a fierce public outcry, and he did even less in the Ninth Ward, which had its own marshal and special dedicated tax to pay for the office. The sheriff's main base was in Ruthberry and the north end of the parish where his supporters lived, his chief campaign funders being the old-money landowners. Some of these families had been in power for more than a century.

The marshal's office could perform any police work in the ward, as well as handling civil papers and security for the Ninth Ward Court in Milltown. Sometimes it seemed that the marshal served as the only real law in the Ninth Ward.

"You got any idea about who did this to my wife?" Tom asked the marshal. He and Brownlow stood outside on the front porch.

The marshal smoked. "Not any leads or suspects. Nothing at all. We got the state police to fingerprint the house, but not a thing's come of it so far," the marshal said.

"I want you to go see Sloan Parnell. I had to knock the hell out of him over at Beam's feed store a couple of weeks ago."

"And you don't like him so you think he'd go and rape your wife? Come on, Tom. That's a far stretch." He snuffed out the cigarette on the porch post and tossed the butt into the yard.

"He's Judge Parnell's grandson, and he's marked with a real bad seed. What's wrong? Are you scared of him?"

"I ain't scared of no man."

"You're full of shit. Every man is scared of somebody."

"I'll look into it."

"You'd better. I might have to go visit him myself one night soon if you don't."

"Tom, you'd do well to stay away from him, if you know what's good for you."

"I've already said it once, and I'll say it again. My hog dog was loose. He broke his chain on the day of the attack. I'd bet a hundred-dollar bill whoever attacked my wife had a patch of skin bit out of his ass." Tom pointed to Jubal where he lay under the tree in the dirt, a thick chain hooked to his big leather collar. The sun was almost down, and the dog seemed to watch the men out of the corner of his eye. Jubal's coat was red-brown like a rich roux and spotted with black, crimson, and white splotches. He had one glass eye that was blue and the other was mud-brown, and his overall build was more in line with a bulldog than a Catahoula. He wasn't an anxious or barking dog, never making much noise around the house, and the other cur dogs were kept far past the barn in a series of net wire pens, but Jubal was always chained near the front of the house under a shade tree to serve as a deterrent to trespassers. If he had broken loose, he would have nailed any stranger who entered the yard planning mischief. Tom believed this fervently. The chain was snapped near his collar for a specific reason, and Tom knew the dog broke the chain to protect his wife.

"Well, it's just another thing to look into," said the marshal.

"I've already told your assistant Wentworth, and I also spoke to a deputy sheriff in Ruthberry by the name of Roberts."

Brownlow looked away, toward the road. He didn't say anything.

"My best guess is the son of a bitch that did this has a big patch of skin missing out of his ass or leg or arm or somewhere from trying to fight off the dog. Jubal'll bite the fire out of anybody except me and my wife and boy, James Luke and Nelda Cate, Corrine Travis, and maybe Martina and Sid Hardin. That's about it. He tries to bite folks, and that's why I keep him on the logging chain when I'm not able to watch him close."

"Like I told you, I'll look into it."

"You do that."

CHAPTER SIX

The sky was gray and dark, as if the clouds were begging to rain. It was Sunday afternoon. Tom and Wesley had dressed for the church services earlier in the day, but Tom decided against going.

He walked to the open backdoor and looked down at the boy who was rubbing Jubal's ears. Wesley rubbed the dog's head and he seemed pleased, his tail wagging. The boy sat on the back steps dressed in a pair of khaki trousers and a khaki shirt like an aged farmer.

Tom stared down at the boy and remembered how he and Sara didn't think they'd be able to have a child of their own. After they'd been married two years and no pregnancy occurred, they went to see a doctor in Pickleyville. The doctor said Tom was almost completely sterile. It was scarcely possible that they'd ever conceive. But then after their third year of marriage, they had a son, and he saw it as a miracle from God, evidence of the Lord's graciousness and answered prayer.

"When will Mother come home?" Wesley asked.

"Maybe tomorrow, maybe the day after," Tom said.

"Is Aunt Corrine going to stay at the hospital with her tonight?"

"Yes, she's there now. Then I'll relieve her for a while later, and afterward she'll come back and stay there for the night."

"Can I go with you to the hospital?"

"No, they won't let you go into the room."

"Why?"

"You're too young. I've already covered this ground with you about the hospital rules."

"Pops, who hurt her?"

Tom was startled. This was the first indication that Wesley knew something truly dreadful had happened to his mother, and she was not simply ill. "Where did you hear that somebody hurt her?"

"School. I heard Mrs. Maxine Bennett whispering to Mrs. Jennings."

Tom wondered exactly how much he knew. "I'm not sure, and neither is the marshal, though I have a suspect."

"Who?"

"I can't say."

"You need to say, Pops."

"No," Tom said.

"We need to figure this out."

He could see the boy beginning to cry, tears sliding down his face. "I need to figure it out. But this is not your concern." He reached down and hugged the boy, held him against his chest for a few seconds.

It started to drizzle. Drops of rain fell across their shirts. "Let's go inside before we get wet. And I'll go put Jubal back on his chain," Tom said to the boy.

Tom had sold a few more hogs that he'd caught by baiting them with corn at Junior Cooper's catch pen deep in the piney woods. The homemade trapdoor gate worked like a dream, but he realized the process of catching the mavericks was going to get harder and slower over time. He needed the money to recoup some of his livestock investment, not to mention the hospital bills coming home like a second assault. The deadline for removing the hogs from the rangeland was December 31st, and it was always on his mind, a foreboding date haunting him.

Before the attack, he'd planned to buy more tools for his carpentry work, a planer and a wood lathe, a big band saw and a drill press. Perhaps he'd start doing odd jobs and fix-it projects for cash money when he wasn't at the brickyard, now that the livestock business was becoming dead to the past. However, the estimated two-thousand-dollar hospital bill he now faced would flag any attempt at investing in an at-home shop. The surgery left pins in Sara's shoulder and arm, and the time in the hospital cost money that he didn't have readily available. The Hardins didn't have insurance, and their savings account at the bank wasn't enough to cover the bills. Tom needed to sell the remaining hogs. So far, he'd only earned four hundred dollars from the hogs and cattle he'd sold, but a number of hogs were still running wild in the woods.

The day Sara returned home, she was a shell of her former self. Her face was still swollen and drawn to the right side, and several of her teeth were missing. Her left eye was bloodshot and her vision blurry. The pain was unceasing. Her broken shoulder was in a brace, and she could hardly walk because of poor balance, but at least she was home, back to the house where she'd lived since shortly after their marriage. Yet this was little comfort since it was also the place where she had been left for dead. Often, she just sat on the couch and wept, drying her tears with her dress. The new television screen showed the gray images of the Baton Rouge station, WBRZ, but she didn't really watch it. Sara never even acknowledged the television set. When she heard footsteps nearing the room, she would cower, trying to hide. Then she'd go stiff as a corpse until she understood who was approaching.

Perhaps the worst of it was the cold shame of the attack, the rape itself. How could the family speak of rape? There were no adequate words for the attack on the homemaker, mother, and wife. Truth be told, Tom and Sara never really talked about anything beyond trivial matters—daily activities and books. Words had not come to them to address the anguish and sense of violation. Silence was its own punishment, and it continued to force more pain on the broken Hardin family like some kind of cosmic millstone crushing them into powder, grinding each of them into the dirt.

CHAPTER SEVEN

W hile Sara slept, Tom stood in the kitchen cutting onions. He was cooking, baking potatoes and a pork roast in the oven, picking up the slack in the housework. This was the first time he'd kept house since their marriage. Corrine cooked a little. Nelda helped out. So did Martina and a few others, women from the Methodist church, friends and family in the Zion community. Mostly, folks brought food to the house ready to eat, but they never ventured beyond the front porch.

Sara slept in the bedroom, an oral tranquilizer causing her to breathe with shallow breaths, the sound of a whisper floating from her dry lips. On days when Tom had to go to work, Martina or Corrine stayed with her all day, and this made Tom feel a little better. She told him the pills chased away the dark shadows, cloudy images of being attacked. Still, when she slept, sometimes the certainty of death visited her dreams, and she'd awake screaming and fighting a ghost.

The phone on the wall rang. Tom dropped the kitchen knife into the sink, wiping his hands on a rag, grabbing the phone just as the third ring hit the first note. He answered it saying, "Hello. Hardin residence." He spoke softly, hoping the noise wouldn't wake his wife.

"Is this Tom Hardin?" the woman asked. Her voice was sweet and youthful sounding.

"Yes. Who's speaking?"

"I can't say. But I need to tell you that Sloan Parnell was the one that raped your wife. He did it to her on account that you whipped him."

"Ma'am, how do you know this?" Tom massaged his temple with his partially wet left hand.

"Sloan talks a lot when he's drinking heavy, and he's always drinking heavy."

"Who is this?"

"I can't tell you. The Parnells are powerful people. And I'm scared."

"How do I know it's true? I don't even know who you are."

"He told me your dog bit his left forearm bad, and it's not healed. He said your father's pocket watch is under his truck seat. It's inscribed with Ansel Earl Hardin on it. Sometimes he gets drunk and calls me."

"I'm not missing my daddy's watch."

"You'd better go check, Tommy."

He was stunned. Almost no one ever called him "Tommy" except for a small circle of friends and neighbors. He couldn't place the voice, and he didn't think the old watch was missing. He kept it in his top dresser drawer. It was there the last time he checked, as best he could recall.

"Lady, why are you telling me all of this?"

"I don't know. Maybe Sara deserves a little mercy for something she did a while back. And the Lord's been dealing with me, chastising me for some sinful ways in my life. He's been speaking to me, talking to me in my prayer times. The Lord said she didn't deserve what she got. But I better go now. I've told you all the Lord put on my heart to say."

The phone went dead. Tom held it to his ear a few seconds and then hung up.

He went into the bedroom where Sara slept, trying not to disturb her.

She spoke without opening her eyes, sounding startled. "Tommy, is that you?"

"Yes, I'm looking for a handkerchief."

He searched the chest of drawers, but the watch was gone. He considered whether he should go directly to Brownlow but decided against it. What would it accomplish anyway? The marshal either wouldn't or couldn't do anything, and Sloan might destroy the evidence linking him to the crime.

Tom contemplated killing Sloan, perhaps shooting him with a .308 rifle, his old Savage 99 lever action deer rifle. Shoot him from the highway as he walked out of his front door to go drinking. Or maybe sucker him into a fistfight and take an oak stick to him, not quitting until the man died. These were twisted images that he sought to dispel from his mind, but the violent vision lingered despite his best efforts.

He studied it a while, considered it all. He would make a reasonable plan to deal with the knowledge and do something. In the meantime, he needed to verify that the watch was still in Sloan's possession.

Tom called Nelda and asked her if she'd be willing to come over and relieve him of his care-giving. He asked her if James Luke was home, and she said he was. Nelda and Tom swapped shifts looking after Sara. Wesley was over at Corrine's house.

When Nelda arrived, Tom drove over to James Luke's house. When he got there, dogs started barking, two yellow curs running from James Luke's barn, a small pole barn that sagged a little in the middle.

From inside the barn, Tom heard a sharp whistle and the dogs settled down a bit. There was nothing moving at the barn, though James Luke's truck was parked beside the building. Tom buttoned his denim jacket. The barn door opened, and James Luke stuck his head out and waved, hollering at the dogs. Tom walked over and found that James Luke was pouring out wheat shorts to feed some small pigs he'd gathered from the woods. The pigs fought over the food, squealing and tussling.

"Damned things are crazy as all hell. I'd say they're feral and would eat me if I fell in the trough." James Luke grinned.

"Yeah, hogs are killers, but not that young," Tom said.

"Hell, years ago I saw a hog eating a half-alive calico cat in a thunderstorm. Old hog carried the cat out into our yard and was eating it under an oak tree. I shot the hog and killed it, but there was no way I was going to eat it after what he had done to the cat."

"That's sick," Tom said, standing with his hands in his pockets. He'd heard the tale once before but doubted its veracity.

"You need something, friend?" James Luke asked.

"Uh-huh," Tom said, stalling a couple of seconds, and then he launched into the story, telling James Luke about the phone call and the pocket watch and the marks left from the dog attack.

James Luke appeared taken aback, one hand gripping the rope handle of his bucket, the other holding a cigarette. "Sloan Parnell is a no-good sumbitch. If he did that to your wife, he deserves some pain. He'll just do it again. Let's go get his sorry ass right now," James Luke said, his face red with anger.

"No, I just need to see if he has Daddy's watch in the vehicle and decide what to do next," Tom said.

Earlier in the year, James Luke had a rift with P.T. Parnell over some money. The elder Parnell had been James Luke's former drinking buddy, and he was some kind of business partner in a venture to raise giant sinker cypress logs from Lake Tickfaw and sell them to the state under Governor Davis, a kickback scheme that Tom never could quite understand. On top of this, there was a large tract of land that he was going to buy for the price of the stand of timber, but P.T. bought the property out from under James Luke. He was always working an angle to make money in a side business. Most of the time it was a fly-by-night scam that included taking someone else's cash. Because James Luke and P.T. had a falling out, he cursed the Parnells daily.

"Why not go right now?" James Luke said. You want to take after him? I say let's ride," James Luke threw his bucket into the feed room where he stored grain in a large steel bin. He took a hard pull on his Camel.

Tom said, "I need more information. Then we can go check his comings and goings, search his truck to see if we can find the old watch."

"Don't ass around. I say let's do something now. He might get rid of the watch. That's all of the rock solid evidence you ought to need. The dog bite on his arm might heal up, make it an invisible scar." He gripped a bottle of beer that had been sitting on a 55 gallon oil drum, and swallowed a quarter of it in two gulps.

"I won't waste any time. But the woman said he's injured on his left forearm, and Jubal must have latched onto him good, which makes sense with the chain broke and all. I know he'd try to bite the hell out of somebody if he wanted off the chain bad enough to break it."

"What do you really want to do?"

"I'd like to bring him to justice."

James Luke sneered. "Justice. What's that supposed to be in this godforsaken place?"

But he never answered.

Tom called the marshal for an update on the investigation. According to Brownlow, Sloan Parnell had a solid alibi. He was in Mississippi cruising a stand of timber all day long for Fitz-Blackwell. He had three nights of hotel receipts from the Rosalie Hotel to prove it, and he was on the company time clock. But the marshal mentioned no eyewitnesses, only Parnell's word and an assignment sheet, a handwritten timesheet from his job and the hotel tickets.

When the marshal told Tom the alibi, he offered little reaction. The so-called proof did not persuade him one bit. He said, "Mighty fine police work. Thank you and good-bye."

Tom was sure that Sloan, by nature, was making other enemies. As a representative of Fitz-Blackwell, he would most certainly face opposition from other farmers and hunters out in the woodlands, the many fires being clear proof of an arson conspiracy, and any number of the men could kill him as easily as pulling a trigger. However, in the overall scheme of things, if Sloan turned up dead, Tom did not want to be a prime suspect, so he decided not to tell the marshal about the woman's phone call.

CHAPTER EIGHT

A t the stroke of midnight, Sloan's family home burned to cinders, the old two-story Parnell place with its dueling cedars at the end of a long driveway. It was torched in the darkness, the stars not glowing, a time when normal people were asleep in bed. But at the witching hour, Sloan was sipping bourbon and Coca-Cola over at the Belt Buckle Lounge. A neighbor drove to the bar and announced that the house was consumed in flames. Sloan had inherited it when his Uncle Bixby Parnell died of a brain aneurism two years earlier. At one time, the home was insured by Lloyd's of London, but Sloan had failed to renew the policy earlier in the year. Instead of mailing the premium, he bought the services of a string of prostitutes on Plank Road in Baton Rouge. He was now out of a fine home and seventy acres of young pines, which were also charred to a crisp.

On the day after the old Parnell place burned, Marshal Brownlow was waiting for Tom at the brickyard parking lot at four o'clock when the yard shut down for the day, the time when most of the workers left for the day. He stood beside Tom's truck.

"How's Sara?" Brownlow asked as Tom approached.

Tom described Sara's condition and her constant pain.

"Judge Parnell called me this morning," the marshal said.

"Is that right?" Tom said. He had heard about the torched home as soon as he got to work, men standing around a burn barrel in the cool morning talking about it, the men trying to stay warm in the chilly air. They were all happy it went up in smoke, but no one claimed responsibility for the blaze.

"That's right. He called me," the marshal said.

"Well, was he asking you to go play some golf?" Tom laughed.

"I don't play no golf."

"Or was he trying to bribe you?"

"That's enough, Tom. You're usually a respectful man. If you don't respect me personally, at least respect the office."

"Why are you calling on me today?"

"The judge thinks you burned down Sloan's house, the old Parnell home place. That's what Sloan told his grandpa."

"Marshal, that's a real serious accusation. Not as serious as rape and attempted murder, though. But you don't appear too worried about that. Maybe I need to go get a corrupt judge to call you. That might prompt you a little more to hunt down the man that tried to kill my wife."

"Tom, you're playing with fire."

"Not literally."

"Literally."

"You got any evidence?"

"I've got plenty of motive against you."

"Motive my ass." Tom did his best to sound incredulous, and he shrugged his shoulders.

"You believe he was involved. And Sloan Parnell was scared to death of you after the fight y'all got into over at Beam's feed store, and now he's mortally fearful after his house burned. Judge Parnell says Sloan's damn near too scared to leave the place where he's staying. He won't hardly go to work. Judge says he's more or less up day and night at a camp on Lizard Bayou, and he's about as frightened as a schoolgirl in a lightning storm. He's drinking heavier than normal, stuck on a barstool at the Belt Buckle when he's not cowering at the camp."

Tom took note of where Sloan was convalescing. "Look, there was hardly a fight. He grabbed me, and I knocked the hell out of him a couple of times. I don't care whether the guy is scared or not. I didn't burn down his house. Last night I was at home looking after Sara. Sounds to me like he's either got a guilty conscience or he's delusional over his own wrongdoing, and I'm about tired of hearing his name come up in every conversation I have."

"Don't go anywhere near him. If you do, I'll have to come after you. I'm going to call on you again about the fire or maybe the state fire marshal will come see you."

"If you need me, you know where I work and where I live." Tom got into his truck and drove back home to Zion.

CHAPTER NINE

Tom felt especially uneasy after the marshal's visit, and he was determined to get to the bottom of his wife's attack. He wanted to seek out the truth. So he drove over to James Luke's place later that evening near dusk, having made a shift swap with Corrine who stayed at the house to watch Sara. He told Sara that he needed to go help James Luke move some hogs into a lot before it got too late. Tom never made her stay by herself, not yet. He never left without someone else being in the house. She could do things for herself despite the shoulder sling, but he did not want her left by herself or made to feel lonely. Plus there was a dangerous assailant still on the loose, still a free man, and Tom's primary suspect was Sloan Parnell.

James Luke met Tom in his front yard as he pulled up in his truck.

Tom got out of the truck and had an angry look on his face. "I'm about ready to go pay a visit to Sloan Parnell," Tom said.

James Luke raised a brow and sneered. "Now you're talking sense. The sumbitch has been the lead candidate from the start," he said. "What you got in mind?"

"I don't know just yet. I need to see if my daddy's watch is in the drunk's truck," Tom said.

"That'll tell you an awful lot, won't it?"

"It'll give me plenty of knowledge."

"If it's in there, you gonna tell the marshal about the watch? I'd say it wouldn't be too wise a thing to do."

"I don't think so. It won't do any good."

"No, it won't. Fitz-Blackwell and Sloan's family have bought the marshal lock stock and barrel. I wouldn't say jack shit to him. He can't be trusted."

"Let's drive down to Lizard Bayou."

"All right. Let's take care of it."

"He's drinking himself blind."

"We can take my truck."

"Okay."

They loaded into James Luke's Chevrolet pickup. Tom noticed the big pearl-handled U.S. Army Colt automatic lying on the seat in a leather flap holster. Neither man said anything about the pistol as James Luke turned the truck onto Lower Louth Road.

There were a dozen cars and trucks in the barroom parking lot. It was dark out. The air was hazy, almost like a dead winter fog, a creepy damp cold. One naked light bulb shone beside the front door of the long clapboard building. The walls were white siding covered with ancient mildew, gray-black with funk. The bar was close to the bayou, and the air carried the dank smell of muddy water.

On the right side of the barroom parking area sat Sloan Parnell's red and white International Scout, a four-wheel drive truck that resembled a Jeep.

"Pull in beside the Scout," Tom said.

James Luke stopped beside it.

"Leave the engine idling. Holler at me if somebody comes this way," Tom said.

"You don't reckon the truck's locked?" James Luke asked.

"We'll see."

The sounds of a jukebox wafted through the thin pine barroom walls. Tom grabbed the flashlight from the truck seat. He left James Luke's pickup door ajar despite the cool air, and he opened the Scout door quietly. He shined the flashlight under the driver's seat, bent down and saw an empty King Edward cigar box without a lid and a half pint of Old Crow. He pulled them out and placed them on the seat, and then he shined the light underneath the passenger side, squinting to see, his cheek pressed against the floorboard. He saw a cotton bag, similar to a flour sack. He reached in and got it. It was chunky feeling and hard. He opened the sack and saw his father's watch, as well as a nickel-plated derringer with two barrels, which he immediately cracked open. It was loaded with a pair of .22 rounds.

Tom gritted his teeth. At that moment he was flushed with enough rage to go inside the bar and kill Sloan with his fists—beat him where he sat on a barstool drinking himself stupid. Tom rubbed his left hand across his jaw and down his neck over his Adam's apple. He stood up thinking. Then he leaned back inside the Scout cab and stuck the cigar box and whiskey back underneath the seat. He carried the cotton sack in his left hand, and shut the Scout door and got back into the truck with James Luke. He dropped the flashlight and sack on the seat. Right then he decided not to hang onto the little pistol, but to throw it out later for safety's sake.

"You find it, man?" James Luke asked.

Tom held up the bag like a prize.

"You want to go get him?" James Luke had his hand on the column shift.

"Yeah, I do but not yet. Let's get out of here before I change my mind and kill him," Tom said, his anger welling. But then he took the pocket watch from the sack. He rubbed the gold cover with his thumb, wondering why Sloan would rape his wife, take the watch, and now sit on a barstool thinking he had gotten away with all of it.

James Luke pulled the transmission out of neutral and put it into reverse. His left foot held down the clutch. "We ought to go confront his sorry ass now," James Luke said. "You know full well he stole the watch out from your house when he tried to kill Sara. Just walk into that bar and shoot him down. Provoke him and end it." He hit his hands on the steering wheel to emphasize the point.

They sat a while in the truck cab, talking, debating how to address it all.

"I think I need a drink. I'm a little dry," James Luke said.

"Me, too. Let's go see if he's in there," Tom said. He was a teeto-taler, never drinking a drop, and he didn't even know where the words came from.

James Luke smiled. "Good. Now you're talking." He turned off the Chevy engine.

Tom knew he'd spoken out of moral weakness. They soured the taste in his mouth as he walked toward the barroom doors. He yielded to anger and hate. When James Luke opened the sagging door, the stench of stale beer, smoke, and rank urine knocked Tom in the face. The bar was not much brighter than the parking lot, as opaque as a snake hole at midnight.

There were a half-dozen people sitting at the bar, another two played at the pool table. A patron stood at the jukebox pushing in nickels. A tune by Wynn Stewart, "Another Day, Another Dollar," careened off the walls.

Sloan Parnell sat at the far end of the plywood bar talking to a woman, the only woman in the room. She wore an amber blouse barely covering the tops of her breasts.

James Luke motioned to Tom, and they took a table against a wall away from the dull glow that issued from naked light bulbs hanging from the ceiling.

The barkeep came over to the table where they sat. He was a one-eyed man named Huey Jenner from Traylor Branch. "What y'all drinking?" he asked.

"Beer. Two bottles of Jax," James Luke said.

The barkeep smiled. "Y'all come way out here to meet up with somebody?"

"Sort of," James Luke said. "You might say that." He lit a cigarette.

"Beer'll be right over," Jenner said.

"Thanks," Tom said.

For an hour they drank beer, speaking hardly a word between them. Tom hadn't drunk a swallow of alcohol since he was a teenager, and the beer created a light buzz in his head. They watched the bar where Sloan placed his hands all over the woman until she finally slapped him in the face. Huey Jenner told Sloan to go back home, that he was a sloppy drunk, and that he had long worn out his welcome. All three of them passed curses and insults: Sloan, the woman, and the one-eyed barkeep. The woman moved to a stool at the other end of the bar and sat down beside a different man. Sloan threatened the barkeep, said he'd climb over the bar and knock him in the head unless he learned to respect his betters.

The barkeep reached beneath the bar and pulled out a crudely fashioned stick made from a cypress knee as big around as a baseball bat at the grip and as thick as a stovepipe on the end. "I'll beat you to death with this lion tamer if you as much as sneeze in my direction," he said. Then he braced himself with it as if to hit Sloan like a batter on a baseball diamond. But Sloan laughed in his face. Then he turned and looked directly at James Luke for a moment, scowling. James Luke stared back long enough to put Tom on edge, despite the beers he'd consumed.

Sloan staggered toward the woman at the other end of the bar. The jukebox wailed the Hank Williams song, "Settin' the Woods on Fire."

About this time, a tall redheaded man came from near the jukebox and grabbed Sloan by the back of the collar. The big man had muscles like hills on his shoulders, mounds of flesh on his arms, and he seemed to squeeze the life out of Sloan with his meaty hands.

"Don't hurt him," the one-eyed barkeep called out, "he's the judge's grandbaby. He's just a big-mouthed sissy. He don't mean nothing by it. I can handle him all right."

But the big man continued to drag Sloan by the collar. Sloan hollered every step.

"What the hell is going on?" Tom asked.

"That's Red Tadlock, and he's going outside to give somebody a migraine. Let me go pay the tab and you follow Sloan," James Luke said.

The patrons were scrambling, folks moving in different directions, most heading toward the door.

Tom followed them out to the parking lot.

Men were swinging and staggering, fighting and hollering, beer bottles flying like falling stars. It was a fracas, and Tom did well to avoid being hit by a fist, a boot, or a bottle.

"I've damn near had enough of you," the big man yelled at Sloan as he threw his whole body into the Scout cab and shut the door, telling him not to ever come back to the barroom.

Then the big man turned back to the melee and began knocking out teeth, busting heads, blows that sounded like timber cracking.

Sloan cranked the engine, revving it to a loud scream. He shouted obscenities from the open window.

James Luke joined Tom in the parking lot after he handed the barkeep three dollar bills.

"Parnell's leaving," Tom said.

A pair of fighting men fell into Tadlock who began to beat both of them like schoolboys. At the same time, the Scout tires threw rocks and oyster shells across the parking lot, the tires squealing when they touched the blacktop road. James Luke and Tom made it to the pickup and followed Sloan into the roadway.

Tom reached for the cotton sack that was on the seat and took out Sloan's derringer. The pistol was about the size of his palm. After they were on the blacktop nearly a mile, Tom rolled down the truck window and threw the pistol into the roadside with enough force to send it across a fence and into a thicket.

"What the hell did you do that for?" James Luke asked.

"Piss on him and his little gun," Tom said, staring toward the red taillights of Sloan's International Scout up ahead of them.

"Man, you should have kept it as a souvenir or sold it for a few bucks."

"I don't need anything he has."

James Luke picked up the .45 automatic from the seat between them and then put it back down absently. "I guess he's headed to his old man's camp on the river," he said.

"I bet that's where he's going," Tom answered.

They trailed the Scout on Lizard Bayou Road. Sloan was flying high, barely making the curves, and James Luke gunned it behind him at sixty miles an hour, looking for the taillights to come into view during straight-aways. The blacktop turned to loose gravel after a while, but Sloan and his Scout kept pushing, speeding away, the distance between the Scout and James Luke's 1958 Chevrolet truck widening. They lost the taillights altogether in a sharp curve and were traveling into the low-lands near Lake Tickfaw.

The roadway came to a "T" some distance ahead at Joe Bageant Road. The night was dark and starless, a black finality in the air as sure as hell itself. As they approached the "T," a faded stop sign came into view. James Luke said, "Parnell's place is to the left."

Tom could not remember if the camp was to the east or to the west. But he said, "Then turn left."

James Luke came to a rolling stop to make the hard left turn.

Tom could see a flickering of red light straight ahead, out across the gravel road and into a palmetto-dotted cow pasture. "Hold on. I believe something's out yonder," Tom said, pointing. He could see a broken fence in the high beams of the truck. A creosote post was freshly sheared a couple of feet above the ground, the barbed wire missing. It was obvious.

"The sorry bastard's run off the road and into the field," James Luke said.

"Either him or somebody else, but odds are it's got to be him as fast as he was driving," Tom said.

James Luke pulled the truck over to the side of the road near the breached fence and stopped. He took his pistol from the seat and held it in his right hand. Tom carried the flashlight. The two men walked quickly down the wood line and into the field.

The Scout motor was no longer running, but the lights were still on. The front end of the vehicle had hit an oak tree twice as big around as a man's waist. The cab was crushed on the passenger side, and it was evident by the damage that the Scout had rolled over prior to stopping at the tree.

Tom aimed the flashlight into the cab. The window was rolled down, the door shut, but there was no driver. Sloan was missing.

"You think he ran off?" Tom asked.

James Luke peered into the empty cab. "No, I don't think so. I bet he got slung out."

Tom thought about his father's watch, and the clear truth of finding it in the truck. Now Sloan's blood guilt was irrefutable. Anger filled Tom's chest. He wanted to bring justice to the man who'd done such harm to his wife and family.

They called out to Sloan and began searching along the path that his truck had taken before it crashed under one of the hardwood trees that dotted the pasture. This was not a good pasture, just a thick area, partly forested, rangeland for scrub cattle, not Fitz-Blackwell property, but private land owned by some dirt farmer by the looks of it. As they walked, wild-eyed cows ran along in front of the wrecked Scout, staring into the headlights.

"I see him," Tom hollered.

James Luke was ten paces behind.

Sloan lay face down over the top of a bramble of briars and vines, his head lower than his torso, his face submerged in a snaky pile of saw briars, blackberry, and fallen limbs.

The two men stood gazing down a moment. Tom's flashlight traced the body. At a distant house a pen full of hounds barked.

"Let's get him out of there, see if he's alive," Tom said. The sight of Sloan's limp body quickened his spirit, and the hate emptied in a moment.

"Shit man, we were about to kill the no-good bastard," James Luke countered, the Colt hanging from his hand.

"We need to see if he's alive." Tom said.

James Luke grimaced. "No, we don't need to see nothing but that old road out yonder."

They argued for a minute. Then the two men fished Sloan's limp body out of the thicket. His face was mangled with deep cuts, and he was bloody. He was unconscious but seemed to be breathing a little. Tom thought he could feel the faintest pulse on his wrist as he gripped it, but he wasn't sure.

"Let's leave his ass be. He won't live no time, the shape he's in. We need to get the devil's hell out of here," James Luke said.

"I'd like to go, but I believe we need to see if he's going to make it," Tom said. He'd come out of his moral stupor. He wanted legitimate justice to be served. He wanted to check the arm for the dog bite, to get more evidence to show the law what he did to Sara.

They stood looking down at Sloan.

Tom said, "I want you to go to the nearest house and call an ambulance and the law for me. That's what I want you to do."

James Luke shook his head. "Damn it, Tom. What the hell are you thinking? Are you crazy? You're going to get us charged with something serious."

"I need to see to it that he is looked after by a doctor," Tom said. "I need to make sure he is prosecuted for trying to kill my wife if he lives. Anything less is a betrayal to Sara. I need to look for some wounds from Jubal's bite. I want to see it with my own eyes."

"Kill him. Or leave him to die on his own. Don't do anything less."

"No, I'll have no part of that. We need an ambulance. You get one or I will."

James Luke stared at Tom. "Then take the damned pistol," James Luke said, handing him the .45 automatic.

"Okay," Tom said, slipping the gun into his waistband, unsure why he took it.

James Luke turned and left for the roadway.

Tom kneeled beside Sloan and thought. After a couple of minutes, he remembered to look at Sloan's left arm for the dog bite. The female caller had said his left arm was injured from the big dog's jaws, so he unsnapped the left cuff at the sleeve. He held the flashlight under one armpit to free up his hands. He rolled the sleeve to the elbow. The arm was unscathed, not one sore or lesion of any kind on it. Nothing was there. He used his Barlow pocketknife to cut the sleeve all the way to the shoulder, and it was as clean as a new whistle.

Confused more now than before, Tom used the pocketknife to cut the right sleeve. He turned Sloan's arm around into the flashlight beam. There was plenty of blood. He cut the sleeve farther up to the shoulder and saw the compound fracture. A sharp bone stuck through his lower right deltoid that almost made Tom retch, but he kept studying the arm. He found nothing there attributable to Jubal's thick jaws. Not a single fang mark left by the dog.

Tom took off his own jacket and covered the man's body. With his handkerchief, he wiped some accumulated blood from the sliced face and neck. It was cold out, and now Tom felt an additional chill. He did not know what to think. It occurred to him to pray, but he did not know what for. His wife's healing? A prayer for this dead man before him? Prayer for his own redemption? Tom became disoriented, and for a moment incapable of doing anything at all. He felt stunned and stared at the man lying prone before him. He wondered how he came to kneel in this place and thought James Luke was one of the reasons.

He stuck his face into his hands until James Luke and the deputy sheriff arrived. Soon after, the marshal and a state trooper drove up, and then some medics from Pickleyville arrived to carry Sloan to the Ninth Ward Hospital.

As the ambulance was about to leave, P.T. Parnell, Sloan's father, pulled into the cow pasture in his blue Cadillac. He was drunk, so hammered that he fell into an armadillo hole and broke his hip and had to be driven to the same hospital as his dying son.

"We just saw the taillights in the woods," James Luke said to the officers. "The fence was busted and down. I reckon he had drunk too much hard liquor. He smelled like a whiskey barrel."

Tom said nothing at all, shivering in his thin shirt, nodding. Agreeing to everything as a witness. His denim jacket was covered in blood and completely ruined.

Sloan Parnell was pronounced dead at the little hospital in Pickleyville ten minutes after his arrival. His neck was broken, the coroner's autopsy would say once it was complete. He was dead from a traffic accident, less than a mile away from his father's camp on Lizard Bayou.

CHAPTER TEN

On the day of the Parnell funeral, Marshal Brownlow drove to the Hardin home. Jubal barked, tugging on his chain, acting as if he would take the tire off the patrol car if he could get anywhere near it. Wesley called to his father who was nailing some loose boards onto a holding pen that he was building for hogs, a temporary place to keep them until he took the last one to the auction.

Brownlow met Tom at the pigpen gate. He said, "I don't know what part you played in the wreck, you and old Cate, but I figure Sloan had it coming. I don't want to follow up on any of it. I'd like to leave it be. I understand Red Tadlock put him in his truck, and he was shitfaced intoxicated when he died. That's what Tadlock told me," the marshal said.

"We had no role in the wreck whatsoever. We just found him." Tom stood with a claw hammer in his hand and a nail apron fastened to his trim waist.

"You were out yonder chasing him. That much is clear."

"I wouldn't exactly say that."

"Look, I just don't want no more wars between you and Fitz-Blackwell. No more fighting between nobody and the timber companies in the Ninth Ward. I don't give a damn what happens in the Sixth or the Eighth Ward or anywhere else. The old ways of free-ranging and traipsing all over timber company land without permission is over. The open range hogs and cattle is over for good in Baxter Parish, and it ain't coming back in your lifetime or mine. Being able to run stock on timber company land is done and finished. It's all gone now. This here is the New South, and the old way of doing things is no more. The man that attacked your wife is dead and buried as far as I'm concerned. The investigation is closed shut. A woman called my office the other day and said Sloan did it and some shit about your daddy's watch that was stole and whatnot, but the watch wasn't in the cab of the truck like she said it ought to be. I checked on it myself. I don't understand it all, mind you. But all of the investigations are over with, even Sara's attack. I spoke to the High Sheriff, and we're done looking into it. As a matter of fact, I called Judge Parnell, and he said that Sloan's heavy drinking was what killed him dead. He was surely surprised that he ain't already died ten years ago from it."

Tom nodded.

"I'm going to trust things are back to normal," Brownlow said.

"Whatever you say, Marshal. Far as I'm concerned, I'm at peace with all men."

"Great to know it. Another thing. Some of us are getting together a hunting lease with Fitz-Blackwell, and I wanted to invite you to join as a charter member—on account of what you've gone through and your place in this community. The lease'll cover all of their land in the south end of the parish. You'll be able to hunt anytime you want, just no running stock. I sure would like you to join. It won't cost more than fifty bucks a year for charter members. You and Wesley can join up together as a family for fifty bucks."

Tom stared at the lawman and was quiet. There was an uncomfortable pause. Then he said, "No, I believe I'd just as soon pass."

"Think on it a while, will you?"

CHAPTER ELEVEN

Sara's body healed in due course, and the family made adjustments to confront their sorrow. They tried to love each other more, tried to make something good come from the tragedy.

Tom caught the last of the hogs and cattle from the woods and sold them at the auction, keeping none back for home use. As the hospital bills started rolling in, he sold all of them. Every last hog. The check was a mere pittance, but he needed every nickel of it.

After dispersing the cows and hogs, he sold his horse Sam, too, as well as his Simco roping saddle. Sara's hospital bill was still formidable, but he worked out a payment plan, largely done through his own integrity and willingness to confront the debt. He visited the chief of the hospital, Dr. Beau Oxford, face-to-face, and they set up a monthly schedule of payments.

But what tore at Tom day and night was how close he had come to killing an innocent man. He couldn't understand how Sloan was not the man who'd assaulted his wife, but the lack of a dog bite told the tale. The crazy phone call from the woman about the pocket watch and the wound made him even more confused and confounded. He didn't know what to make of it. It vexed him like a sore tooth that wouldn't stop worrying his mouth. If not Sloan Parnell, then who else did it? Who or what did he have to defend against? Who might come again to attack Sara and his family? It was as if a spirit had come into their lives and left to return in the future.

One morning he went out to feed Jubal and the other dogs some scraps from the kitchen, leftover bread and bones soaked in bacon grease. He stood in front of Jubal and rubbed his head and ears, the dog smiling a wide bulldog smile, more interested in the affection of his master than the pan of food. Tom spoke to him like a friend. "Jubal, who did it? What happened that day?"

The dog answered with the same silence that he got from Sara, the same silence from the marshal, and the same silence coming from the dangerous act of trying to get the truth out of Sloan Parnell. Tom did not know who was out there lurking and stalking. No answer came, nothing but silence with its desperate finality.

The whole landscape seemed to change. Sometimes Tom could hear saws and machinery working on the new interstate that was being built a few miles away from Zion, a section of the Eisenhower National Highway System. Day by day the open range conflict began to fade into the distant past. Truth be told, there were few young pines left to burn, and folks simply gave up the war in despair of challenging the new stock law or stopping the killing of the oaks. Fitz-Blackwell won, and the people lost.

One evening during a late December chill, Tom sat at the kitchen table with his head in his palms. The gas heater burned in the corner of the room, a blue flame sharp and warm. He had never been a man given to melancholy, but there were times after Sloan's death when he was overcome with disorientation and guilt, as if he faced a solid wall with no way to go around it or scale it. He wondered if Sloan had realized that he was being followed, and if he'd responded by burying his foot down on the accelerator. Tom remembered how Sloan looked over at James Luke before he left the bar, and Tom saw his face when he acknowledged James Luke's presence. It was the look of petrifaction and instantaneous acknowledgement of his own mortality. Perhaps their presence in the bar might be reason enough for him to believe he was being followed, even if he never saw them trailing on the roadway.

"Tommy," Sara said, "it's over." He looked up at his wife who stood in the doorway between the kitchen and the living room. Her shoulder was out of the sling, and a dental bridge was made to cover her missing teeth. Her hair had been a deep auburn, but it was becoming gray, turning silver, a physical reminder of the attack.

"What's over?" he asked.

"My rape and Sloan Parnell's death, and if you keep dwelling on it all, you'll pine away and leave this world dying an early and needless death. You're no good to me and Wesley like this."

Tom was dazed. Neither of them had ever said the word "rape" before in the company of the other, never once. His head shook in self-recrimination and bewilderment.

She stepped closer. "It happened to me, not you, and I've got to go on with life and so do you."

He stood and embraced Sara, knowing that this hell needed to be put away, the brokenness mended. For the first time, he understood that he needed to bury the past. Right then he resolved to leave behind the business of free range livestock and the old grudges. He resolved to leave behind Sloan Parnell's death or to try his best to let go of the violation against his wife and home.

After a minute passed, he let her go. He stared at her face and hair, and he promised her that he'd leave it all behind and quit grieving over the past.

She stepped back. "I'll say one more thing. If I can get well enough in my mind, I'm going to get a job in town. I'm tired of sitting in this damned house day after day, year after year. I won't sit here the rest of my life."

"Okay," he said.

They embraced again, kissed, and soon went to bed and to sleep.

The following Sunday, Tom, Sara, and Wesley returned to Little Zion Methodist Church after almost two months away. They sat in their regular pew. Tom could see the marshal where he sat next to his wife and daughter several pews ahead of them to the left, across the center aisle of the sanctuary. It was the Brownlow family's turn to light the

Advent candles. Donald, Mary Anne, and their daughter Priscilla gave a short Bible reading, and they played their part in the service, lighting the candles to mark the season.

The piano played Christmas carols and hymns, and the song leader stood waving his arms to the music. They sang "Hark the Herald Angels Sing," "Away in a Manger," "Silent Night," "The First Noel," and "Joy to the World."

After the congregation finished the hymn singing, they listened to a sermon by Reverend Poole as he preached of God's eternal faithfulness, his fidelity and sacrifice, and our need to be holy and faithful in return, all of it bound together in a bloodstained tapestry of mercy, grace, and love. He said none of it made sense without God's gift to the world through the birth of a little baby laid in a Bethlehem manger.

It was the Sunday before Christmas, 1964.

CHAPTER TWELVE

It surprised Tom how he prospered after removing the hogs and cattle from the woods. The world was changing, and he changed along with it. For seven years he had worked at the local junior college as a journeyman carpenter, and served for the past three years as the foreman of the shop. Sara worked across campus at the library, having begun her job in August 1965, several years before he took the position at the college. Tom worked at the Ponderosa, a maintenance complex based in and around a giant Quonset hut that had been salvaged from World War II surplus. The shop was named after the home of Ben Cartwright's ranch on Bonanza. As a civil servant, Tom gave an honest day's work for a day's pay. As a carpenter, he worked at the college but was never really a part of the town and gown. More than once he discussed with his wife the possibility of completing his associate's degree, but he hated to submit himself to the arrogant professors, who came in two varieties: those who held maintenance workers in contempt and those who did not even recognize their existence as human beings. He was willing to work for them, but not study under them.

Monday, May 20, 1974, was Tom's fiftieth birthday. Sara had made him a German chocolate cake and brought it over to the shop for lunch to share it with the men who worked there. Harvey Shaffer, a carpenter, brought fresh fillet catfish and fried them on a propane cooker outside the building, the fish turning golden brown in the big black skillet. Hours later, Tom was still full from the hearty meal.

Dub Freeman, a student worker, helped Tom steady a sheet of plywood. They stood at the table saw in the Quonset hut. It was hot inside the metal building, even with two five-foot tall fans blowing at each end of the shop. In front of them lay the sheet of plywood he was trying to cut, ripping it down the middle with a ten-inch table saw blade. Tom flipped the switch to the electric motor on the saw. The blade whirled, and it screamed when it entered the wood, the sound stinging his ears. He was careful to make the cut smooth, keeping the plywood as steady and as tight as he could on the big table. He was aware that a careless move could cost him a finger or worse.

After it was split down the middle, he placed one of the pieces on the back of a frame he'd built for a professor's bookshelf. He was fashioning this solid, functional shelf for a faculty member's office in Rayburn Hall. He wished he had the budget to buy oak or perhaps birch, which stained nicely, instead of this god-awful pine, but he did the best he could with the materials the college could afford.

Because he was such a meticulously detailed man, he served as the lead cabinetmaker at the shop, and during his off-duty time, he was a handyman and general carpenter for the junior college faculty and staff in their private residences. Not long after taking the position at the college, he converted his old horse and cow barn into a shop. This was where he now worked on projects at night and on weekends. He no longer had any cattle, hogs, horses, or chickens on the place, and he didn't even own a dog. Jubal had died of old age five years earlier, and Tom had long ago forsaken the hunting and farming he used to do until the mid-1960s. From time to time, he'd plant a garden, but he hadn't planted anything in several seasons.

Wesley, who was now twenty, worked alongside his father on projects at home, and he was essential to keeping their little business going. Soon to graduate from the junior college himself, he studied nearly free on his father and mother's staff tuition exemption, which covered everything but his textbook rental and lab fees each semester. Now he was planning to study architecture at the University of Southwestern Louisiana in Lafayette. It was his dream to become a professional architect, a designer and builder of homes and businesses, schools and churches. The university was a hundred miles away, and going to the university would mean he could no longer help with his father's projects. Tom said he planned to cut back on his outside work as a result, knowing he couldn't do any large jobs without Wesley's help.

At closing time, the carpentry crew left the Quonset hut and punched the time clock with paper cards. Tom turned off the lights and pulled down the big garage doors and locked up the shop. He was at the tail end of the line of men leaving the Ponderosa, the time clock made a loud cha-punt sound as he placed the card into the slot for the stamp. It read 16:34 in faded blue ink. He dropped the card into a slot on the steel cardholder at the end of a long hallway in the main administrative building near North Oak Street.

"Have a good weekend and happy birthday, Tom," Shaffer said.

Tom thanked him for the catfish meal, and they walked to their trucks. Dust billowed as the vehicles left the parking lot in a line entering the street.

He was not going directly home but to the Claiborne House in downtown Pickleyville. It was Dr. Howell Claiborne's family residence. Tom and Wesley were to meet with him about a project, designing and building a home study. He knew that Dr. Claiborne had left the junior college administration under a dark cloud. Most everyone at the college had heard about his affair with Charity LeBlanc during his wife Eliza's prolonged illness.

Tom also remembered Charity from the 1960s. She ran with men in town, business men and the local Sicilian mafia, even dated Sloan Parnell. Tom guessed that she was in her early thirties now, and he'd seen her on campus twice in months past.

The rumor mill said that the president had retired because of three consecutive scandals. First, he started the indiscretions with Charity and moved her into his old family home downtown while his wife of more than forty years was in the hospital for a surgery. Second, a short time after his wife died of a subsequent stroke, he married Charity in Nevada, the dirt hardly settled on his first wife's grave. And third, Charity brought him to shame by carousing with faculty men as a newlywed, the worst scandal occurring not a month after their Las Vegas wedding and extended honeymoon in Japan.

The president's new wife got caught by campus security having sexual relations with an English professor in his campus office. A night security guard was making his rounds checking locked doors for the evening when he happened upon them. Part of the tale that made the story more scandalous was that the male college faculty member in question was widely believed to be a homosexual, and this added plenty of satire to the whole fiasco. Dr. Claiborne was sixty-six years old and healthy, not ready to retire, but he was forced to resign by the college trustees in order to avoid a very public termination hearing based on Charity's antics.

The woman had moved up in the world as the new wife of the "retired" president of Baxter State Junior College. Dr. Claiborne was a man more than thirty years her senior and the son of a United States Congressman from the early part of the century. The house they lived in after being kicked out of the campus mansion was a two and a half story place in Pickleyville, the stately Claiborne family home that was once owned by the demagogic politician.

Dr. Claiborne and his first wife had been prominent members of the Federated Presbyterian Church a block away from the old Claiborne House, and Charity joined the church soon after their marriage. Dr. Claiborne was an elder and a member of the church session, a ruling board for the congregation, and his first wife had played the organ for services and was a conservatory-trained musician.

Tom was uneasy, even though he liked the old man well enough and agreed to come and talk to him about the job when he'd called the Ponderosa. Dr. Claiborne hired both Tom and Sara years ago, and he had a measure of loyalty to the man for that reason alone.

Wesley was going to meet his father at the old Claiborne House. He was nearly finished with his associate's degree with a double major in art and drafting. He had only one class to finish, a shop-based independent study project for graduating students during the summer session. Wesley's degree requirements would be completed by the first week of August, though he wouldn't be able to walk at commencement until December. The young man was adept at drafting, and he was more than able to work as a journeyman carpenter as well, especially as a cabinetmaker and finish carpenter. At the meeting with Dr. Claiborne, they needed to find out what the old man had in mind, to start a discussion of what the project would entail in order to offer an accurate bid on materials and labor. Wesley's primary role was to render a model for the project with specifications, and his father would provide the bid and on-site supervision. They'd work together on the project at their little home-based shop in Zion.

As Tom drove to the Heller-Reid neighborhood where Dr. Claiborne lived, he passed houses on city streets under a canopy of hardwood trees, the foliage green and rich. He thought about his son and the promise of additional schooling in Lafayette. An architecture degree would make him a white collar worker for the rest of his life. Regardless of what he might learn at USL, Tom knew that Wesley had the practical expertise necessary in carpentry and the building trades to be successful, and that this would give him an edge over students with only book-learning. Tom, on the other hand, didn't have Wesley's artistic and drafting skills, a disadvantage that the boy helped him overcome in their work together. He might have to hire a part-time helper after Wesley left for college, though his son promised to work on weekends and during school breaks. But Tom realized that Lafayette over in Acadiana would be a whole new experience, something different from living at home and going to the nearby junior college. He'd miss his son and companion in the carpentry business, though he wished him great success.

When Tom stopped his truck in front of the big Claiborne House, he saw Wesley's two-door Ford Maverick coming toward him on the street. Wesley pulled in front of him toward the curb and they parked nose to nose.

Tom was pleased that Wesley had arrived on time. Tom had always found the president a nervous fellow who didn't quite know what to do with himself, and he didn't want to make the old man wait and have to spend much idle time chatting. He hoped Dr. Claiborne's new wife wouldn't be around. They got out of their vehicles and met on the sidewalk.

"Did you bring your sketch pad?" Tom asked. He gestured to Wesley's big portfolio under his arm on a strap over his shoulder. Inside he carried pencils, as well as plenty of examples of their work with some drawings.

"Yes, sir. It helps to keep track of what the paying customer wants," Wesley said, sounding like a student in the Commerce Department at the junior college. He wore thick sideburns like little brown lamb chops, but his hair barely touched the collar of his shirt. He was in many ways the physical equal to his father. However, he stood three inches taller, and was just as wiry and strong, quick and fast as Tom. Wesley ran cross country in high school and could have done the same at the junior college had he wanted to try out. Wesley's bell bottom jeans were worn but not ratty, and they covered his leather shoes. His belt was tight around his waist, and his clothes fit his frame. He was meticulously clean, conservative for the times.

The pair eased up the brick walkway toward the house, a large white colonial with lap siding. Gas lamps lit the sides of the front door to cause a dull illuminated glow around the red entryway.

Tom knocked on the door, three steady wraps with his knuckles. He waited a moment. Before he could tap on the door again, it opened wide. There stood Charity LeBlanc Claiborne smiling. She wore a linen gown that showed her pointed breasts, the split up the thigh revealing her shapely leg.

"Welcome gentlemen," she said.

"We're here to see your husband," Tom said. He was trying his best to hide his antipathy toward her. He did not trust this woman and did not like entertaining her presence.

"I'll be handling this project, Tommy. Dr. Claiborne is at a history conference in Nashville at Vanderbilt, and then he's coming home for the pre-Memorial Day picnic at Baxter State, and directly afterward he's going to spend time doing research at the Library of Congress in Washington for most of the summer. He's doing some research for a book he's writing. As a matter of fact, he wanted me to go with him, but I have so many important projects here in town that I needed to stay," she said.

They stood awkwardly at the door. Wesley looked at his father.

In an instant, Tom made a decision—one that he realized he might regret later. "Ma'am, I was supposed to see Dr. Claiborne today, and I planned to work with him on the project at his request. But if he is out until the picnic, then I suppose it'll be a few days before we can get back together on it. Please let him know I came here today, and I'll come back at his leisure," Tom said, watching her for a reaction.

Charity's mouth screwed as tight as a prune all of a sudden. "Well, Tommy, I suppose we'll need to find us a new carpenter, won't we? Damn you." She stepped back and slammed the door in their faces, the heavy wooden door closing so fast and hard that the frame rattled and the gas luminaries flickered.

"Well, I guess it's time to go home," Tom said, resigned. He turned toward the brick walkway and the automobiles.

"Pops, don't you think that was a little harsh?" Wesley said.

"Harsh? I don't think I was rude. I said 'ma'am' and never raised my voice. I tried to tell her I'd come back as politely as I could."

"That was easily a thousand-dollar project, and I need the money for the year at school."

"We can handle the tuition money."

They walked back to their vehicles parked at the curb.

"Dang it, Pops, what's wrong with this job?"

"That woman is a blight on the soul of this town, and I don't want anything to do with her. Not if I can help it, and I suspect that I can help it."

"That's it, then?"

"As far as I'm concerned, it is."

CHAPTER THIRTEEN

T he next day was Tuesday, and Marshal Donald Brownlow sat in his office chain-smoking, drumming his thumb on the edge of his ink blotter, his oak desk cluttered with duties that he was putting off. He'd marked the days in red ink on the calendar. He picked up his cigarette from the ashtray and took two quick drags, and then crushed it. The brown ashtray was shaped like a bloodhound's head with long ears. It was a gift from his wife, something she bought for him on vacation in Gatlinburg, Tennessee, a few years earlier. He was stalling, brooding, thinking, allowing a woman he did not want to see to cool her heels in the front office with his secretary. It was ten minutes after twelve, and he had failed to get lunch. The woman had been in the building for at least fifteen minutes.

He buzzed his secretary on the intercom. "Mrs. Lott, please send her on in," he said.

"Yes, Marshal," she said over the speaker.

He lit a new cigarette with his Zippo and did not stand when the woman entered the room. He motioned for her to sit. Brownlow was keenly aware of her reputation. As a result, he was guarded, as if a hungry weasel had just entered the chicken yard and he was a plump hen.

"Glad you could find time to see me as busy as you must be today. I had a real urgent need to speak with you this afternoon," Charity Claiborne said.

"Shame to hear about your father. I offer my deepest condolences," the marshal said. He noticed her blouse was unbuttoned at least two slots lower than what was respectable. She was the daughter of the infamous philandering Church of God preacher, Brother Penrose

LeBlanc, a full gospel minister who was, by all accounts, an unredeemed rascal, a parson well known to prey on women in his congregation. Local folks speculated that he'd been molesting Charity and her sister along with other women in his church for decades. Penrose had died earlier in the year. The marshal hadn't gone to the funeral, though he did read the obituary in the Pickleyville *Star-Register*.

"He died peacefully in his bed. Sugar diabetes pursued him almost from the gates of hell," she said. "But praise God, because of his death, I have been saved and rebaptized. The Apostle Thad Hussert at the Flaming Sword Church laid hands on me, and I now have the Holy Ghost for the first time in my life. Like Daddy always said, unless a grain of wheat falls to the ground, it can't flower and grow." She stared at the marshal.

"Well," he said, unsure how to comment on her new-found faith. Brownlow had been diagnosed with diabetes recently. He was taking shots in the stomach, and his eyes were ailing from high blood sugar. Right then he was having trouble focusing. The edges around Charity's face seemed fuzzy.

"My Lord, it's real smoky in this place," she said.

The marshal crushed his newly lit Winston cigarette in the ashtray. "Ma'am, why are you here today?" He didn't mean to be abrupt, but he took note of his own sternness of voice. "As you said yourself, I'm busy and need to get back to my work."

"Marshal Brownlow, I'm here because I have a confession to make. Something that has been gnawing at me for almost ten years. When I was saved, the Apostle Hussert said to get everything right before man, so my sins can be right before the Lord, and I'm here with you for that very reason."

He felt a shot of pain in his back, a sharp jab. His lower back was a source of chronic antagonism, almost like a bad deed done in the past now returning to haunt him, and it was getting worse lately. He felt assaulted from all fronts: from the diabetes, herniated disks in his back, and high blood pressure. He felt flushed in his face. He waited for her to speak again.

"Ten years ago, I made some telephone calls that I believe might have led to a person's death. It was Sloan Parnell, Judge Parnell's grandson. We used to run together, date a little. We had a very jealous relationship, him and me. Uh, marshal, you mind if I smoke?"

"I thought it bothered you."

"It does, but I really need a cigarette."

He offered her his pack, but she waved him off. She retrieved a pack of Kool Filter King cigarettes from her purse along with a lighter. She lit a cigarette and exhaled out of the side of her mouth.

"Please go on," the marshal said. "Like I said, I have some business to attend to." He leaned forward and put his hands on the desk, attempting to ease his back pain.

"I called you in November or December of 1964. It was about Sloan Parnell and Sara Hardin's attack. I said that Sloan was involved, but he wasn't alone. Not at all. Like I said, we used to run together. Do some drugs and drink liquor. Nothing serious, just a little whiskey and pills. I came to find out that Sloan was seeing Sara Hardin on the sly, and she was seeing other men besides her jackass of an old man, Tommy. I was only seeing one man, just Sloan. But she was seeing Sloan and James Luke Cate, too. Sloan got drunk one night and told me he was two-timing me with Sara Hardin. I got real pissed, and it kind of got out of hand. I called James Luke Cate at work and told him what was happening, and before long James Luke Cate tried to kill Sara and beat her almost to death. I called Tom and said Sloan did it to his wife, just to set a little trouble in motion. I always liked to see the pot stirred, and I know the Lord forgave me for it when I got born again. The last time I saw Sloan, he told me he believed Tom burned down his house and all the young pine trees he had planted out there. He was mortally afraid, scared to death. He told me he believed he was a marked man and that Tom Hardin was trying to kill him," she paused a moment and took a deep drag from the menthol.

She exhaled smoke and continued her story. "Anyway, I believe Tom and James Luke killed Sloan after I called. I'd wager James Luke baited Tom into going after Sloan and maybe they faked it all like it was a bad accident. I know this sounds kind of strange, but it's how it happened. All because I made some anonymous phone calls. I feel so bad about it now." She took another pull and blew a slim line of smoke above her forehead.

"Ma'am, you're a born liar," the marshal said, remembering the details of the rape, and Parnell's death, even the anonymous phone call. "You're just a bold-faced liar. The case is closed shut. And if you think I believe this horseshit about some kind of love triangle with Sara Hardin and Jim Cate, you're beyond damn crazy, pardon my French. Tom Hardin a murderer? You're plumb goofy and ought to go see a head doctor."

The woman's face turned crimson. She crushed her cigarette into the ashtray. The butt had a lipstick mark as red as her face. She left it circling in a whiff of smoke in the marshal's ashtray. "You'll do well to listen to me, if you know your place," she said.

"I won't listen to another damn word of it." The marshal stood from his desk, stiff in his back and legs, his knees hurting from perennial gout. He loomed over Charity with an intense anger that overshadowed her. "This is the devil's own nonsense, Mrs. Claiborne. I don't have no more time to throw away on your craziness. But have a nice afternoon." He walked to the door without speaking and gestured with his hand for her to leave.

She gathered her purse from the floor beside her chair and stood abruptly, staring the marshal in the face. She was tall and fine-looking, somewhat intimidating and intense. "If you don't bring these men to justice, then I'll go visit Judge Parnell myself. You do recall his family estate burned? His grandson was killed. Me and the judge have a long friendship going way back. Do you hear me, lard ass? Don't dare underestimate me. I'll help clean your clock come election time. We'll get somebody else elected in your place," she said, a look of scorn on her face.

"Lady, to start with, there's nothing to investigate here. And if there was, you'd be the first one I'd need to interrogate and throw into a jail cell. That and I'm planning to retire from this office next year, so I don't give a dog's damn about the judge and his old money. I don't have to deal with rich politicians or squirrelly women like you anymore. So please don't let the front door hit you in the rear end, Mrs. Claiborne. But do try to have a real nice day," he said.

The woman shook her head in anger and hurried past the secretary and toward the door, her heels clicking on the terrazzo floor as she walked.

"Marshal," Rita Lott said as Charity left the building, "I don't believe she left here happy."

Brownlow looked at his secretary from his office door. He seemed quizzical, one side of his mouth almost grinning. "No ma'am, I don't reckon she was happy at all."

The rest of the afternoon, Brownlow and Mrs. Lott looked through the Ninth Ward Marshal's Office general file and junk room, hunting for anything on Sara Hardin and Sloan Parnell. It was late May, humid beyond words and scorching hot. The file room and storage, mildewing in the back of the marshal's headquarters, had no air conditioner. After a half an hour of moving boxes of Christmas decorations, a tinfoil Christmas tree, as well as various ephemera, they found the box of files from 1964. The two of them were perspiring. The marshal sweated profusely, almost unnaturally. He looked like a Hereford bull in the summer sun. His back tortured him to such a degree that he felt faint.

"Marshal Brownlow," Mrs. Lott said, "you're lucky I don't cuss." She wiped her forehead with a napkin, a line of sweat and dirt at her hairline.

"Your dedication is always appreciated," he told her. He looked at her blue blouse, which was dusty, almost gray with grime. "Put a dollar or two extra in your check to dry clean your clothes."

"I will," she said, not offering the slightest thank-you.

The marshal stayed after closing time. At five o'clock Mrs. Lott left for the day. His old notes were written with a black fountain pen, and they jogged his memory well enough. But despite this reunion with the past, there were no real leads in the file. Nothing new. Police work was less advanced in 1964, he reasoned. The coroner's report on Sloan Parnell said his neck was broken at the third cervical vertebra. No other trauma was visible except for what appeared to be a laceration on his face from tree limbs in the cow pasture, and a compound fracture on his upper arm, the bone struck through the skin. No other noticeable damages were noted.

No matter how hard he tried, he did not understand this woman, Charity LeBlanc Claiborne. Why dredge this up? Why now?

In his many years in office, even as a deputy marshal before being elected the marshal himself, he had known that guilt could work on someone's insides. Under the pressure, people might make guilt-induced confessions. However, he didn't see in Charity's eyes an inclination toward guilt. Sins of the flesh were a matter of course for her, but a visit to a lawman to recall tales was not the typical outgrowth of her nature, especially with the implication that other people had done the crimes, and she was the innocent trigger to all of the death and destruction. This woman seemed like a special case all to herself, and her set of motives were all her own.

Before him were the old files, mere scraps. But he needed to make something of them, so he continued studying them like a worn copy of the Bible. It occurred to him that his whole career was made up of such scraps, and with these scraps he fashioned a life's work. From his experience as a peace officer, few people ever gave the whole truth and nothing but the truth—at least if they were somehow connected to a breach of the law. Even honest people offered only partial truth at such times. Many folks lied to him out of general principle even when they had no dog in the fight. He came to realize that obstruction of justice was routine, a way of doing business in Baxter Parish and elsewhere. There was an old principle that he learned early in his work: If folks are talking to the police, they're guilty of lying until proven innocent. Nine times out of ten, the principle was gospel true, he thought. It was a shame, but that was all he had to work with. He had to make sense of things and do his job despite the common deception.

The marshal placed the files in his top left desk drawer, the spot where he kept a pint bottle of gin to knock the edge off the occasional stress of his work, diabetes be damned. He locked the building and left into the late evening sun, traveling toward his home a mile away. But he changed his mind and turned around near the driveway and headed toward the interstate to leave the south end of the parish. He drove north to Pickleyville, a Winston cigarette dangling from his fingers, his hand resting on the patrol car door, the smoke trailing out of the cracked window.

Then he turned off I-55 and headed east on Highway 190 toward Pickleyville. He drove to the new shopping center where Radio Shack sat in one corner of the new Town and Gown Shopping Plaza. He parked in the asphalt lot. The marshal felt tired from digging in the storage room files, from heaving box after box of cases long closed. When he got out of the patrol car, he dropped a spent cigarette on the ground and smeared it flat with a boot heel.

Across the lot he saw a blue pickup truck squeal its tires like it was on a racetrack, careening onto 190. He reached for the car door as if to pursue the truck, but he immediately relented, reminding himself that this was not his jurisdiction. The ward he was duly elected to serve was several miles to the south.

Brownlow walked into the store to buy a cassette tape recorder. The electronics clerk said a particular machine was a good one, the premium grade, a portable recorder. Normally, he would have sent his deputy,

Freddy Wentworth, or Mrs. Lott to buy the item, but today he decided to take care of it himself, and had come up with a strategy on his own for dealing with Charity Claiborne's little challenge, and he wanted to keep his plans as quiet as possible. He needed to get folks on tape immediately.

He paid for the tape recorder with petty cash, just under one hundred dollars. He thanked the cashier and walked out of the store with the box under his arm. He placed an unlit cigarette in his lips as he went to the patrol car.

But the hot parking lot seemed even warmer now than when he was working in the storage room fighting file boxes. The sun was lower. He knew it couldn't be any hotter. Yet it felt like the kind of heat that will trick the eye, as if the asphalt was molten at a distance, mirage-like, and sweat gathered in his hair and neck and around his collar all of a sudden. He noticed that his shirt at the armpits was soaked. He began to feel nauseated, his throat thick. A hard panic engulfed him. Air was difficult to take into his mouth. He wanted to vomit or fall to the ground. He began staggering and almost lost control of the cardboard box under his arm. He dropped the unlit cigarette from his mouth, which hit the asphalt. He lumbered a few more steps to the car and placed the box haltingly on the roof. He grasped the car's warm steel with both palms.

Brownlow tried to breathe. He released his hands from the roof and fished for the car keys in his pocket, opening the driver's side door, the backseat, and put the box inside. After he opened the front door and pulled himself inside the cab, he felt even more ill. He sat down hard in the seat and leaned out of the open door to the ground, vomiting violently, a projectile. The second volley of vomit caused vessels to burst in his right eye.

"I think this is a good day to pass on," he said out loud.

Instead of dying, he had the presence of mind to drive himself over to Dr. Dan Danly's office. The doctor was about to retire after a day seeing patients. He was locking the glass doors to his office when he saw the marshal turn into the lot in front of the building. The marshal looked half dead, and the physician checked him as he sat in the patrol car in the parking lot. He called for an ambulance with the marshal's police radio, knowing that the man was in the early stages of cardiac arrest.

Ten minutes later, a pair of medics placed Brownlow into the ambulance and put an oxygen mask on his face. They transported him to the Ninth Ward Hospital Emergency Room where he was treated by the doctor on staff, his world uprooted and sprung like a giant oak tree caught in a tornado, the entire landscape a dark pall.

CHAPTER FOURTEEN

James Luke Cate's hair was black except for some distinguished hi-lights of silver around the edges close to his ears. He lived with his third wife in Natchez, Mississippi, on South Pearl Street. The house, built in 1852, was called the Slocum Cottage. It was named after his wife's maternal ancestors. Natchez was a city on the east side of the Mississippi River, a notorious river town with a seedy reputation, a sordid past that never seemed to die.

He had been away from Baxter Parish for almost a decade, ever since he left his first wife Nelda in the spring of 1965. He fled the parish and had almost no contact with anyone from the area since his departure. At first, he lived in the capital city of Baton Rouge, where he worked for the state highway department headquarters. He moved in with a wealthy woman from Baton Rouge, or "the red stick" as it is translated into English from the French.

The woman was only one of the reasons for his departure from Nelda, and it didn't take long for him to marry again. His second wife caught him with another woman from Natchez, and she divorced him, too. But not before he could steal an ample amount of her money. He took the money with him to Natchez and his new job as a civilian manager with the Army Corps of Engineers, working on the levees on the Mississippi River floodplain. His ex-wife's assets left him a solid business stake, and his profitable holdings grew rapidly.

In Natchez, he continued his love affair with the old money divorcee, Heloise Tartt. They married following a torrid romance. Her money did nothing less than compound his power and influence. His background in the military and years with the Louisiana highway department, followed by the job in the Army Corps of Engineers in Baton

Rouge, not to mention his wife's father, a scion of Natchez and the South, played heavily into his rapid advancement in the Vicksburg District of the Army Corps. His father-in-law lived in a mansion overlooking the river and was a banker, the son and grandson of Natchez and Vicksburg bankers. The family was prominent even before the siege of Vicksburg in 1863, a time when townspeople ate dogs, cats, and even rats to stay alive.

Today, James Luke was fishing in the brown silt-filled Mississippi River, the water the color of worn saddle leather. He stood on the bow of the fiberglass boat and cast his lure into a bramble of treetops on the edge of the bluff. He'd caught three small bass and tossed each one back into the water, none of them worth keeping.

He cast the stiff rod with a hard flick of his wrist, and the line lobbed out into the water about fifty feet. On the end of the line was a spinner bait with stainless steel hooks as sharp as a new razor. The bait fell into the bramble. He thought he'd gotten his lure stuck on a limb, so he began to troll over to the half-submerged treetop using his battery-powered electric motor. He jerked the rod a few more times. He felt the lure give way, and he started cranking the pricey Abu Garcia reel, the fastest model for sale at Downtown Natchez Sporting Goods.

The line went as taut as a steel guitar string, and the rod bent. The fish took the line back toward the bramble. James Luke set the hook with a mighty jerk of the pole, and he was able to fight the big fish, pulling him from the bramble with his arms stressing the pole's strength. He tugged on the rod with the bull bass on the other end of the line, fighting it, and twice the fish broke the water's surface as if to spit the bait and treble hooks into James Luke's eyes. But the barbed hooks held and the gear was strong and the line was kept tight through his determination and unfailing luck. James Luke finally got the big bass to the edge of the boat after about five minutes, and he reached into the brown Mississippi River water and lifted the lunker with his thumb in his mouth, an index finger under the lower jaw.

He gave a successful smile when he held the largemouth bass at eye-level. He removed the hook with a pair of needle-nose pliers and placed the big fish into an ice chest. It weighed more than five pounds, the biggest bass he'd caught in the Mississippi River, not a true monster, but a fine one.

He opened a second chest, ice covering Budweiser cans, a dozen of them. He'd drink all of them by dark. It was ten o'clock in the morning, and he lit a cigarette and embraced his first beer of the morning.

Just a few miles away, North Natchez was a hilly slum out of sight, out of mind, an area practically nonexistent to the gentry and middle classes, a community east of the river's bluffs where the elites—with their mythic pretense of Mississippi history—wouldn't have to view it. It was a forlorn landscape of abject poverty. Despite the civil rights movement, nothing much had changed there since Reconstruction. James Luke thrived because of the stringent inequality and contradiction of Natchez and the surrounding areas. No group or individual was equal to the gentry class, to which his wife's mother was heir. However, James Luke was getting ahead faster than almost any other man in Natchez, a far more rapid ascent than an outsider was allowed to make.

Across the river from Natchez were the small Louisiana farm towns of Vidalia and Ferriday. Ferriday was the loathsome home place of the piano player Jerry Lee Lewis and the preacher Jimmy Swaggart. Mickey Gilley, the country singer, was actually from Natchez, but he had his musical roots in Ferriday. All three were cousins and professional musicians. In 1974, only Jerry Lee Lewis was a household name, though his two cousins were gaining in notoriety. Lewis ran off with his thirteen-year-old cousin and besmirched the disreputable town until he made it big banging on the piano and singing "Great Balls of Fire."

On both banks of the river, James Luke thrived. His father-in-law made the business go well, and his job with the Corps helped him peddle influence and grease the wheel for lucrative contracts, which gave him steady tax-free cash kickbacks. From concrete work to livestock grazing, there was money to be siphoned off the government and its business partners.

He began making gains as a regional slumlord, buying up shotgun shacks in North Natchez and out in the country. These tarpaper and clapboard houses were mostly located in the black quarters. However, some were in white ghettos, and he'd started the first trailer park of any real size in North Natchez and filled it to capacity with hardly room to park a car between the mobile homes. These were hovels, tin shacks, most still on rubber tires, trailers with dented and gapped aluminum siding. He rented many of them from week to week—sometimes for cash, sometimes for drugs or stolen property, and sometimes for sex.

The more money he made, the more he wanted. The more power he acquired, the more he sought. His father-in-law was impressed with his holdings and entrepreneurship, his innate friendship with capitalism. James Luke knew this by the way he carried on and on about his Louisiana son-in-law, bragging about his many acquisitions and profitable exploits.

Recently, James Luke had become the freshman member of the board of directors of the Planter Class Bank in Natchez, the first non-native Mississippian to hold the post in anyone's memory. He was also on the board of the Natchez Adams County Republican Party. In fact, the Party of Lincoln was rare in Natchez, but James Luke could see the future turning toward the GOP like a crystal ball, and he believed Mississippi whites were within a decade of going Republican en masse.

He drove a 1973 Chevrolet Suburban four-wheel drive, a long-bodied truck that was can-like in its capacity, a panel truck that he used to carry workers who cut grass and did maintenance on his rental houses. Much of his work in rentals was done while on the clock for the Army Corps. As a field supervisor with the Vicksburg District, James Luke had the freedom to come and go as he pleased, simply needing to tell the secretary that he was "in the field," which could be anywhere in the large district. A low profile in the towns up and down the river was essential. When he wanted to do something truly nefarious, however, he had to be wary of onlookers and witnesses. He knew that in time his identity as a businessman and a Corps employee would cause public exposure. He was becoming more and more recognizable, and he knew it was a potential problem.

During the afternoon following the fishing trip, once he'd put away his boat at his house, he drove across the big river bridge to a Louisiana duck hunting camp. It was a swampy area known only as "The Wash," a lawless region of derelict Cajuns and poor blacks south of Vidalia that seemed stuck in some kind of historical malaise. The Wash was beginning to receive some of the South's first shipments of cocaine, and James Luke was one of the chief financiers of its distribution along the Mississippi River. Likewise, he was setting up pot growers with seed and even lamps to raise it behind closed doors, such places as hay barns and homes and hot houses. One of his "associates," as he often called the men he worked with in the drug trade, had put out over one thousand marijuana plants on a secluded Corps property across the river from Natchez. James Luke was just beginning his ascent as a drug lord, but he liked to think of himself as an entrepreneur and a business pioneer. He worked on the drug project like it was a full-time job, and he was getting ready to expand his business to other states.

He drove his Suburban out to The Wash, the land as flat as the bottom of a raccoon's foot. He'd gotten overheated while fishing and was running the air conditioner in the vehicle, nursing an ice cold beer in his lap. The Wash passed beside his window like a bad memory, all darkness and poverty maintained by government welfare, monthly checks and benefits, which could only be received if the residents remained in poverty. Crippling poverty was a tool used to keep the labor cheap, usually day wages paid in cash, and men like James Luke enjoyed the status quo of their social class as if it was established natural law.

Local governments refused to tax the landowners enough to provide adequate schools or services, keeping the structure of poverty and wealth as rigid as a corpse, so fixed and immutable that it rivaled the

Divine Right of Kings. However, the local taxpayers were always obliged to build prisons to house the worst rabble-rousers and offenders to keep the public safe for democracy. The place gave the term "vicious cycle" clear and concrete testimony for anyone with eyes to see it.

James Luke steered the vehicle deep into a rice field, the roadway nothing more than grass and ruts. He wondered if he'd make it to the camp without getting the truck bogged down to the axles. But he had four-wheel drive and all terrain tires. After skidding and sliding in the muck, he pulled into an old hunting camp nestled in a stand of cypress at the back of an open field. He was glad that he wouldn't have to be extracted from this gumbo mud that some misguided fools referred to as a road.

A dozen vehicles were parked in the camp yard. The building was set atop cypress blocks about three feet off the ground. Both the yard and porch were busy with movement. On the porch sat several black men hovering around a table throwing cards. They drank liquor and smoked joints, barely lifting their eyes to James Luke and his long blue Chevrolet Suburban. He saw them focusing on their fast moving card game, and he could hear the Godfather of Soul pulsating from the turntable, "Say it Loud - I'm Black and I'm Proud."

"Shit," James Luke said. "I'll do well to keep from getting stabbed. The sorry sumbitches." He got out of the automobile and walked to the porch. One man looked up from the cards and nodded.

"I need to see Took. Is he inside?" James Luke asked.

"He up in the house. You got any rooms to let? My lady friend need a place," the man said. A wicked scar passed from his jaw to his temple, and he wore a sagging blue shirt that showed a thin collarbone.

"I might," James Luke said.

"I'll tell her to go see you," the man said, dropping a playing card on the table.

Inside the old camp, Tucker "Took" Newbill stood over three racks of ribs at the kitchen sink. He rubbed the ribs with both hands covering them in a concoction of red spice. A big box fan blew swampy air through the room. The air floated with the sharp smell of cayenne pepper and garlic. The music was muffled inside, the speakers on the front porch pushing bass thuds and thumps into the yard. James Luke nearly heaved from the smell, his eyes watering.

"How's it going, Took?" James Luke asked. They were the only two men in the room.

"It ain't nothing but a thing," he said, hardly glancing at him. The racks of ribs were red and heavy, and he worked in the red rub like a pit master. "You staying for dinner? We got plenty. I got some barbeque on the pit now, and it'll be ready before long."

James Luke could see the tableful of washed vegetables—piles of onions and carrots, bell peppers, tomatoes, and a giant pot of boiling water on the propane stove. "No, I need to get on back to the house."

"You here to see the supply?"

"Yeah."

"It's in the bedroom." He pointed to a closed door.

"How much?"

"Five kilos."

"I thought we'd agreed on six?"

"We got less. Sometimes it just be that way in this hard business. Just pay me for five."

"No, I want six." James Luke saw the butcher knife beside Took's right hand, a long knife with a wooden handle. His thoughts focused. He believed Took was cheating him, holding back a kilo of marijuana for his own sales. "How much off for the kilo?"

"Same as the rest. Prorate it," Took said, stuffing a clove of garlic into a slice cut in the ribs.

James Luke did the math. "Okay, I'll give you twenty percent less, but you're going to need to tell me what happened to the rest of it." He was nursing a growing element of rage, but he viewed the butcher knife as an imminent threat.

"I'd go get the reefer for you, but my hands is all nasty." Took pointed again to the door not far from the refrigerator. "It's by the bed in the tote."

James Luke went toward the door.

Took said, "There might be somebody in there, but pay 'em no mind. They just kids. The reefer's in the canvas tote."

James Luke nodded. "You know I don't carry no dope in my tuck. You're going to need to be here this evening for Sonny Boy to come for it." He put his hand on the door knob and pushed it open. A faint light entered the otherwise dark room. He could smell the strong odor of green marijuana. In the bed, a pair of bodies was grinding under a white sheet, a slim man and a fat woman. They never stopped.

He raised an eyebrow at the sex but said nothing to them. He found the sack on the floor and pulled it over to the light in the doorway and untied the top of it. He removed several paper bags that were filled with leaves and big stems. He crammed the bags into the sack and carried it into the kitchen.

Took gripped the knife in his hand where he was cutting garlic at the table. "How is it?"

James Luke threw the rucksack at him with all of his might, and the blow knocked vegetables off the table and onto the floor. The knife fell, too. And in a second, before Took could react, James Luke rushed him and started beating him upside the head with a pair of brass knuckles that he'd pulled from his back pocket. "Don't lie to me you damned boon. Don't you ever dare try to pass this shit off to me again. You said this was bud, but it's ditch weed." He beat Took with the brass knuckles and his fist, knocking the man down. As he lay on the floor, James Luke continued to swing.

Took's mouth made a cruel gesture as if he could see his own death, the destiny of judgment, the sulfuric fires of everlasting torment, an abyss encroaching and surrounding his spirit like a band of fallen angels. He was terrified under the steady onslaught of the man's heavy blows.

James Luke snatched up the butcher knife, but he hardly slowed the iron-clad fist. And Took's screams did nothing to stop the attack.

The loud blows summoned the man and the woman from the bedroom. They emerged through the doorway, their naked bodies wrapped in sheets. Other men began to file into the front room from the porch. They watched, gawking, the intensity of James Luke's rage surprising them, turning everyone into impotent witnesses.

He left the bag of dope. With one hand he grabbed the sharp butcher knife, and with the other he gathered Took's shirt in his hand. He began to drag Took by the collar, pulling the sweat-covered body toward the open room, away from the kitchen as he attempted to crawl away to escape the rage.

"He lied to me, and he had it coming. I'm going to drag his black ass to the truck, and if any one of you as much as peeps, I'll cut his throat and yours, too," James Luke said, meaning every word of it.

The blacks gave him room, pushing to the sides and away from James Luke and Took. They watched as he pulled the semi-conscious man out the door to the porch and down the rickety wood steps and into the yard toward the Suburban.

From the porch, the onlookers stared at James Luke as he dragged his prey. There was an uncanny stillness and hatred in their eyes toward this spectacle, but a measure of unchained terror had set in. They were witnessing a one-man lynching of their friend by a monster. That's how these onlookers would remember the event the rest of their lives. This was the ignoble wrath and consummated horror of an enraged white man against his enemies.

Once at the Suburban, James Luke let go of Took and opened the door. The black man fell flat on the ground. James Luke slung the butcher knife over the cab of the truck and into a briar thicket, and he pulled out his Colt .45 automatic from his truck seat and brandished it for the men on the porch to see. Then he started the big engine and drove away down the muddy lane.

CHAPTER FIFTEEN

There were times when Wesley could not comprehend his father's decisions, which came to him like a slap in the face. He and his family had been saving so that he could attend USL and study architecture, but a good portion of the savings went toward the down payment on the Ford Maverick that he drove. Wesley was pleased to have missed the military draft being twenty years old with the war coming to an end. He could see the Vietnam conflict dying on the vine with a whimper instead of a roar. The draft was effectively ended, and because he was born in 1954, he was never really in line to go to Southeast Asia. The authority to induct anyone ended on June 30, 1973, and Wesley felt safe. The only drawback was that he wouldn't have the GI Bill to pay for more college.

He needed the extra money from the job at the Claiborne House, not for the fall term but for the spring. He pondered it Monday night and was unable to sleep. So on Tuesday evening, while working on his summer school project at the Industrial Arts Shop on campus, he called Charity in an act of defiance against his father. He felt boxed in by Tom, and he didn't like it at all.

Over the telephone, he apologized for his father's actions, making up a tale about his father being on a strong medication for his blood pressure that affected his judgment. On and on, lie after lie, tall tale after tall tale.

Charity invited him to come over and bring his portfolio of work. They set a time of six o'clock on Wednesday. Nothing would make him happier than to get the project started, he said.

The excitement, the forbidden fruit, and the prospects of doing the work alone was a challenge. It almost made him too high to think at all.

He could use the college's shop—not the one at his father's maintenance department, but the facility in the Industrial Arts Shop used for students and classes. He and his teachers were good friends, and he was on solid enough terms to do personal projects any time he wished, day or night. He was the only student in the program to have a staff key to the building.

Wesley arrived at the oak-lined street a minute before six on Wednesday. He was conscientious like his father, even while he was secretly rebelling against his father's rules. As much as he was a drafting student, he was also an art student, and he told himself that he was going to let his hair grow a little longer once he arrived in Lafayette, maybe sow some wild oats, have a good time, party a little in Cajun country, and as the French say, *Laissez le bon temps rouler!* He wanted the good times to roll in Acadiana.

He carried his big brown portfolio under his arm just like the last meeting, walking to the front steps of the big house, the same place he'd visited on Monday with his father. His heart beat irregularly, almost skipping beats. Dissent from the rules was a great motivator. He overcame his momentary fear and rang the doorbell.

The door opened. Charity Claiborne stood tall. She was buxom yet fit, elegant for a woman of her background, an unlettered vixen who got by on her sexual prowess and willingness to use it for gain. She exercised often, playing tennis at the country club near the little local airport, and she swam daily in the backyard pool, often nude. This evening, she wore a Japanese gown, which she'd bought tailored in Okinawa on her honeymoon with Dr. Claiborne several months earlier. The gown was tight around her hips and pelvis, and it made her look like a model in *Esquire*. Wesley read the magazine from time to time at the college library where his mother worked.

"Please come in," Charity said. "I was watching from the window, waiting for you to get here. Did you circle the block to make it at six on the nose or do you have great timing?" she asked as a German cuckoo clock rang the hour in the living room.

"No, I just planned it right," he said, stepping into the foyer.

She shut the door and stood near him beaming.

Wesley looked at a painting on the wall that resembled something by one of the Dutch masters, an oil painting of an aged man at a small table, his face long with a pronounced nose and a flamboyant wig. It was hung opposite of the front door and was framed in exquisite gold that seemed to be wrought iron or forged and covered with leaf.

"This is really nice," Wesley said.

"Oh," she said, touching the frame. "That is the portrait of the explorer Pierre Le Moyne, Sieur d'Iberville. He's an ancestor on Dr. C.'s mother's side."

"That's interesting," he said.

She led him into the large formal living room. Wesley blushed slightly at the split in her dress showing her long legs. He thought it was funny that she referred to her husband as "Dr. C." But then he realized what she meant—chiefly by the way she raised her eyebrows when she said "Dr. C.," as if he was in the next room and busy with some important task or perhaps dying in a hospital bed or recently buried, as if he was under her nose and she was not at all pleased with it.

In the living room, she babbled about art pieces they owned, turning her head around to face him when she spoke. She pointed out pieces hanging on the walls as she bragged.

Wesley felt awkward. He wondered if she cared at all about the carpentry project. The woman asked him questions about his college major, his plans for the future, and what he carried inside the portfolio. When they walked into the informal den, which abutted a glass sun porch, she invited him to sit on the couch, a comfortable tan velour couch that overlooked the backyard. He bounced his foot and his leg unconsciously like the beat of a metronome on top of a piano.

She sat sideways watching his right leg bounce. Charity smiled. "Don't be nervous, Wesley."

He stilled his leg, embarrassed that she'd picked up on his anxiety.

The woman continued. "I would like the room to be fitted with adjustable bookshelves on all walls with cabinets on the bottom, something British-looking and fancy but not too fancy. Wood that's stained dark. I want them to work with a sliding ladder like the one I saw on television once. The ladder rails should be near the ceiling and have wheels at the bottom to move it along. In fact, Dr. C. has ordered a ladder with a brass rail. It should be here by the end of the week. Dr. C's still at Vanderbilt in Nashville and won't be back until the early flight first thing in the morning," she said, winking.

Wesley opened his portfolio and took out a black sketchpad and a pencil. He also had an aluminum tape measure. He showed Charity black and white photographs, 8x10s that he'd taken of projects, film he'd developed at school. Kitchen cabinets, bathroom cabinets, a desk, and a set of bunk beds built for a cousin in Packwood Corners. The photographs were interesting and artfully done for local work. Wesley was an accomplished photographer and could develop the photographs to his advantage. He could tell she liked the work.

Charity held these pictures in her long fingers and studied them with her bottom lip bit slightly and crimped in her teeth. "These are marvelous. How much was your father involved in building these?" she asked.

He'd expected the question. "My father is employed full-time at the junior college, and I work in our shop on all of the projects. I do it at least forty hours a week on top of school. It's all my work. My old man helps, but I do the jobs from design to installation, and I can do your job from beginning to end and provide you with a finished product just like you want. I'm going to USL in Lafayette this fall to study architecture," he said.

"You're confident, Wesley. Maybe a little cocky. I'll give you that much," she said. "How much will you charge us?"

"I go by a simple formula. The cost of materials times two, plus ten percent. I assume you want oak. I'll do a draft, get your approval, and then come back with two quotes on materials from hardware stores in town. That'll give you the price based on the lowest material cost," he said.

"Great. Oak is fine. Just stain it dark brown. How long will it take?"

"Well, I'll have the rough sketch and quotes on materials within a few days. I'll need about six weeks at the most if I'm working alone, start to finish for a good job, barring some kind of unforeseen problem. I'm taking my last class at Baxter State, an independent study course with Mr. C.J. Kirby, which won't take much time. I'll devote all of my waking hours exclusively to your project. Can I look at the room where you want the study built?"

"Absolutely. Follow me," she said.

Wesley stood up, gathering his things and placed the photographs into the portfolio. He noticed her knee again, the fit and strong leg slipping out of the dress, and he tried not to stare as they walked to the study, down an open hallway across the room. She pushed down her dress where it rode high on her hips, the split on one side showing plenty of thigh.

The study had two chairs and a large roll top desk that appeared to Wesley like an expensive antique. There were a couple of pine book shelves that were crudely built and full of double stacked books. Other books sat in piles on the floor. He began to measure and write the dimensions of the area in his sketch pad. He asked Charity to hold the end of the tape measure. He took copious notes in his book. All the while, she was chatting about her ideas for the room.

When he was done with the measurements, Charity said she might want Wesley to draw up an additional plan for a new cabinet for a double washbasin in the master bedroom. She wanted a double instead of the single basin that was presently in the room. But her husband had not agreed on the bathroom renovation project yet, she said. She wanted a written plan to show Dr. Claiborne. This would help her persuade him to do more renovations on the old house.

Wesley followed Charity down the hall and up some stairs to the master bedroom. She turned on the light. He was a little unsure of the situation. For a moment, he almost regretted coming to the house in defiance of his father. He followed her deep into the bedroom where a queen-sized bed was made up with silver linen sheets and yellow pillows with frilly edges.

They stepped into the bathroom. It was at least three times larger than the bathroom at Wesley's family home, the one he'd helped his father build onto the back of his parent's bedroom. It had a porcelain vanity and wall-to-wall mirrors, an oversized tub and cabinets. He looked at it carefully, and got his sketchpad ready. His hand shook a little, nervous to be in the bedroom suite alone with the woman.

Charity said she had some good ideas for new cabinetry from Southern Living magazine, and she'd find the issue for him. Then she asked if he had a girlfriend and he said no. He answered directly and respectfully as possible but focused on making quick sketches and writing measurements in his pad.

When he finished looking over the room and doing a final check on his measurements, they walked back into the bedroom. She dimmed the lights. He was surprised and more than a little uncomfortable.

"How much will the bathroom project cost, and can we get a discount for both?" she asked.

"I'm not sure, but it won't cost too much. I don't think anyhow. You're going to need to have a plumber to run the double pipe, which might cost a good bit. Plus the new washbasin and fixtures. I'll quote you a fair price and stick to it. How about that?"

"Cool," she said, putting her hand on his upper arm as they stood at the foot of the bed.

He nearly recoiled but stopped himself short.

She instantly took in his shock. Her face was radiant and warm with heat. "Please sit a minute, Wesley." She was still holding his bicep. "I promise I won't bite you. Relax. I just want to talk about our little project."

"Ma'am, I think we'd better go downstairs, and I really need to go home."

"Sure, we can do that, but don't call me 'ma'am.' I'm hardly any older than you." She let go of his arm, and they left the bedroom together.

CHAPTER SIXTEEN

Sara was at her desk in the campus library. It was time for the pre-Memorial Day convocation at the Wilcox Hall auditorium. This was also the annual picnic held on the Friday before the holiday. The library director had asked all of his staff to attend the event to make a good showing for their department. Classes were not yet in session, though summer school was soon to be underway. Thelma Doolittle Memorial Library was going to be operated by several student workers and Miss Lemuria Lund, a woman whose age, poor eyesight, and inability to walk kept her stationed at her desk in the back of the library where she catalogued books. All of the rest of the fulltime employees were required to attend the convocation. Sara left the building a few minutes after most of her colleagues. She had been preparing a large fiscal year-end book order and could not easily leave the work. The time got away from her, and she feared she'd arrive late.

This was the first major campus ceremony hosted by Dr. Myles Polk, a long-time dean who had risen up through the ranks to become the new president of the junior college. Dr. Polk was a local man who had gone to the laboratory high school in Wilcox Hall, and he was the grandson of a founding professor of rhetoric and logic. He was a natural comic, his humorous speeches much anticipated at gatherings where he was scheduled to speak. He was always a hit because of the otherwise seriousness of the stiff-shirt administrators on campus, a school largely run by accountants and schoolmarms.

Sara followed the crowd of people into the end of the building where the assembly was to be held. A man spoke to her, Dr. Harper Nelson, the head of the Agriculture Department. He had been summarily fired but recently rehired after he took the junior college leaders to court. He held the glass door open for her, and she walked through to the hall of the old laboratory school where children used to study in the heart of the college back in the days before parish desegregation killed it, shutting it down in 1969. It was by far the best school in the parish but all white. Oftentimes the graduates went to Yale and other Ivy League schools. The Baxter State Lab School had boasted one of the highest college placement rates of any Louisiana public school. The political elite refused to integrate. A red-hot controversy exploded over white high school girls dating black boys. This led to a complete meltdown of common sense. Instead of doing what the federal law required, the junior college shut down the only college preparatory school in the parish. Families with money sent their children to the local "academy," a segregated private school on the edge of town called Southern Pines Christian Academy. The best high school in Baxter Parish and one of the finest in the state died. Close it rather than integrate it seemed to be the sentiment of the elite.

"How was your morning?" Tom asked his wife. He was waiting for her near the stairwell.

"Just fine," she said.

Tom took her hand, and they walked into the crowded auditorium. He was dressed in a white shirt and black trousers, which were clean and pressed. He wore a bolo tie with a sterling silver keeper. Sara was conservatively dressed, her hem two inches below the knee.

The auditorium seats were tight with narrow aisles. Tom and Sara saw Wesley near the front where he had saved two seats at the right side of the stage, and they joined him there.

The program began with President Polk welcoming dignitaries, the mayor, city councilmen, three state legislators, and several wealthy patrons of the college, big donors and money people. Some had given tens of thousands of dollars in donations over the years. A few of the men were members of the Sicilian mafia, so-called business owners who could hardly read their own names but bought and paid for attorneys, judges, and college officials to do their reading for them. These illiterate mobsters were sons of strawberry and pepper farmers, and their children would go to Baxter State for free on scholarships before transferring to Loyola in New Orleans or Louisiana State University in Baton Rouge to complete their college degrees.

One donor was acknowledged for his recent endowment gift. Darfield Blahunt, a Hungarian businessman, was running a Ponzi scheme unbeknownst to Dr. Polk and many of his investors present. Blahunt stood to be acknowledged. He didn't know that he was the target of a federal corruption probe and would soon find himself held without bail to face charges of securities fraud among numerous other crimes.

After recognizing Blahunt and his wife as true "Baxter State Bobcats," Dr. Polk said, "Ladies and gentleman, the only thing short about my talk today is my punch line: we need your money, and we'll be passing the hat before we're done." From behind the lectern, Polk pulled out a "hat" made from a five-gallon bucket with a wooden hat brim and decorated in Baxter State green and gold. Tom had made it for Dr. Polk earlier in the week and the campus painters had painted it. The crowd roared when Dr. Polk ceremoniously and begrudgingly dropped in a dollar bill out of his own wallet, the billfold wrapped in a red bandana like a hobo's stash.

The Hardins sat together as a family. They watched the convocation festivities. Tom was stone-faced during the whole proceeding, finding very little of it funny.

President Polk called Dr. Claiborne and Charity to the stage to bestow upon him an emeritus title. Dr. Claiborne was dressed in a lime green jacket with a gold "BS" logo on front, and Charity wore high heels and a dress that gave plenty for public view.

The former junior college president accepted the wooden plaque. He asked his wife to hold it for him. Smiling wide, he grasped the edges of the lectern. "Now, I'm not going to teach today, because Mrs. Claiborne said we'll be eating barbeque shortly, and it would take me at least three hours to get through the first half of my lecture on Louisiana's contemporary political traditions and their origins in eighteenth-century France."

One unruly student in the back hollered, "Bring out the guillotine!" The crowd of college teachers and staff cackled like crows.

"All scholarly lectures aside, I should say how much this fine institution means to us and how much this president emeritus title means to me personally. I'll be here to teach a course as a scholar-in-residence this fall, and each of you have made a lasting contribution to my professional success for thirty-one and a half years. We thank you from the depths of our hearts," he said, eyes misty, his voice strained with deep emotion.

The room broke into applause. Then came a standing ovation. Sara stood, followed by Wesley and then Tom.

Charity waved her hand as she stood on stage next to Dr. Claiborne, the diminutive festival queen hand wave. She still looked like a pageant winner, one who'd long lost her innocence—if she ever had any to begin with. She was the same age as her husband's daughter who lived in Tallahassee, Florida. The father and daughter were estranged and no longer spoke to each other. Dr. Claiborne and his wife held hands as the crowd continued to clap for ten seconds.

When Dr. Polk returned to the lectern, the applause stopped. "We honor this great man's faithful service. We are certainly thankful and appreciative of his hard work, and he shall be sorely missed in his capacity as president by every faculty, staff, and student affiliated with this grand institution. He shall not fade away. On the contrary, we believe Mrs. Charity will make him live forever and ever," he said, a brief pause and a rueful grin on his face. A few people murmured, and others gouged their neighbors' ribs at the backhanded compliment.

One professor shouted, "I'd sure live forever." It was loud enough to be heard across the auditorium, and the place erupted in more hissing and chortling.

Dr. Polk went on unflappably. "And we welcome you back to teach history as long as you both shall live," he said deadpan to a few chuckles. Then he offered gushing praise for the faculty and staff, and he welcomed one and all to the Civil War Memorial Park behind the auditorium where a country band was soon to start playing music and barbecued chicken would be served free of charge, compliments of the Alumni Club.

The campus chaplain at the Baptist Student Union, Reverend T.B. Owings, climbed the stairs to the stage and requested everyone to bow in prayer. He asked the Lord's blessing on the food, on Dr. Claiborne and in his future journey through life, and a special blessing on his new wife, as well as the upcoming summer term of study. When he said "Amen," the attendees left the auditorium in a congenial rush.

Outside, Sara took a picnic table underneath a tall loblolly pine, a tree that would have made a sturdy electric pole. Tom and Wesley stood in a long line holding paper plates. It was hot, eighty-seven degrees, with little breeze. The school band played the Baxter Parish fight song, and the cheerleaders held their pom-poms at the ready. Under the shade of an aged live oak tree, a country band tuned their instruments.

Local politicians and dignitaries milled around the crowd. One octogenarian tax assessor had been elected to office for nine consecutive terms, the longest-running assessor in Louisiana history. He glad-handed everyone and walked up to Sara. "Hello, I'm Martin Wayne Chester and how beautiful you are today, ma'am. Surely this day is not nearly as pretty as you," he said, never slowing his step to greet yet another potential voter.

Out across the grassy student union park, Sara could see that her husband had gotten two plates and was walking toward their table, Wesley following. Tom balanced two cups of sweet tea against his chest. He said little as he handed her the tea. She could tell he was fuming about something but couldn't figure out what had happened.

Wesley didn't say anything at all, just looked down at his chicken and coleslaw, baked beans with bacon. He appeared sullen.

"The chicken looks tasty," Sara said.

"It'll do under the circumstances," Tom said.

As the Hardins ate their meals, Sara saw Dr. Claiborne and Charity moving toward their general direction. She did not know anything about the rupture between Tom and Wesley, or the conflict over the Claiborne project.

The Claibornes were visiting tables, shaking hands, hugging necks, and talking. The president sidled up to the Hardin table, which was covered in a red and white checkerboard table cloth.

Sara could hear the country band. It played "You are My Sunshine," a song brought to worldwide fame by Louisiana Governor Jimmie Davis. There had been a discussion in recent years of changing the name of the school from Baxter State to Jimmie Davis State Junior College, but the state legislature was uninterested in allowing the change. It could let loose a torrent of college name changes throughout the state, many of them bought through cash bribes.

"How are the Hardins?" Dr. Claiborne said. He reached out to shake Tom's hand.

Tom stood, quickly wiping his hand on a napkin, and he shook Dr. Claiborne's hand, which was cushy-soft, the skin unmarred by calluses like Tom's hands. "We're all right. Congratulations on the retirement," Tom said. He sat back down again at the table.

"Thank you," Dr. Claiborne said.

"How's the good librarian Mrs. Sara and how's Mr. Wesley?"

"We're fine, President Claiborne," Sara said. She noticed that Charity had split up with her husband and was across the little park a few tables over, speaking with a faculty wife, her palm on the woman's shoulder, strutting around as if she were outfitted in a pageant sash and a tiara.

"Hope you enjoy your new title," Sara said smiling.

Wesley nodded sheepishly.

Dr. Claiborne tried to downplay the honorific. "Truth is, emeritus is Latin for 'he's served his time and now he's all washed up.'" He laughed. "Thank you for sharing your husband's fine craftsmanship in renovating our home study," Dr. Claiborne said.

Tom's brow furrowed. Wesley squirmed, turning red, putting down his piece of chicken on the plate. Sara sat with an uncertain look on her face, knowing immediately that there was some kind of trouble.

Tom spoke up. "We did go out to your house last week, but we're unable to work on the project at this time." He was stiff-looking, his palms flat on the table cloth.

"I do believe my wife said you and Mr. Wesley were moving forward and were bringing back a price by early next week, as well as a rendering of the plans. There must have been a miscommunication of some sort. I'll go get Mrs. Charity to straighten this out." The old college president marched two tables down the row where his wife was chatting with some women.

"What is Mr. Hardin speaking about related to them not doing our little project, honey?" Dr. Claiborne asked his wife.

Sara could hear them talking above the band. President Claiborne was almost shouting.

"Tom, what happened?" she asked.

"We went over to look at the job, but I decided against doing it," Tom said, not whispering, but speaking in a calm voice. "Isn't that right, Wesley?"

Wesley stared down at his plate just as silent as a deaf mute.

There was a dark quiet for a few seconds. Dr. Claiborne brought Charity to the table leading her by the hand. Lateral lines pronounced on the old man's forehead, and a bead of sweat popped up on Charity's brow.

Sara felt ill all of a sudden.

"Now I have Mrs. Charity here to clear all this up. Isn't Mr. Hardin preparing a bid for our new study? You said it would come with a draftsman's likeness of the work?" Dr. Claiborne gazed at his wife.

"Why, yes, dear," Charity said, her eyes gone steely, a tried and true poker visage across her face. This was the fulfillment of years living by deception at every turn. She was able to confidently defend herself no matter the scandal or accusation.

Sara wanted to leave, to go back to her familiar spot in the library where her comfortable sweater was draped over the back of the wooden swivel chair at her desk. She wished she'd never come to the barbeque. She knew she was stuck, and the tension was gaining depth and breadth like an expanse of kinetic energy, a social force that causes lasting cracks in human relations.

"No," Tom said. "I'm not sure that we do. We've decided against the job and wish you the very best in finding a carpenter to do the work, but I'm afraid it won't be us."

Dr. Claiborne was flushed, clearly furious. He made a fist at his side and then released it to an open hand.

His wife pointed to Wesley. "This fine young man came over to the house by himself on Wednesday of this week, and he says he's going to do the job alone. It will be his own personal project," Charity said.

"Not while he sleeps at my house," Tom said, shaking his head.

"Oh, please, Tom," Sara said. She knew the junior college pettiness, the personal politics, and she feared for both of their jobs. Despite Dr. Claiborne being retired, one phone call and both of them could be fired from their permanent positions.

"Dr. and Mrs. Claiborne, I guess I've done all of the picnicking I can handle for one afternoon," Tom said. He stood and tossed his cup of iced tea, half-eaten plate of barbecue, coleslaw, and pork and beans into the garbage can just across from the table. "Yes, sir, I've had about all of the good company I can take for one day. Time to go back to the shop and get some work done," he said as he walked away.

Sara stood and made frantic apologies for his behavior, saying he had not been himself lately, and that it was all a big misunderstanding. Then she followed her husband out of the park.

Wesley sat at the table and never looked up, and the Claibornes glowered at him with their jaws clenched tight.

Sara caught up with Tom about a hundred feet away at the edge of the Student Union.

"Please, please Tommy. Wait," she called out to him. "This is serious."

He turned and looked at her but never stopped walking. "It sure is. But I'm not discussing it now. We can talk about it tonight," Tom said.

"We'd better," she said.

They went in opposite directions to their campus jobs, both walking with their heads down, shoulders stiff, as if the dead had gotten up from their graves and were traipsing the earth. Sara felt like the wind had been knocked out of her, almost as bad as the attack in 1964.

CHAPTER SEVENTEEN

Wesley was mad enough to bite the head off a tenpenny nail. He tore out of the gravel parking area at the Industrial Arts Shop and headed north on Oak Street, a narrow blacktop road that bordered the edge of campus. The little Maverick six-cylinder motor whirred. When he passed the Quonset hut where his father worked, he wished they would have bought a Dodge Charger or something with real power, and right then for the first time he hated the little car that he'd once loved so much since his parents bought it for him. Now he wanted a Barracuda or a Challenger or a Duster when he passed his father's workshop heading toward downtown.

As he shifted into third gear on the column shifter, he had no idea where he was going, but was certain he was leaving the campus and his hardheaded old man behind. Wesley knew Tom was dead set against the Claiborne job and wouldn't back down for anything. The young man drove, wandering aimlessly and thinking.

He was even more livid by the time he reached Dead Man's Curve at the Pickleyville crossroads. The disagreement with his father was churning inside of him. To make matters worse, he had not gotten to eat his lunch at the picnic, and he was hungry. He stopped at the National Grocery to buy a Hubig's Pie and a Nehi Orange Crush. Inside, he spent twenty-seven cents on the cherry pie and a quarter on the Nehi. He drank and ate while standing under the store overhang outside. It was hot even in the shade, Wesley's back resting against the brick wall. He began to calm down a little and tried to compose himself. He hadn't intended to loiter, but he was unsure where to go, wondering what to do next. The fried pie settled his stomach. When the pop bottle was empty, he went back inside and placed it in the return rack and got a nickel back from the cashier. He looked at it and realized it was a 1934 Buffalo nickel. He rubbed it between his fingers, stuck it in his blue jeans pocket, and hoped his luck was changing somehow. Then he threw the Hubig's bag into a garbage can outside and left the grocery parking lot.

As he drove back downtown to see a buddy, Nate Forrest, Wesley planned on asking if he could stay a few nights. He didn't want to go back home right away. He went to South Spruce Street near the old First Baptist Church, a decaying building with mammoth concrete steps that led to the second-floor sanctuary. Forrest lived in a ratty garage apartment across the street from the church. When Wesley pulled into the drive, he almost didn't bother to knock on the door. Nate's bicycle, his only means of transportation, was not on the second floor stoop where he usually kept it. But he climbed the steps and knocked on the door anyway. There was no answer. So Wesley figured he was at work.

Wesley's class work was almost done for the summer even before the term started. He'd nearly completed the independent study project by working on it in between the spring and summer terms. The class consisted of a drafting project, a sample house plan, and blueprints for a brick ranch-style home. He decided to go back to the Industrial Arts Shop and work on the Claiborne job for a while, so he drove the Maverick in a big circle from one side of town to the other, still worrying about the mess he'd gotten himself into. He went to the building and let himself in and started working on the Claiborne drawings. No use in fretting when I can do something constructive, he thought. I'll do some work, get something done at least.

By dark, Wesley had finished at the shop, accomplishing all he could do at the time without the prices on the lumber. With the list of materials and rough drawings for a quote on Monday, he'd be ready to submit the price to the Claibornes, though he was unsure if Dr. Claiborne still wanted his business.

Some students were beginning to gather at the Industrial Arts Shop for an evening welding class, a night track to help local men find work in the industrial trades.

Wesley packed up his portfolio and drove back to Nate's garage apartment. The bicycle was now chained to a post at Nate's second floor stoop. When he got out of the Maverick, he could hear guitar music playing inside. The windows were open. He climbed the steps and beat on the door.

Nate opened the door and welcomed Wesley inside, and then he sat back down on the couch. He picked up the old Harmony flattop guitar that was leaned against the cushion, and started strumming a few chords of Lead Belly's "In the Pines." Then he dropped his tortoiseshell pick on the coffee table. "What's going on? You don't look so good."

"The proverbial shit has hit the propeller," Wesley said.

"Why? You get the clap? Knock up the little girlfriend you don't even have?" asked Nate.

"No, I got myself tossed out of the house."

"Whoa, Nellie. That's not good. And you're one of the decent guys here in P-Ville. You must have screwed up."

"Well."

"Let me guess. You're at my place to sleep on the couch?"

"Nate, you're a prophet."

"Yeah and what all happened?"

Wesley told him the whole story, including the visit earlier in the week to Charity's bedroom.

"Now if you're not stuck in the creek and can't climb up the bank. Your old man's still gonna pay for school, huh?"

"I don't know. He's mad as hell, really pissed."

"Have you gone back home?"

"No, I'm putting it off as long as I can. Let Pops cool off and take some of the edge off everything, I hope."

"I bet you're scared to face him again."

"A little."

"Okay. Stay here tonight. But tomorrow you'll figure out how to deal with it. I'd tell the Claibornes to find somebody else to build the shelves. Keep the peace at home. My daddy says all the time it's a whole lot easier to keep the peace at home than to fight foreign wars abroad. Wesley, I'd rather be sewed inside a bagful of dog turds before I'd get into a fight with your old man. The man does not play and has no sense of humor."

"Thanks for the advice. I'll take the couch. You got an extra pillow?"

The next morning, Wesley woke up more tired than rested. He had barely slept, his mind too anxious with thoughts of the conflict and what had gone on, what was left to do to salvage things. He smelled bacon frying in Nate's iron skillet. Nate worked as a cook at the P-Ville American Diner, and college kids liked to hang out with him because he was always cooking something good to eat, playing the guitar and singing some kind of song.

At the table, Wesley said, "Why don't we work on the Claiborne job together? We can split the profit after materials."

Nate swallowed a mouthful of coffee. "I'm no carpenter, but how much are we talking?"

"Maybe two or three hundred dollars each. I need help with installation more than anything else. I don't know. I could just pay you for coming over and helping me move the cabinets and shelving and installing them. I could pay you by the hour, if you don't want a big commitment. I know you've already been working a lot at the café." Wesley not only needed physical labor, but he wanted a buffer to help deal with Charity.

At the sound of cash money, Nate's eyebrows raised slightly. "I'm your man for a few hours of work. Just pay me the same as I make at the diner, which ain't much. But I can't mess around a lot or I'll flunk my algebra class. I've got Dr. Rawlings for Math 161, and she's hard as hell. I took her last spring and dropped the class. If I get behind this summer, I'm screwed. I've come to realize that she's worse than a co-bra."

"How's that?"

"At least a cobra has the mercy to spit in your eyes and blind you before he kills you. And Rawlings wants you to see everything she's writing on that damned blackboard when she tries to maim you."

Wesley laughed.

"I can help you a little when you need it. Maybe a couple of evenings as long as it doesn't foul up my class, my work schedule at the café, or my back. I'm already working forty hours a week at the café this summer, and Dr. Rawling's math class is going to start next week. But God knows I could use some extra bread."

Nate handed Wesley a plate with three eggs sunny side up, toast, and two strips of crispy bacon. He ate ravenously. He remembered that he'd never eaten any supper the night before. The last meal was the Nehi and Hubig's Pie at the National Grocery. He thought about his plans for the remainder of the summer, the move to Lafayette, and trying to get the work finished before the fall semester started. The rift with his father could derail all of his future plans—if Tom took away the car or failed to give him the college money. He didn't want to back down on the Claiborne job. It was a matter of principle and pride.

Nate placed the hot skillet into the kitchen sink and it sizzled. He sat down with his own eggs, and ran a slice of toast across the top of the yolk making the egg break into a watery spread. "Life is wonderful until the darkness surrounds you like an abyss," he said, smiling wide. "I think Albert Camus said that."

Wesley didn't even care to ask what he meant by the comment.

CHAPTER EIGHTEEN

During the evening after the picnic, Tom and Sara argued as never before during their marriage of twenty-three years. In the low light of the living room, they battled about Wesley and the Claiborne job and Tom's harsh rudeness at the campus picnic.

Tom tried to leave it alone, but Sara followed him, hounding him from room to room offering her bill of indictment. It was as if she had been storing up past acts for this very moment. She reminded him of his failures in life and served as his personal prosecutor.

More than once, Tom wondered if she would strike him. She had taken up Wesley's cause saying Tom was narcissistic, utterly self-centered. She said she'd known this character flaw over the decades, but she kept her mouth closed about it until now, but no more.

"You are hard-hearted, self-righteous, and unwilling to compromise. It's your way or no way. The sun and moon must take their cues from you, Tom," she said, her eyes blazing with contempt, her finger pointing at him, shoulders square. She stood in the living room and he sat in his chair. The television played in the background.

"I think the constellations do just fine without my help," he countered.

"Not even Almighty God knows how to run the world without your guidance," she said.

"The Lord isn't asking me to do this job. I simply do not want to work for that woman, Charity Claiborne. I want nothing to do with her. She's corrupt."

"Why?"

"She's a liar and a harlot, and I don't trust her. She's deceived Dr. Claiborne into marrying her. But she won't deceive me. That's for damn sure."

"You've worked for plenty of sinners before. It's never stopped you from cashing a check."

"I still don't have to work for her."

"No, you're expecting her to walk on water. You've been made perfect like some of the Methodist ministers believe of themselves."

"Sara, I'm sure you've heard that she literally drove the first Mrs. Claiborne to the grave."

"Eliza died of a stroke. She had terrible health problems for years. Heart attacks, surgeries. She was not well for the longest time."

"Sure, she had some health troubles, but it was made worse because Howell was shagging Charity every chance he could get. That woman was even hired as a receptionist at the Marble Palace, for Christ's sake. She worked in the President's Office while they were involved."

"I've heard about all I can stand. It's all just nasty rumors. I don't know what they did or did not do. But I do know that Eliza Claiborne died, and they were married shortly thereafter. Who cares? It's your unbending rules of decorum that place burdens on people beyond what they can carry. Now, you've turned on Wesley. This is nothing but a little carpentry job to pay for his college tuition, and it won't cause you to lose your good morals and sterling reputation, I promise." She put her hands at her sides and walked out of the living room where Tom sat staring at her back as she left.

Tom did not think he was nearly as cocksure as Sara claimed. He was heartbroken over the rift with Wesley. He sat in his chair in the living room, one foot on the floor and the other on a padded Ottoman. A worn copy of William Faulkner's *Absalom, Absalom!* sat on the end table. He picked it up and tried to comprehend an infinitely long sentence a dozen times, but his mind would revolt from his reading and go right back to the fight with Wesley and Sara. He tried to read a few pages during the course of an hour, comprehending little.

Sara never reentered the room, and she spent the rest of the night in the bedroom. Tom tried to sleep on the couch, but his restless mind left only the knowledge that his attempt to do the right thing had caused a rupture within his family.

Wesley was a good kid, Tom knew, and he hoped his son would follow the right path back home, make his way toward better judgment. But he was unsure this hope would come to pass. He knew he couldn't force the boy to make the right decision.

He also hated what Charity Claiborne stood for, the sense of entitlement that she displayed because of her good looks and because of her new place in the upper class of Pickleyville, the town and gown clique that ran the city. Tom couldn't see how the money made from working for her was worth the indignity. How could taking on this project accomplish anything good? There were other jobs and other people he could do work for on the side. He didn't have to take every job offered. This was the right and privilege of any craftsman. Tom's goal was to protect himself and his family from the corrosion of Charity Claiborne, and to get Wesley through architecture school over in Lafayette. He wanted to keep the family unity, too, and he'd never leave his son high and dry moneywise. If he had to work multiple jobs by himself to help Wesley become an architect, so be it. He'd always been a blue-collar worker, and he would do whatever was necessary to allow his son to become white-collar.

This was the most serious threat to his family since the long day in 1964 when his wife was raped and almost killed by a still unidentified assailant, a ghost perhaps, some entity that entered into their lives like a wisp of smoke and left as mysteriously as when it arrived. There was no light in this darkness. He now felt a certain kinship to former times with the accompanying sense of dread.

It was as if some bad epoch in history had repeated itself, the resounding echo of fate. Tom couldn't understand the insanity, the chain of events leading so quickly to the estrangement with Wesley and Sara. Certainly, he didn't care to return to the past—not ever.

So Tom got up from the couch an hour before dawn. He woke up early even though he didn't have to go to work. Not a word was said between him and Sara after the fight and her departure to bed the evening before. He left the living room in darkness wearing only a T-shirt on his back and a pair of boxer shorts. He walked down the hallway and opened his son's door and turned on the light. He knew Wesley hadn't come back home before he opened the door. The bed was empty. He realized that he and Wesley were too much alike for the other's good. He hoped the boy would come back home and they could reconcile. Tom turned the bedroom light off but left the door open when he exited the room. He went to the kitchen and lit the gas stove to heat the aluminum percolator coffee pot. The local station no longer played old-time music and jazz during the day or night. He turned on the radio. Now the station only played country records. He listened to Glen Campbell's version of "Galveston," and then "Begging to You," by Marty Robbins. And when the Robbins song quit playing, he turned off the radio in despair.

No matter his desire to stay away from the past and never to return to it, there were times when he regretted the current age, despite the relative peace he'd lived in since his wife was physically healed from the assault and took the position as a clerk at the college library.

By this time of the morning, he used to hear roosters crowing in the coming dawn, and he took great comfort and reassurance in the daily sound, but now none of his neighbors kept chickens any longer. He liked the fresh eggs, but some time after Sara went to work at the library, she made him get rid of all of the chickens. After a stray dog killed several in the yard, she threw a fit. She said, "I'm working a job, a full-time job, and I'll buy my own damned eggs before I deal with all of this stress." So, Tom gave the remaining birds to a neighbor who cooked them with dumplings. Now his coffee, eggs, and milk and all the rest of his food came from a grocery store in Pickleyville.

Tom sat in the cool light and drank his solemn cup of coffee. Nothing seemed right in the world. Nothing appeared to follow logic and common sense, and nothing was more important to him than his wife and son, yet both were in exile away from him.

After the first cup of coffee, he got up from the kitchen table and took a cold biscuit from the refrigerator and put it in the toaster rack in the gas oven. Strawberry jelly waited in the refrigerator. He sat thinking about Wesley, Sara, and their conflict. He thought about the little .22 magnum pump in his bedroom closet, how it hadn't been fired three times in almost a decade. He should have been taking Wesley squirrel hunting somewhere during all of these years, even if they needed to drive up to Mississippi to hunt like some of the local men had started doing. I should have carried that boy hunting, he thought. All we ever did was work in the shop at home. We were together, but it wasn't leisure. It was always work, and I'm not sure it was right.

Sharp regret on his mind, Tom spent all day Saturday in his carpentry shop behind the house. It still looked like an old barn on the outside, despite his renovation on the inside. It had a wood floor made of salvaged pine boards and hardwood walls with shelves and stacks of lumber, as well as the tools of the carpenter's trade hanging from nails. On one of the overhead beams sat an ancient McClellan saddle from the Civil War, a ragged wooden saddle tree with a few scraps of blackened leather and brass. The saddle was something his father had kept in the barn, and he never threw it out because it reminded him of the old man.

His current project, a cedar chest, was a birthday gift from a college professor to his daughter. Tom was facing a deadline, the professor having paid his deposit months ago and the birth date was coming within a week. The party was set for the following Saturday. Tom had fashioned strips of cedar and laminated them. Wesley had helped join the pieces together using dowel pegs, and the bottom of the chest was placed on thin wooden rails. The box was two feet wide and four feet long, and two feet deep. The laminated wood slats showed different grains—red, white, gray, hues of amber—and they would be pretty when the lacquer was applied.

Tom placed a dowel rod into a hole on the bottom. The hole was filled with carpenter's glue, and he tamped the rod down with a wooden mallet. The mallet was made from a fallen hickory tree in the yard, the head fashioned from a limb that he'd shaved down to size. He wished Wesley was there to help him install the hinges on the box lid. He smelled the cedar. It was even more profound after drilling the hole to insert the dowel, and he felt sad that he could not share it with his son.

On Sunday morning, Tom attended the service alone at Little Zion Methodist. They sang hymns: "What a Friend We Have in Jesus" and "O for a Thousand Tongues to Sing." He listened to a sermon taken from the Book of Hebrews preached by Reverend Poole, a local pastor. He worked part-time at the church and taught Senior English at Milltown High School. He had one foot in the world of religion, and the other in the ongoing battle to defeat comma splices, sentence fragments, and incoherent paragraphs. Poole had earned two graduate degrees, one in theology from Southern Methodist University in Dallas, and the other in English from LSU. As a bi-vocational pastor, he stood on the bottom rung of the Methodist clergy ladder, but this suited him well enough. He often said that the proper role of the clergy was that of a servant and not a master, and staying as a local pastor and never getting ordained as an elder prevented him from entering the Methodist rat race toward larger churches and the bishopric.

Tom thought that having a public job allowed the minister to empathize better with the parishioners, since he worked full-time outside of the congregation like everyone else. At least it shielded him from charges of only working on Sundays and not knowing what it was like to function in the real world.

CHAPTER NINETEEN

Wesley's back throbbed from sleeping two nights on Nate's couch. It was a hard plastic couch, something Nate bought for three dollars at a yard sale in LaPlace, a small town south of Pickleyville where he grew up and where his parents lived. Though Wesley had decided to go home and get some clothes, he first worked out an arrangement with Nate to stay the rest of the week. Wesley offered to help out with the rent money and the cost of food.

It was Sunday afternoon, and Wesley closed down the Industrial Arts Shop at four o'clock with his key. The campus was empty, not a car in the lot except for his Ford Maverick. Wesley's stomach was in his throat just thinking about going home to get his things. His eyes twitched, and he couldn't be sure how his father would react when he asked for the tuition money, but he was determined to do it. Around seven hundred and fifty dollars was in a special bank account from what he'd been told by his parents, and he wanted to be sure that he had the money for the fall term squared away. The Claiborne job would cover most of the spring semester's tuition and fees. With a part-time job in Lafayette, Wesley figured he would be able to return in the spring and continue his studies uninterrupted. In the summer, he could find full-time work and sock away enough money for the following fall.

As he walked to his car, the big art portfolio under his arm, a red Mercedes turned down the side street and into the parking lot and honked. Wesley could see Charity's long black hair, her sunglasses and ivory-white smile gleaming in the driver's window of the sleek convertible. The car came to a smooth stop. She leaned out of the window and Wesley bent over to talk to her.

"Hey, Wesley. I drove by to see if you were on campus. It's great finding you here. C.J. said you're always at school working. I saw him yesterday." C.J. Kirby was Wesley's favorite teacher and building supervisor at the Industrial Arts Shop.

"I'm working on your project today." He held his portfolio and squatted beside Charity's door, looking at her face, seeing her flawless skin and tan neck.

She took off her sunglasses, and for the first time, he noticed her deep blue eyes. They looked completely true and sincere, honest and beautiful eyes. They seemed to Wesley more inviting than any eyes he'd seen before.

"I'm so sorry about how we handled the problem with your father on Friday. I should have explained more to Dr. C. beforehand. It caught him off guard, and he reacted like he was surprised by it, I guess."

"Me, too. My father has more or less kicked me out of the house."

Her eyes widened and her brows rose. "Oh my! He's kicked you out. He's that mad about the job?"

"Yes, he's plenty mad that I took work without telling him. He's wound pretty tight and doesn't like to be surprised."

"Wesley, do you want to just drop the whole thing? I'll pay you for the drawings and get someone else to do the job. I don't know who, but somebody'll do it. Maybe you know a good carpenter in the area who can help us." She looked resigned, her hands on her lap. The Mercedes purred, idling like a big old cat.

"No, I need the money for school at USL."

"Come to think of it, the president of Southwestern is a friend of my husband. Dr. C. knows President Van Broussard well over in Lafayette. They've known each other for decades. I think they went to college together or something. I've been to the mansion twice. I bet we could pull some strings and get you a scholarship. We can sure try."

"That would be super. It would be helpful, very helpful."

"Wesley, where are you staying?"

"With my buddy, Nate. But I don't know what I'm going to do until my dorm opens in August. I'm sleeping on his couch. It's as hard as a rock wrapped in rawhide."

"Wow. You know, we have a pool house out back, a little furnished guest cottage. It's got a nice new bed. When we moved to the family home after Dr. C. retired, we figured we'd get a helper to stay there. It had been a caretaker's quarters years ago before the swimming pool was added. It's totally furnished, a studio apartment. I think we could work something out for you to stay with us while you're renovating our study. Just until you leave for Lafayette," she said.

He thought for a second. At that moment, he was standing at a crossroads. One life was on the left and another life lay on the right. He didn't like the choices ahead, but he felt like he was being forced by his father to take one pathway or the other. At least it could sever his relationship with his father, but not his mother. She'd stand by him. An opening was pointing the way toward Charity's world, and he knew to distrust it, but he decided to take the risk anyway.

"Wesley, are you still there," she said, putting her hand on his arm.

"Yes," he said.

"You seemed to zone out on me."

"I'm still here. The apartment sounds fine to me."

"Super. We'll work something out for the rent easily enough. When do you want to come see it?"

"I'll come by tomorrow, if that's okay. I'm going to get some of my things from the house this evening and stay with Nate tonight."

"Excellent. Just call me. Or better, if you see my car under the carport on the side of the house, stop by. Maybe after lunchtime. Dr. C.'s gone to Oxford, Mississippi, doing research. Then he'll come back for one day, and then fly up to Washington to the Library of Congress. He'll be there for a few weeks. But I've already talked to him about having someone stay in the pool house. We were about to run an ad in the school newspaper for a student to live in the guest house and help out around the place, but you can have it until school starts in the fall."

"That's great. Thank you so much."

"I'll see you tomorrow, right?"

"Absolutely."

"You're so sweet. Bye-bye." She drove off waving her hand out of the window.

Wesley felt troubled, as if his back were against a wall. Yet here was a door open wide, and he was going to walk straight through it and deal with the consequences later.

CHAPTER TWENTY

My best guidance will fall on deaf ears, Tom thought, as he waited for Wesley to come home. Despite this knowledge, he prepared a little speech for his son. Both Friday and Saturday night, he waited. Sara was angry and worried, and she was still not speaking to him. The world was often dominated by indifference to hard decisions, benign ambivalence, but this was a rebellion counter to his faithful leadership, kicking against the pricks like St. Paul, an affront to his authority and wishes as a father. Tom knew that Wesley was now twenty, and he was able to make it on his own terms and live by his own lights if he wanted to.

To Tom this was a new age, the dawn of Babylon, brother against brother and child against father. Indeed, it was the kind of world brought to America courtesy of President Richard M. Nixon, a man fit only to lie, a sleaze in an expensive suit with a band that played "Hail to the Chief" every time he strode down a sidewalk. Tom wondered if this was the era when no one had loyalty beyond his own self-interest. He believed this was a time not unlike the Book of Judges in the Bible, a time when "every man did that which was right in his own eyes."

All he wanted was a good life for his son and security for his family. But as much as he wanted to be reconciled with his son, he also wanted Wesley to repudiate Charity Claiborne for his own good, and for the overall welfare of the Hardin family.

It was afternoon. A cold supper waited for him in the refrigerator, surely a silent supper, as his wife had turned off the conversation like a spigot. He got up from the table and went into the yard and walked around a few minutes, and then went to the front porch to think. After a while, Tom started reading a massive book by T. Harry Williams,

Huey Long, a biography of Louisiana's most infamous governor. During a peaceful evening, he could read for hours, but this was no peaceful evening.

Tom heard Wesley's Ford Maverick turn onto Lower Louth Road, just around the corner. He could tell Wesley's car needed a new muffler. The car was only three years old, and they'd just paid it off, and already they had to start making repairs. He put the book down on the bench beside his cypress rocker. The gravel crunched under the car tires as he pulled into the driveway toward the house.

Tom stood. He watched as he got out of the car, several empty cotton sacks in his right hand. "Where've you been, son?" he asked.

"Here and there, almost everywhere, but nowhere in particular," Wesley answered, looking at his father square in the face.

Tom's forearms were tight with muscle as he closed them at his chest. The cavalier tone slapped him, the smart mouth, the lack of a direct and straight answer. "Boy, I'll knock your teeth straight down your throat. You want to come here to the house, you'll show a little respect."

"Yes, sir." Wesley looked down at his feet briefly.

Tom wasn't sure of the sincerity. "Where've you been staying?"

"Over at Nate Forrest's place. On the couch."

"Why didn't you call? Your mother's been worried, and you have a good bed in your room."

"You gave me an ultimatum, Pops. You told me to quit the Claiborne job or don't come back home."

"But you're here now."

"I'm here to get some clothes, if that's all right with you."

"Have at it. What about the Claibornes? You'd be wise to leave them be. Charity is nothing more than a homewrecker. She's got a dark and vicious heart. It's cold as ice beneath that pretty veneer that you see, the hair and makeup and pretty legs, and that German car she drives around like she owns Pickleyville."

"You don't know her well enough to say all of that."

"I know about her well enough. Since way back, she and her people, the LeBlancs, were always a blight on the landscape, even her preacher daddy, and she's the reason old man Claiborne's first wife is dead today. I fervently believe that."

"Are you saying she's some kind of murderer? Come on, Pops. Then why did we go over to the house for the job to start with, if she killed Dr. Claiborne's wife or something?"

Sara gazed through the window in the living room. She held the curtain aside and watched. Tom could see her looking from the corner of his eye.

"I went over there to deal with Dr. Claiborne himself out of common courtesy. He hired your mother in 1965 and me in '67. Now I'm not saying she murdered Mrs. Eliza outright, but that Charity drove her to an early grave by relentlessly pursuing Dr. Claiborne. It was a public disgrace and a true scandal at the college. Not to mention her affairs with that fruity English teacher right after they got back from the honeymoon."

"You blow everything out of proportion."

"I'm telling you, she drove his poor wife to her casket. Mrs. Claiborne was a real sweet lady, too. She was the mother of their children, taught piano lessons in town. I've been inquiring about it all. Charity was set up in that big house where you plan to work even before Mrs. Eliza was dead. She was his mistress. And it was her constant scandalizing that caused the old man to be forced to step down from Baxter State. That's the God's honest truth."

Wesley turned his head away from his father, and Tom thought for a second that he might be able to get Wesley to reconsider. Tom wanted him to change his plans, leave the Claibornes alone. But when Wesley turned back his face, he knew it was not the boy's plan to do the right thing. The young man clenched his teeth and set his jaw in outright defiance.

Wesley said, "All you give me is criticism. I've never done anything in my life that you were happy with. Nothing's ever correct. I give up.

The only thing I want from you is the money for the fall tuition. I need this job for the spring tuition and you know it."

"We have enough money set aside for this coming semester. It gives us another four months to come up with the funds for the spring. And you're not being fair in your assessment of me. I try to do what's best for you and our family at all times, and right now, I don't believe we need the job or any money from Charity LeBlanc or Claiborne or whatever she goes by nowadays," Tom said.

"You're unwilling to compromise. I've had plenty enough of it. I want my tuition money, and I want to leave with some clothes and my car."

"First thing, I need to know what your plans are. Are you planning to stay with Nate Forrest?"

Wesley was almost shaking with rage. He wanted to lie, just tell his father that he was moving in with Nate, and avoid additional conflict. But then he blurted out the truth: "I'm moving into the guest house at the Claiborne place for the next few weeks until the job is done, and then I'm moving to the dorm at USL."

Tom's face was reddened by his son's words, his cheeks hollowing and the blood leaving his head. Rather than arguing, he backed up and sat down in the rocker. He was instantly reminded that he and Wesley built the rockers seven years earlier. Tom was stunned. His body could not feel the cypress wood against his blue jeans.

Wesley began to rant, trying to provoke his father's wrath, knowing there was a vast gulf between them that could not be bridged. It was as if all of the care and friendship they had between them had been for naught.

Tom said nothing. He sat listening on the porch, letting Wesley gripe, make his petty charges.

Now the boy reveled in the permissiveness and kept going on with his complaint. "You're more interested in your own spotless reputation, more interested in your own silly perfection and righteousness than us. That's always your highest priority. It's just an idol that you worship, bottom line. And I'd like to have my college money right now," he said, ending his diatribe with a direct request.

This brought Tom back to Wesley's little speech. He hadn't heard three-fourths of what the boy said. "I wish you wouldn't move in there. It's going to end badly. I guarantee it," he said.

"That's your opinion." He stared at his father and wiped away a stream of tears with his forearm.

"I'll give you the money, but it's in the bank."

"Good. I'm going to pack my clothes."

"Do whatever you think you need to do."

Wesley went to his bedroom and packed enough clothes to last him until the fall, including his winter coat in case he didn't come home for Christmas. Sara followed him into his room talking about trivial things. She acted as though she knew nothing of the trouble with the Claibornes. She stood at his door making small talk as he packed his cotton rucksack, brine tears occasionally slipping from his eyes. She hugged him before he left, and she told him to come home for supper and that she'd wash his clothes any time.

Tom stayed seated on the front porch as Wesley went into the yard to his Maverick. He watched Wesley pack the trunk. "Where do you want to meet me for the money?" he asked.

"How much is it?" Wesley said.

"About eight hundred dollars, I think."

"I'll meet you at the bank on your lunch hour tomorrow. The new drive-through branch over on Thomas Jefferson. At noon."

"Well, tomorrow's Memorial Day. It'll be closed."

"Then make it Tuesday."

"Okay." Tom watched his son go to the car, get in, slam the door, and grind the starter. It wouldn't crank. He could see Wesley pounding the steering wheel with his palms, and he almost went out to help, but then the Maverick engine caught, and the boy left the yard fast, up the gravel driveway and onto the blacktop road.

Tom scanned the yard, which seemed empty and void. At that moment, he felt washed up as a man, never amounting to much, never really accomplishing anything to speak of. He never left the old home place, the little piece of land and house he'd inherited from his father. His mother died when he was nineteen. When he married Sara, she moved into the family home with Tom and his aged father, who died six months later. Over the years they remodeled the house and updated it, much of the work done with Wesley's help. They'd built an additional laundry and den on the backside of the house, as well as the master bath. It was a good and adequate home, and he hoped to leave it to his son one day. Even if it wasn't much, it would be a little something. But this did not show much accomplishment or exhibit a great deal of ambition. Home was all he ever wanted, a good home place. That was his chief ambition in life, to make a home and keep it. Now it appeared to be falling apart at the seams like a cheap pair of boots.

He did not want to deal with Sara's scorn due to his stance against the Claiborne job. Now for a moment he wished he could return back to the old days when he'd go check on his cows or ride his horse into the woods and hunt, maybe call James Luke and go find some raccoons at night with a good dog, maybe have a Catahoula bulldog chained in the yard to guard the place. Nelda and James Luke split two weeks after Sloan Parnell's wreck. Tom lost one of his closest buddies. Truth be told, he rarely thought about James Luke except in rare moments. Now the past didn't add up, nor did the present. Tom had no horse and no hunting dogs, no place to hunt on open range, all of the timber company land now leased to hunting clubs. Much of the old hunting land sold for developments because of its close proximity to the interstate highway. Now trailer parks and a few poorly planned subdivisions dotted the old hunting grounds. He never joined a hunting club. Perhaps for the first time, he came to look at the period of the 1950s and early 1960s as the good old days, but then he recalled his broken wife and the dead body of Sloan and questioned even that memory.

He longed for something else. Perhaps a little peace and quiet, a little tranquility of home and hearth. He wanted to shake Charity's image from his mind altogether. He wondered if he was going to lose his wife, too, in addition to his son. They'd not passed a kind word between each other since the picnic. Trouble was all around him like a haunting for past deeds coming back to find a resting place.

CHAPTER TWENTY-ONE

The marshal was aggravated and cranky. He didn't like being stuck in bed and unable to do anything, laid up like an invalid at Pickleyville's two-bit Ninth Ward General Hospital. The hospital was within his jurisdiction and funded by the same taxes as the Ninth Ward Court and his office. He told everyone who came to visit that he was unable to rest with nurses poking him and prodding him at all hours of the day and night, the hospital stay a type of unfettered harassment.

The doctors said he was lucky to be alive. More than once he wished he'd died from the pain in his chest. He was on the verge of open heart surgery, or so the cardiologist from New Orleans told him, and his arteries were tight with blockages, as tight as a boxer's fist. But he didn't want his sternum cracked open like the shell of a boiled crab. Worse, unlike a crab, he wouldn't receive the charity of being dead before the cracking. They would have to send him to New Orleans or Baton Rouge to do the procedure. The doctors thought he might get by without a surgery, but he had to lose weight, nearly one hundred pounds, quit smoking immediately, and begin taking medication for the blockages. In addition to the heart condition, his sugar was high and staying that way, often resting at three hundred points. He was not a well man, his body a case study in premature morbidity.

His wife Mary Anne was at his side constantly and rarely left him. But Sunday afternoon, she went home for a rest and to do some house work. He could still see the deep concern across her brow when she departed from the hospital room, as if he could tell that she still thought she might lose him.

However, the marshal had a sense that he was not yet ready to finish the race. He had some work left to be done, and he had an accusation of murder and the bizarre testimony of Charity Claiborne to deal with. Not to mention, the whole case of Sara Hardin's attack had come back into focus, a case long closed that needed to be responded to as soon as he was able. To get to the bottom of all of this would take time and effort. No one else would do it. He was sure of that.

He prayed to live on. Others prayed fervently, plenty of others. He was on every church prayer list in the Ninth Ward of Baxter Parish, both Protestant and Catholic, black and white. To clear things up with Charity's ongoing fiasco, he had to be fit to work. He swallowed hard, the drip needle piercing his skin and stinging, the tape holding down the stainless steel spike on his bruised hand.

At first, he was glad that Mary Anne spent time at the hospital. But he was happy now whenever she left him alone for a while. He needed a break from her hovering. She crocheted and tried to engage him in talk, but he did not want to chat aimlessly. After thirty-three years of marriage, he'd about run out of unnecessary small talk. She told her husband that the preacher called the day before and said he was coming to visit in her absence. He asked Mary Anne to tell the preacher to bring Tom Hardin along for the company. Brownlow was simply ambivalent about the minister and his approach to the church and community. He'd seen Methodist preachers come and go at Little Zion Church. Some were good, others fair, and two or three were honest to God rogues by the marshal's own estimation. Poole had been the longest tenured minister at the church by far, and this was attributed to his job as a high school English teacher. He didn't want to leave town or his job teaching, and the bishop chose to keep him at Little Zion. This minister wasn't bad, but simply average. Despite his lack of enthusiasm over the preacher, at least he might have something different to talk about for a little while, something other than Mary Anne's constant chatter.

He hoped the minister could persuade Tom to come to the hospital, which was important for his latest investigation now stalled by a heart attack. He wanted to get a feel for where Tom stood on the events in 1964. All of this could wait. Brownlow was tired. He closed his eyes and tried to take a nap, tried to get a little rest if at all possible before the preacher and Tom arrived.

Late Sunday evening, Reverend Poole drove his Oldsmobile to Tom's house from the parsonage and then to the hospital. In the car, Tom spoke about his work at the junior college campus. He never brought up the struggle with Wesley or the conflict over the Claiborne project. He'd never really confided in Poole or any other minister at the church over the years. There was a private nature about Tom that often prevented him from seeking guidance or help from others.

But there was nostalgia in Tom's mind. He and the minister reminisced about the old days when he used to run cattle and hogs in the woodlands and the period afterward when he made the transition from jack-of-all-trades and woodsman to civil service worker at the junior college maintenance department. Tom rarely spoke of the period, the pine tree wars, or the simultaneous damage to his wife and family. Today, he was stuck in a quandary and was trying to find his way out of it by looking to the past.

"You think Donald's going to pull through?" Tom asked the minister, as he looked out of the Oldsmobile window at the roadside desolation of a Baxter Parish sunset. He rarely went to the hospital except for visiting with the minister when someone was sick in the church.

"There's no way to tell, but I think he's going to be okay. I spoke to the cardiologist and he seemed pretty hopeful. Donald appears to be coming along, but he's not out of the woods yet. Biggest thing is, he's got to push himself away from the table and give up the smokes," Poole said. Reverend Poole was a slim man and the only person in Zion to take up jogging in the 1970s. He was the closest thing to being a health nut in the area.

"Do you ever get tired of going to hospitals and visiting sick people?" Tom asked.

"Well, sometimes I get a little weary of it, distracted mostly. But this is about all I know to do. Preaching is the easy part of my work. A hair-lipped spider monkey could be trained in homiletics, but visiting the sick and the soul-worn is one of the few authentically Christian things that I ever do except for conducting funerals. Most of my work is administrative, and that's not even real ministry at all. It's bureaucratic. I try to stick to doing visitation and sometimes let the other work slide. My most important ministry is dealing with the ill, the dying, and the dead. Like John Wesley said, 'I am always in haste, but never in a hurry.' I take time with these issues. Both my father and uncle were Methodist ministers, and I knew well what I was getting into when I accepted the call to service and went into the parish ministry."

Tom followed the minister through the hallways, his mind elsewhere, his thoughts on the challenges at home. The hospital halls were antiseptic, institutional white in color. The air was cool on Tom's arms, even though he wore a long sleeve dress shirt, the same clothes he'd worn to church in the morning.

He was worried about Wesley. They'd always worked together, spent time together on projects. For all intents and purposes, they were business partners since his son turned twelve years old. They were close, he thought. Wesley had never before entered into a particularly rebellious stage, and Tom felt a measure of uncertainty over the conflict. He'd never faced anything like it before. This problem originated with Charity Claiborne. This much was sure. Why couldn't she leave well enough alone, leave the work arrangements to her husband? Tom was not sure he'd handled it properly. He began to think that he should have humored the crazy woman and taken up business matters later with Dr. Claiborne. Maybe he could have dealt with it all by tripling his fee. Force them to pick somebody else to do the work. If they accepted the exorbitant price, he could contract out the project to another carpenter—

give the work to Lucky Smith, a subordinate at the maintenance department who was poor as a barn lizard and in need of money for his wife and seven kids.

He wished that he'd handled things differently, though he still didn't regret declining Charity's business. He did not want to work directly with her under any circumstances, and he had certain prerogatives and rights as a craftsman.

The minister checked in at the nurse's station. The dour woman at the desk never spoke. She just nodded as she counted ink pens, and he walked to the room, Tom behind him.

The marshal eased up in his bed to greet the visitors, a broad scowl across his face. His supper sat uneaten on the stainless steel tray beside his bed. He looked at the meal, staring at it briefly. "Either of y'all want to eat this stuff? It's so bad it would kill a wild boar dead in his tracks."

"No, I think I'll pass," the minister said, smiling. "You need to eat so you can keep up your strength."

Tom shook his head, frowned.

"I'm not sure that a root hog would eat it, Reverend. An old hog might have to chase the nurse down the hall to get something of virtue to eat," the marshal said. He winked and made a crooked smile.

"You holding up okay, ready to go back home?" the minister asked.

"Might as well be holding up. Dying won't do me no good. Fact of business, being dead'll make a whole bunch of people I don't like happy that I'm finally gone. So I intend to stick it out a while. At least till the Lord's ready for me."

The two visitors sat in chairs and made small talk, telling a few stories, listening to the marshal complain about the hospital, hearing him recite the petty indignities of being ill. Reverend Poole tried to act upbeat, chipper, sounding as positive as a Fuller Brush Man standing at a widow's front door trying to make a sale. Being upbeat was a Methodist preacher's primary vocational requirement.

After twenty minutes, the minister said he needed to go see Mrs. Inez Jones, a church member facing gallbladder surgery in another hospital ward. He led Brownlow and Tom in a brief prayer for healing and strength.

Tom stood to leave with him, but the marshal waved for him to stay. "Look, if it won't be an undue hardship, Reverend Poole, I'd just as soon have Tom stay right here with me while you go down the hall for your other ministry visit. We can talk here while you're visiting the sick."

Reverend Poole glanced at Tom. He said he'd return shortly and left the room.

Tom thought that this was a little odd, but he didn't mind waiting. The fact that the marshal had asked the minister to bring him along in the first place must have meant that he wanted to talk about something. He sat down in the straight-backed chair, and took a deep breath.

There was silence as if the two men were sizing up each other for a contest of some kind.

"We got us a real problem," the marshal said, "and I was tending to it when I had this damned heart attack. Serious trouble is brewing."

"What is it?" Tom asked. The grave look on Brownlow's bloated and puffy face caused him alarm. The marshal seemed to be in some form of distress talking about the trouble at hand.

"These doctors aim to kill me to make me better. If it wasn't for my wife and daughter, I'd tell them to leave me the hell alone so I could roll over and die like an old dog. Well, that's not true. I've got plenty to do yet, and I don't reckon I'll ever get caught up with it till I die or retire. And I plan to be retired at the end of this year. Not too many people know it yet." The marshal pushed himself up higher in the bed and almost smiled.

A nurse barged into the room and the marshal told her to turn around and leave. He was involved in official police business. She stayed a few seconds to let him see that she was offended, but left without saying a word.

"Don't let 'em kill you," Tom said.

"No, I plan not to. But I'm glad you came here today. When I was hit with the attack, I was intending to call on you. Tom, I'm going to go on and put the cards on the table for you. Charity LeBlanc, that damned hellacious woman, and I won't dare call her a lady, came to see me," he said.

Tom didn't like the turn in the conversation. He hated to hear Charity's name, especially after the mess at the barbeque on Friday and the trouble with Wesley, everything flowing from it like feces rolling downhill. He began to think of her as his mortal enemy, an absolute foe. He gripped the edge of his chair with his right hand, the veins in his forearm.

"She's caused me some grief recently," the marshal continued. "It's not the first time, but she's gone and done it again. What she says is she's been hit with the Holy Ghost at Brother Thad Hussert's church in Milltown, them sons-a-bitching Pentecostals, no offense intended to anybody's religion. That Brother Hussert calls himself 'The Apostle,' if you dare believe it, and according to what she says, her newly revived faith has got a hold of her, and she's now started confessing her past sins. She came to my office on Tuesday of last week to lay down a burden, and she claims that she made some anonymous phone calls to me and you back in '64, and that it caused all kinds of violence. I ain't completely clear that's what it was all about, but I don't hardly know anymore. People are so damned crazy nowadays." He was taking short breaths from talking too much.

"What have I got to do with her?" Tom asked. Now both of his hands were clasping the arms of the chair on each side of his thighs. He squeezed the wood tight, gripping and then releasing. He realized she'd gone to see the marshal one day after he and Wesley had gone to the Claiborne House and refused the job.

"Tom, I hate to tell you some of the nutty-assed allegations she said about you and your wife, but it's been dropped into my lap, and I've got to go address it straightway. I don't even want to bring up the old history, now long passed. But I've got so little choice left," Brownlow said. He rubbed his finger on his forehead to remove a line of sweat. "She says that Sloan Parnell did not rape your wife."

"Okay. What's new about that? I pretty much figured that out myself."

"Well, instead she says you and Jim Cate killed Sloan, and Jim raped and beat your wife himself. That's a real hard pill to swallow. She says Jim and Sloan Parnell both were sleeping with Sara, some kind of love triangle, and that Jim did the raping and beating on Sara when he found out that she was running around with Sloan, too. On top of all that, she accuses you of killing Sloan and burning down the old Parnell place, and she's going to tell Judge Parnell directly."

"It's all a lie. It's just a damned lie," Tom said. He stood up without thinking. "My wife did no such thing." He pointed at the marshal with his index finger.

"Tom, please sit on back down," Brownlow said. "We're just getting started."

Tom sat. He appeared ashen, one lone tear emerging from the duct in his right eye and staying there, never falling. His jaw trembled.

"Did you burn down the old Parnell place?" asked the marshal.

"No, I never burned anything, not a single pine tree," Tom said.

"Do you know who burned down the Parnell place?"

"No."

"She says Sloan was sleeping with Sara, and she told Jim about it during a phone call one day. Then Jim tricked you into going after Sloan out of pure revenge. Undoubtedly, Jim coaxed you into doing it to cover up for what he'd had done to Sara, maybe. Charity says Jim was championing Sloan's death—and that either you or he did it alone or both did it in some kind of a conspiracy. I don't know what to think. Of course, I looked into Sloan's death back then and found it to be an accident. This is all a bunch of trouble. Now I've got to investigate the accusations. I don't know what to believe, but there's bound to be some truth in it somewhere. There's always a little truth in every damned lie. What

I've got to deal with more than anything is if you had any part of Sloan's death. That's the big question I've got to answer."

"The answer is no. Neither James Luke nor I had anything at all to do with Sloan's death. We were together, but Sloan ran off the road on his own accord, driving ninety to nothing and blind drunk at midnight."

"Then why in the hell were you at the barroom that night, and why the hell were you in the woods where he wrecked? Y'all were there and following behind him. Jim was a heavy drinker, not you. You're no barfly. It makes no sense to me."

"I was there to see if he had my father's stolen pocket watch. I got an anonymous call from a woman that I couldn't identify by listening to her voice. Until this day, I've had no idea who called me. Now I know."

"Did Parnell have it?"

"Yes, he did."

"And you tried to kill him over it? Or was it over what he did to Sara?"

"Neither. He was drunk and ran off the road. He didn't even know we were anywhere behind him."

"But had he not run off the road, what were you going to do?"

"I don't know."

"Y'all were ramming him with your truck bumper, weren't you?"

"No, I said he drove the Scout so fast we weren't anywhere near him. The motor must have been hopped-up or something. We were at least a half-mile behind him when he ran straight through the "T" at Lizard Bayou and Joe Bageant Road and out into the woods. We couldn't have caught up to him if we'd wanted to."

"How sure are you of this?"

"Dead sure."

"Well, we sure have us a dead man, so being dead is plenty appropriate. What about Jim and your wife?"

Tom grew quiet, stiff, and his eyes watered more. The story carried a devilish sting. "I don't believe it. I don't see how it makes any sense.

I just can't believe it. How does this Charity woman know any of this to be true?"

The marshal shrugged. "Charity is the underbelly of Baxter Parish, and she's gone from the bottom to the top. Crazy? Yes. A liar? Uh-uh. But like I said, there's a kernel of truth to it. She says Parnell did some confessing of his own to her. His tongue tended to run free when he got some whiskey on it, she said, which is true."

"I can't believe a word of it. It defies all common sense, everything I know to be true."

"Tom, there was a lot of peculiar things happening in the '60s. Things went upside down. I barely understand it all myself. Hell, somebody told me the other day that J. Edgar Hoover wore a dress and was queer as a three-dollar bill. The man that told me this had a brother that worked for the FBI. My God, Tom! J. Edgar Hoover, head of the Federal Bureau of Investigation, in a dress? What in the hell was happening back then?"

"I agree, some things went haywire back in the 1960s, but that doesn't mean my wife ran around with these men. At the time, James Luke was my best buddy. And my wife sleeping with some shitbird like Sloan doesn't add up. Charity came to you with all of that crap because I wouldn't build them a set of shelves and cabinets at their house on Thomas Jefferson Avenue. I turned down a job at their place on Monday of last week. It got kind of nasty at the college barbeque on Friday, too. They took mortal offense to my not accepting the job."

"So y'all had some kind of disagreement?"

"We did. This past week was a circle in Dante's hell."

"Dante?" A puzzled look came across the marshal's face. "Look, I don't mean none of this is absolutely true. I surely don't. I'm not accusing anybody of nothing. But there's some questions arising that ain't nobody has ever asked. As a matter of business, where was James Luke the day your wife was attacked?"

Tom was gray-faced, too shocked to be angry. His hands were limp and wet with sweat in his lap. "I recall he was off from work that day. It never was clear what he was doing. I never asked."

"You sure?"

"I remember clearly that he was off work. That much I know."

"Didn't he divorce Nelda soon after?"

"Yes, he did. He left town a few months after the attack on Sara. They divorced, and he moved to Baton Rouge."

"Why'd they part ways?"

"The story that was passed around was that he was cavorting with some woman at the highway barn from what I recall, a secretary or something, and Nelda found out. Again, that's what I understood at the time. They split up. Nelda married two years after they divorced and lives in Dahlonega, Georgia, with her second husband."

"Where's Jim living now?"

"I never heard from him since he left, but I was told he's a bigwig with the Army Corps of Engineers in Natchez or Vicksburg, Mississippi."

"Tom, I mean no disrespect to your wife and family, but I've got to get to the bottom of this thing before Charity goes to the Parnells about Sloan's death and stirs up something from bad to worse. I'd just as soon you keep a lid on everything."

"All right. No disrespect taken." Tom was too shocked to take immediate offense.

"I need to interview your wife."

"Okay. When?"

"It might be a while. I can't do a damned thing till I get my ass out of this hospital bed and get my old sea legs back underneath me."

"I could bring her over here."

"No, we'll wait on it. I'll be in touch. Tom, you give me your word that you won't talk to her about any of this or talk to anybody else either?"

It was quiet in the hospital room for a moment. He ran a finger over the IV in his hand. The marshal stared at Tom.

Tom buried his face into his hands. "Do I need to go see a lawyer about the wreck that night? Neither I nor James Luke had anything to do with it. Sloan was blind drunk, and went off the road on his own accord. That's just the way it happened. In fact, I made James Luke call an ambulance when we found Sloan in the pasture."

"I believe you. I don't think you need to see no lawyer. It's consistent with my investigation back in '64. But I know y'all were up to no good. That doesn't mean anything illegal took place. No, I don't reckon you need to go see no lawyer. So have I got your word? You won't talk to nobody?"

"I'll keep quiet. I won't speak to Sara or anyone else."

"Then don't say nothing to nobody. But how in the hell did Jim Cate become a bigwig?"

"He had a lot of ambition deep down. He went to the Noah Pickens School of Commerce and Business in Baton Rouge back in the late '50s for some kind of certificate, and then he went to work for the highway department, and then migrated up to Mississippi. From what I heard, he married a rich man's daughter in Natchez, after he divorced his second wife. Seems like he was only married to his second wife for a short time. Nelda never had any money to her name, but James Luke married up every time."

"That'll do it. Marrying a bigwig's daughter'll make you a bigwig as fast as Roger Bannister can run a mile. Been my experience it's the easiest way in the world to get wealthy in this country."

About this time, the minister entered the room. As was the local custom, all real conversation stopped when he said, "Hello, gentlemen."

CHAPTER TWENTY-TWO

On Memorial Day, Wesley was glad to find that the downtown hardware store was open for business half a day, as was the hardware and lumberyard owned by the Sicilians on the edge of town near I-55. He got two quotes on the materials for the Claiborne project, and he wrote everything up as a formal bid, putting together the estimate using a typewriter in the Industrial Arts Shop.

He was a young man trying to make his way in the world. The disagreement between Wesley and his father had been brewing over time. It was not just the one thing, though the casual observer might think it was. Rather, it was the many unspoken rifts between father and son over the years that led to this crescendo of resentment and anger. He'd never bucked his father openly. Instead, he took whatever was dished out, always staying quiet no matter the rule or request.

After eating some pork ribs that Nate had cooked for lunch, Wesley drove the Maverick a few blocks through Pickleyville's streets from the garage apartment to the Claiborne House. He pulled onto Thomas Jefferson Avenue where the Claibornes lived. Several of the houses on the street looked like antebellum mansions, and others were large places with five or six bedrooms, some with guest houses out back for servants. Most places were built in the Midwestern style by merchants who came down the Illinois Central Railroad to recreate a town exactly like the ones they'd left in the Midwest during the 1920s. The houses were built for the merchant class, spacious family homes on large square and rectangular lots similar to the ones they'd parted from in the cold Iowa air as they moved to the sunny Gulf South. Typically, the houses had second stories and some had third floor lofts with windows overlooking the street. These homes were constructed in the heady years before the

1929 Stock Market Crash, and many of the places in Pickleyville had been lost to the banks during the rise of the Great Depression era.

A moment of fear seized Wesley as he turned off the car ignition. At no time after sitting near his father at the picnic had he felt this kind of anxiety. It was choking him. He was both excited to take the plunge toward Charity but also worried about the danger inherent in dealing with a married woman with her reputation. He might have disagreed with his father about the woman and the job, but he knew his father couldn't be completely off base in his assessment of the woman. She was just too forward, too friendly.

He looked across the manicured lawn up to a brick walkway that led to the wooden front door. A plaque stuck into the lawn announced that it was the May 1974 Garden Club award-winning landscape. The door was painted red, almost the same shade as the Mercedes parked under the carport. No other cars were there. He wondered if he should leave the safety of the little Maverick, knowing that there was a dangerous liminal space to cross. He felt like he was seeing a Monet painting where the image was blurred. He no longer saw the closed front door. It opened wide and Charity Claiborne came down the steps to meet him, bounding on her toes like a school girl in the afternoon light. She wore a blue mini-skirt and a tight blouse, and she smiled, calling him out of the car. She insisted on helping him carry his things to the little guest house beside the swimming pool, and she apologized that the daytime workers had gone home and couldn't assist with the bags. This being a holiday, she let them go home early, she said.

Wesley carried his portfolio and two rucksacks, and she packed a small bag of books. He eased into her domain like a runt wolf lost in an enemy pack's territory. But for the first time in his life, he felt like a grown man.

CHAPTER TWENTY-THREE

T om grew pensive after the trip to the hospital. On his day off for the holiday, he went to his shop out back early in the morning before Sara awoke. He did not want to see her face. He worked on the cedar chest. The lights were on inside the shop, a bright and crisp contrast to the utter darkness outside. He tried to work into the predawn, but he did more sitting and thinking than actual carpentry.

Few families farmed for a living any longer in Zion. There were a dozen small strawberry farmers out east of Milltown, but that was about it. Only a small fraction of the region was planted compared to a decade before. Some folks kept hobby gardens, but most privately owned farmland was planted in pine trees or overrun with brush, scrub trees like Chinese tallow. A number of local men fished in the lakes nearby, running crab pots in Lake Tickfaw and shrimping in Lake Ponchatoula. Everyone else bought all of their food at National or A & P in Pickleyville, or at Burke's in Milltown. There was still a fruit stand on Highway 22, and people sold vegetables on the roadside out of the beds of pickup trucks, fruits and vegetables from pickup beds, produce they'd bought elsewhere, often in Mississippi, and sold as retail. One man on Pine Street sold vegetables near the Catholic school. He had a white hand-painted sign that read: THESE VEGETABLES ARE HOME-GROWN... AT SOMEBODY'S HOME. MAY GOD BLESS YALL FOR STOPPING BY.

Now the fortunate people held a state job, and almost no one made their livelihoods from the woods and swamps except for a few timber men. The forests were impassable thickets, no cows or hogs to clean up the underbrush, which became uncontrollable and impenetrable. Fire was the greatest enemy of these thickets, but the burning was fought tooth and nail by the timber companies and the state foresters. In the old days, fire preserved the forest, but not anymore. The risk to the young pines and nearby homes was too great for regular burning. The old longleaf pines were resistant to fire, but not the loblolly. Now houses and trailers could be threatened as the underbrush became a hot flash of burning debris. So the state foresters cut fire lanes throughout the woods with a bulldozer equipped with a large plow on back to make furrows in the ground that would prevent fires from getting out of hand.

Tom could see that the world was going soft. Men began to grow as obese as corn-fed sows. Immobility of body was evidence of opaqueness of mind. Time now fell away with the frivolity of television, which required nothing more than personal isolation and consumption. Little good was left to be accomplished in a given day except waiting for death.

Because locals no longer worked on farms, ran cattle, or tended their gardens, men became interested in the timewaster called "mowing the lawn" with little toy tractors. Loud and obnoxious substitutes for real John Deere farm tractors. Tom realized that in due course these people would only have violence to entertain them.

He picked up his claw hammer. His nails were in the cotton pouch tied around his waist. He fastened a decorative strip to the front of the chest with some small brads. The claw hammer was a tool he'd used for many years. It had a hickory handle that had been strangely notched when he bought it at an estate sale in Ruthberry for two bits. He never knew why there were carved notches, the grooves placed in the handle near the butt end like mementos cut into pistol grips. He knew such a tool could become a formidable weapon if not being used for its intended purpose. In a state of purposelessness, any good tool could become a weapon. If folks quit caring and let the land return to weeds, stopped tending their own spiritual and physical home places and gardens, Tom believed, even a claw hammer became nothing better than a tool for evil. He wondered what was going on in the world.

However, Tom understood some change was necessary and good. Yet not all change was right. Much of what he read in the Pickleyville *Star-Ledger* was nothing more than Chamber of Commerce ideology and feel-good nonsense. There were some other changes he could not agree to, the general lack of respect that had overtaken society. Tom wished these changes to the community had never taken place. It was the death of neighborliness and familial love that seemed the worst of all. The death of common courtesy. He believed it started with the Vietnam War, a program of conquest that sought nothing less than to rip the country to shreds.

He opposed the war quietly, which bothered him sometimes. He was not showy and never considered going to a war protest. There was only one protest in Baxter Parish, back when General Westmoreland came to the junior college in 1968. Eight people showed up with placards and were run off by the ROTC. In disgust over Westmoreland's invited speech, Tom stayed at the Ponderosa during the general's visit and never left the building despite being asked to attend by his foreman.

In a manila folder, he kept a couple dozen letters, letters to his senators and congressmen over Vietnam, typed letters written on Sara's little Olivetti, a letter a year to the elected officials since J.F.K. had been President, all to no avail. It seemed that only a total lack of will by politicians to pay for the war itself could do any good. His vain letters were mailed but received no reply. He couldn't even bring peace to his own family, much less stop a war in Southeast Asia.

Tom was happy that his son would not have to go to the deadly war. He was no pacifist but could never wrap his mind around this conflict in Indochina. When he joined the navy, he could commit himself to stopping Hitler and Tojo, but he never could reach the slightest understanding of the war in Vietnam. He couldn't understand it no matter how hard he tried, no matter how much he gave his government the benefit of the doubt.

It was the American struggle against the war, too, that lowered the threshold for temperance and respect. It was as if all sense of propriety went missing from the country. How could any person cry, "Burn baby burn!" like they did in Watts? He could not fathom it. Either the seeds of McCarthyism or Woodstock were coming home to roost, maybe both.

In all of the freedom talk and harping on civil rights, he saw little progress, the exception being the ability of blacks to register to vote, go to a decent school, and avoid a lynch mob. He could see very little forward progress in the world. Though he was in favor of civil rights, an inevitable and a necessary change to society, he believed it was the failure of the American Way of Life not to end slavery over 100 years ago and head off the bloody Civil War. Now the common good went nowhere beyond a person's self-interest. No sense of purpose, no sense of hope, no sense of shared destiny. There was no public sense that to harm a neighbor is to harm oneself.

These chaotic times were truly cruel and hard on a man's soul, times when son took arms against father. In general, folks acted as though they were happy, but Tom thought their happiness was a false light in a dying and darkened world. His family, he thought, had enjoyed happiness for years before Sara's rape, but since that time he'd seen a harsher world, more daily pain, a hard world with less mercy in it, less love and little honor. Upon hearing the words from Marshal Brownlow at the hospital, he wondered if everything he understood about his family life was a sham, a mere charade, maybe just another gigantic American lie like Vietnam.

He and the family always seemed to look over their shoulders since 1964, unconsciously looking back at the trouble that haunted them. Perhaps a time was coming for another shoe to drop. Tom realized that the shoe was already dropping when the marshal told him of James Luke Cate's possible connection to his wife's assault. Maybe it was Charity offering her little confession that caused hell to make a personal visit to Zion. He wondered if this current trouble was going to be the final blow as he stared at his hammer about to tap down the little brad into the cedar wood.

CHAPTER TWENTY-FOUR

O n Tuesday at five minutes after twelve, Wesley met his father at Tickfaw State Bank to get his college money. It was the first bank branch in Baxter Parish with a drive-through window. Wesley arrived early, and he stood waiting outside for his father.

The young man gritted his teeth when Tom pulled into the lot with his truck. Tension seemed to pass from one to another, their faces radiating heat through their bodies. They walked stiffly, not saying a word as they entered the little bank branch.

Once in the lobby, Tom said, "Son, I'll do what you want. I'll build the cabinets and shelves for the Claibornes, but I don't want your help. And I surely don't want you living over there. Move on back home today, and I'll do the whole project by myself. Stay away from that woman and the house, and we'll make our peace. How about that, son?" He was surprised by his own offer, his mouth open and his cheeks gray.

"No, I don't want you to do that. I just want the money for college, and I'll complete the project myself. It's long past the time for me to move out on my own anyway," Wesley said, perturbed by his father's conciliatory gesture.

Tom grimaced.

Wesley could see the disappointment issuing from his father's eyes when he turned to walk up to the teller's window. Tom gave the woman his account number and asked for all the money in savings. He said he wanted everything that was available, which came to eight hundred and twenty-seven dollars. The savings account was drained empty, and the cash was counted out and placed into Tom's palm. He handed it to his son.

"Thank you," Wesley said, and he walked away from the bank and his father without saying anything more.

At the pool house in the Claiborne's backyard, Wesley put all of the money he'd received inside an envelope and slipped it between the pages of Ayn Rand's *Atlas Shrugged*, his favorite book, which he'd read the summer before. It was one of a dozen books he brought to the pool house. The envelope was marked with the date and dollar amount: "5-28-74 - $1012." It was all of the money he had saved plus the money his family had been putting away for school, the eight hundred and twenty-seven dollars. He was going to ask for the first half of the money from Charity, minus his rent. She said the rent would cost him fifty dollars per month, phone and utilities included. He planned to stay a month or two at the most and then leave as quickly as he'd arrived.

Wesley was placing his clothes in the empty cedar chifforobe when he heard a metallic noise outside and went to the window shade and saw Charity squaring a chaise lounge with the edge of the swimming pool, her terrycloth robe placed across the waist-high wrought iron pool fence. Her back to him, she was dressed in a green bikini top and bottom with a towel over her arm. A magazine and a pack of Kools were in her hand along with a small brown bottle. Her breasts were large, skin almost golden. The word "perfect" flowed in and out of Wesley's mind like a guilty dream.

He watched her sit down on the chaise lounge and untie her bikini top and gaze out at the blue water. Then she turned her face toward the pool house and winked at him, gesturing to him with her chin, opening the magazine to shield her bare chest from sight.

Wesley jumped away from the window, the blinds closing abruptly where he had bent them back to gaze out. He was rattled and embarrassed. He put the heel of his palm against his head. "Shit, I'm busted bad," he said out loud.

Wesley composed himself for a few minutes, trying to forget about being caught while gazing out of the window shade. He sat on the bed to get his nerve up and then gathered his carpenter's toolbox to go over to the house to begin prepping the room for the work. Rather than looking out the window before leaving, he opened the door wide like nothing had happened. He could see Charity now on her stomach sunning, her straps down, and back open. She turned her head toward him and grinned.

"You don't have to worry. I'm not going to get up. What are you planning to do today? And what's in the box?" she asked.

"Uh," he answered sounding stupid, unsure what she'd just said. "Oh, I'm going to start work on the study, if you don't mind. These are my tools."

"Sure. But please do me a favor first."

"Ah-ha."

"Put some oil on my back, would you, Wesley? I'm trying to tan, not burn, and I can't reach it all." She picked up the brown bottle from the ground near her side and held it up, her head turned toward him.

He knew better, but he put down the wooden box and reached for the bottle of oil anyway. He poured some of it on her back and began to rub it in. After a second, he got down on his knees and kneeled beside her to reach across her long back, the smell of coconut filling his head. He wondered if perhaps this was the temptation of the Garden of Eden set in Pickleyville on Thomas Jefferson Avenue.

That first evening, Wesley and Charity went out to eat a late dinner at the Firefly Inn across town. Afterward, they had drinks in the informal den of the big house, and they listened to some of Charity's rock albums on the hi-fi. After a few hours of drinking and dancing to the music, he and Charity went to bed in the upstairs room. A line was crossed while she was poolside, the moments when he was watching her from the window. He had been a virgin. Sex with her made him weak-minded and giddy about his new found pleasure and great luck. The night in her bed made him tired and excited, like a hound near the end of a hunt, and he could only hope for another chance.

CHAPTER TWENTY-FIVE

Once a year, James Luke and his third wife, Heloise Tartt Cate, went to the black-tie fundraiser for the mayor of Natchez on the Fourth of July. James Luke owned a tuxedo with a big bowtie, which he only wore when he was forced to. He hated the annual event. The mayor was vying for his third four-year term. James Luke had plans to grow his business into a more respectable real estate venture on both sides of the Mississippi, investing in property acceptable to genteel Natchez elite rather than continuing his slumlording north of downtown in the black quarters. He would need the mayor's office to acquire easy permits for his real estate investments, and the mayor needed his contribution to the campaign.

The party took place at the Rosalie Hotel ballroom, a great hall adorned with red, white, and blue. The couple spoke very little on the way over in part because neither of them wanted to go to the event. The Cates lived in a prominent part of town, a somewhat modest but adequate historic home that Heloise had inherited from her maternal grandparents. James Luke married her for the money, and the fine cottage was just one advantage to marrying up in the world. They both despised the pretense necessary for life in Natchez, but making appearances was the price of doing business, or at least a major part of success was buying a ticket and showing up. They wanted to escape, but there was no escape in gentrified Natchez.

The mayor said, "Hello there, Mr. Cate," as he greeted folks at the front door to the ballroom where he stood in the receiving line. James Luke shook his hand, and Mayor Cecil Pearce kissed Heloise on the cheek. "Y'all been staying busy?" he asked.

"Real busy. Just to pay my city taxes, I've got to work three jobs," James Luke said, partly joking, but trying hard to jab the mayor where it might hurt him.

"Well, y'all go enjoy some good music and food inside," the mayor said. He didn't bite on James Luke's tax comment, and he shook hands with the next couple in line as quickly as possible.

James Luke and Heloise walked into the ballroom as the band played "The Night They Drove Old Dixie Down," the song a well-loved local anthem of the Lost Cause. The musicians covered both traditional country and Southern Rock tunes. The drummer beat the cymbals, metallic noise clanging, and the sound was accentuated by the bass guitar and strong vocals. Amplified Rock and Roll rhythms pulsed through the room. It was obnoxiously loud like the sounds of a pounding hammermill. Political supporters and their teenage children were there for the fundraiser, and some young people danced on the open floor.

The Cates made pleasantries with everyone they encountered, etiquette befitting James Luke's wife's lifelong social connections. He took a mixed drink from a black waiter's silver serving tray.

The band ended the set and left their instruments for drinks and cigarettes. The noise was grating on James Luke's nerves, the amps turned several notches higher than necessary for enjoyment.

Someone tapped James Luke's shoulder sheepishly from behind. He turned around and saw his father-in-law, Franklin Tartt, acting coy. They shook hands. James Luke's wife and mother-in-law were already sitting at a table drinking cocktails, visiting and complaining about the deafening music now on a short break.

"You clean up pretty nice for the public," Tartt said. He was a third generation money-handling banker, the kind of man that spends his entire day trying to beat a customer out of a dollar, and then patting him on the back and calling his prey his best friend.

"I try. I always want to look like I have a small portion of your holdings," James Luke said, laughing.

"Come on now. You've got every bit of three times my money."

"No, you're white collar, and I've still get dirt on my boots every damned day of the week."

"Hell, you own two-thirds of North Natchez. Folks say you're going to run for mayor when this jack-legged clown finishes up his next term."

"My word, I don't even own a percent of the places in the quarters, and I'd have to be brain-dead to run for public office. Besides, the mayor's post ain't worth a bucket of dried horse dumplings. All he does is listen to people bitch about their water bills and the coloreds day and night, but I do hate to see that asshole Pearce get reelected year after year, even if I did give him three hundred dollars for this campaign fundraiser to do business around town. All the bullshit you've got to go through to work in Natchez. I'm already neck-deep in bureaucratic crap with the Corps of Engineers."

"Well, I still think you want to be the mayor." Tartt acted as if he knew James Luke well. Yet he remained an enigma. The closer he got to James Luke, the farther away he was from the heart of the man. Most people in Natchez, Tartt had no idea how distant he was from true knowledge when it came to James Luke Cate.

Sometimes at night he sat awake plotting his plans like a moribund chess player trying to win a championship. But he did not play by any set rules other than the ones he made up to further his own intrigues. There was no guidebook to follow unless he created it himself *ex nihilo*, out of nothing. His only constraint was the will to power, his willingness to stick a fist in another man's face if necessary. James Luke trusted his wrath and decisiveness, not empty talk, not book learning, and he believed direct action created more wealth and privilege than an entire university business department working overtime. He was the Friedrich Nietzsche of Natchez, and no one fully comprehended it.

"James Luke, you need another drink?" Tartt said.

"Yeah, whiskey sour."

"Me, too." Tartt was a lush, plastered most evenings after six o'clock, usually falling asleep in his living room chair with a glass of whiskey neat. He said to the waiter, "Boy, go get us a couple of whiskey sours." He then turned to his son-in-law. "That old waiter looks almost as good as you in a tuxedo." Franklin Tartt laughed as he lit a cigarette.

James Luke faked a smile and let the comment slide.

They endured several windbag political speeches, the rallying of the troops, faith unchecked in the upcoming administration, promises as empty as cotton candy to the crowd of paying constituents, the price of democracy. The money was a pittance compared to what James Luke would make in the drug trade alone, not to mention the slumlording, all of which was helped along by a clean reputation as a hardworking Natchez-area businessman. This was all part of his strategy to expand wealth and domination. He was fifty-three years old, and he wanted to score big. He always heard that any man who could count all of his money and assets did not have nearly enough to brag about or be content with. Real money was weighed like overdrawn metaphors, the conspicuous symbols of large estates, tens of thousands of shares of stock, percentages of corporate ownership, but not cash tender. Let others estimate your worth from a distance and envy it. He didn't have the assets to afford such comfort, but he was determined to get filthy rich or die in the process.

At home on South Pearl Street, the housekeeper had taken a telephone message for James Luke while they were at the campaign event. It was a note written in pencil on a slip of yellow paper. "Mr. Cate, please call Mr. Marshall Brown Low at his home in Louisiana."

When James Luke read the note, he chuckled.

"What's funny?" Heloise asked.

"Oh, nothing, just Beulah's spelling. The way she wrote something down." He stuck the note in his pants pocket, and loosened his cummerbund.

"What's it about?"

"There's an old boy down in Louisiana that's called about a dog. But hell, I ain't raised hunting dogs since I moved to Baton Rouge.

Something about owing him a puppy from a litter's stud service. He'll give me a hundred dollars' worth of hell about not getting him his pick of the litter. And it's been a decade at least. I guess something's got in his craw," James Luke said.

"After all of these years?" Her frown was slightly crooked, askance, and questioning.

"Yeah, stupid people always get obsessed with what's too late to change. The man called me six months or so back, and I heard an earful about not giving him the pick of the litter on a redbone hound or some such that he claims I promised him years ago. Truth be told, I have little memory of it. I said I had a purebred black and tan litter coming along in a month's time." James Luke smiled and grabbed his wife and hugged her, squeezing her bottom until she giggled.

"But you don't have any hunting dogs to give him a puppy. What can you do for him now?"

"Nothing."

"So you're lying to him?"

"No, I'm stalling. Eventually, he'll say he's coming up here, and I'll go fetch him a puppy from the city pound over on Liberty Road, a hound-looking mutt maybe, and give it to him. Promise him the papers in a week, by mail, of course. Then he can kiss my freckled ass good-bye. The postal service ate them papers and shame on them for it. That was my only set. Blame Uncle Sam. You can't lose in the South blaming the government."

"You're so bad," she said.

He kissed her on the neck and whispered into her ear: "'Bad is good,' my daddy liked to say."

The next morning, James Luke sat on the screen porch of his antebellum cottage and stared at the slip of yellow paper in his hand. "Please call Mr. Marshall Brown Low at his home in Louisiana." He pondered it, went through his options.

Despite the sly assurances he'd given his wife, he did not know ex-actly what this man wanted, but he figured his years of criminal activity in Baxter Parish were finally catching up to him. There was no need to guess what it was about, he reasoned. If the marshal wanted to arrest him, he would get his lawyer to fight it. A good lawyer fashioned the law for his client like a pimp setting up a prostitute with a john. That's what he'd learned since moving to the state of Mississippi. It was just a transaction based on need. The more money he made, the more he used his lawyer to take care of everyday problems as they arose.

It had been almost a decade since he'd lived in Louisiana, and he figured the statute of limitations ought to soon take care of nearly eve-rything. He had not killed anyone, so he wasn't worried about a capital crime without a limitation of years. He'd call the marshal to see what was going on. No use in running away from it. His wife was now off his trail, and she wouldn't ask any more questions. She was highly pre-dictable, and he knew he had her stiff-armed on this one—at least for now.

James Luke remembered the fires. He didn't care anything about the hardwoods or the hogs in the woods. But he hated the Parnells, hated P.T. and Sloan who beat him out of a tract of land in Kilgore that he was going to buy and pay for by selling the trees. The two hundred acres of land was owned by a black family in Biloxi, and they didn't know the value of the trees. When he tried to contract with a local timber man to clear cut the property, Sloan got wind of the deal and his father bought the land out from under James Luke. It was a grudge that ate at James Luke like a cancer.

He started to systematically burn Parnell and Fitz-Blackwell prop-erty. Much of it was done in his truck, riding through the country roads with his coon dogs chained in the bed. He had several packs of ciga-rettes loaded with matches below the tobacco. He'd light a cigarette, take two drags and toss it out of the truck window. The matches would catch when the fire hit the sulfur tips. The cigarettes started roadside fires, and the arson was impossible to trace back to James Luke, a simple hunter in the woods.

But he also rode Diablo, his black horse, slipping through swaths of timber company land at night, young plantation pine trees laid out in rows like corn. A cotton rope trailed behind the horse. The rope was tied to a special D-Ring on the back of his saddle, a tool he often used to drag hogs. James Luke fastened a collection of greasy rags doused in lard and kerosene to the end of the rope, which he lit. He rode Diablo between the pines. With a slow breeze blowing, the fire spread through the pine needles. The wind urged the fire to grow as the horse pushed deeper into the woods, walking his natural gait. The young pines began to burn behind him. Finally, the fire consumed the cotton rope itself near the back hooves of the horse. When James Luke saw the fire closing in, he'd dismount and stomp out the little fire from the remaining rope with his boot. Then he'd gather the rope, wrap it into a circle, and place it in a croaker sack taken from his saddlebag.

Once he made a wide circle through the woods, he'd ride up to a friend's house and visit a while, drink a few beers.

After eating the breakfast Beulah had cooked, he opened the pages of the *Natchez-Democrat*. Though the fundraiser was mentioned, it would be the next day before it was covered and his picture published. The editorial policy required that everyone put down their drinks before the social page photographs were snapped. At least he knew he'd look proper in the paper.

James Luke had important business to take care of today. The telephone message was a nuisance, a distraction. He started to call his Louisiana lawyer, Salvatore Arnone, a bottom feeder with an office in Vidalia and a clientele of mobsters working in the rackets. He was a ham-fisted meat-eater who was never without words or petitions when James Luke needed them, pleadings produced like rounds from a machinegun. Salvatore was a criminal defense attorney with connections to the Cosa Nostra in New Orleans. His reach went as high as Carlos

Marcello, the Mafioso, and he was kept on retainer by James Luke and many others. Salvatore was licensed in Louisiana, as well as Mississippi, and he was just a phone call away.

Nothing I do will matter, James Luke thought, unless I say too much. But I won't paint myself into a corner. If I get the attorney involved too early, it'll show I'm scared. Trying to hide something. I'll be okay alone unless the marshal gets out of hand. Okay for now. At least the marshal ain't too bright no way.

He swallowed the last of his orange juice and went to the bedroom to retrieve his .45 pistol, which was kept in a dresser drawer when he wasn't carrying it. For safety, every morning he placed the pistol in his aluminum lunch box for his travels and workday activities. He checked the clip and the magazine, and wrapped the Colt in a red and black handkerchief and put it in his lunch box before he left the house.

On Saturday at his little second floor business office on Texas Street in Natchez, the place where he ran his slumlord operation, he called Marshal Brownlow. No one answered. "It would be a damned shame if anyone ever needed the law down there," he said out loud.

He waited a minute. Then he tried the marshal's number again, a second number listed, which Beulah had recorded on the yellow slip of paper below the first number. On the third ring, the phone was answered by a woman, the marshal's wife. She went to get him.

"Hello," Brownlow said.

"Hello marshal. This is James Luke Cate, your old neighbor. Returning your call."

"How's Natchez treating you?"

"Natchez is a beautiful city in a truly historic state."

"You sound like you work for the Chamber of Commerce."

"I'm a member in good standing."

"Great to hear it. You still employed by the Corps of Engineers, is that right?"

"Yes, sir. That would be some mighty fine police work you've done checking on me here."

"You've moved up in the world."

"I suppose you've been asking around, have you?"

"A little checking is a good thing."

"Marshal, how can I help you this morning?"

"I need to see you about some things. Conduct an interview."

"I don't suppose you'd mind if I ask why I'm due the honor."

"A rape, a beating, and a murder. An unsolved case from the 1960s."

James Luke's head throbbed for a second as if hit by a brickbat. But he pushed it out of his mind immediately, the pain taken out by his will and deliberateness. His right cheek quivered, but his head did not hurt anymore. "You've been thinking some strange thoughts, have you? When do you want to talk?"

"I can drive up to Natchez today. How about meeting me at the Rosalie Hotel this evening?"

"I'm kind of busy this weekend."

"Meet me in the hotel lobby at five o'clock. I'll buy you supper, and we can chat."

"I said I'm all tied up."

"Mr. Cate, best to see me when I'm in a real cheerful mood like I am right now. Never can tell how long it'll last. I'll see you at five in the lobby." Brownlow hung up the phone.

Ain't that some shit, James Luke thought, as he dropped the telephone into the cradle.

CHAPTER TWENTY-SIX

Marshal Brownlow sat in a comfortable wingback chair in the Rosalie Hotel lobby. Before he left home, he called the Natchez Chief of Police, letting him know that he needed to investigate an unsolved crime that had occurred in Louisiana and interview one of his citizens. He had never spoken to the chief before, but the call was amicable. He was granted permission to interview James Luke Cate, but if an arrest was needed, he should call the Natchez police station to handle it.

He drank a cup of coffee from the restaurant, coffee taken black with no cream or sugar. His chest still ached at times, the heart attack now almost two months behind him, but he came to believe it was nothing other than anxiety. Earlier he'd checked into a room, took a two-hour nap, and showered. Now he was dressed in a fresh uniform. Since the heart attack, he'd lost fifty pounds, largely from lack of appetite. By the time he returned to work, his old clothes would not fit him, and they were beyond alteration by his wife. New uniforms had to be ordered, as well as a new black leather belt to carry his revolver. The only things that still fit him properly were his hat and cowboy boots. People told him that quitting the cigarettes would cause him to gain weight, but this never happened. He wondered if the weight loss was going to kill him faster than smoking and eating. So far, he had not lit a cigarette since he was struck with the coronary in the Radio Shack parking lot.

When James Luke arrived at the Rosalie, the men shook hands and exchanged awkward pleasantries. The marshal didn't trust James Luke Cate and it showed by the way his shoulders and hands remained stiff and guarded when they spoke, though he tried to appear nonplussed.

"Would you like a cup of coffee?" Brownlow asked.

"Yeah, I'll have one," James Luke said.

They walked into the restaurant together. The marshal carried a big brief case with his tape recorder inside. A waiter showed them to a table, bringing menus and two porcelain cups and pot of coffee.

The marshal said, "You want something to eat? I hear the veal cutlets are mighty good, and I'd like 'em myself but I can't eat nothing I want. I had a heart attack a while back. See, nothing that tastes good is good for you. That's something I've learned."

"No, I don't want nothing. I'd just as soon eat at home."

"Suit yourself. Waiter, I'll have me the tuna salad. He's just drinking coffee."

"Food be right out, sir," the waiter said.

"You don't mind if I tape this, do you?" The marshal reached for the brief case beside his chair.

James Luke recoiled. "Like hell. If you're taping this, I'm out the door. I don't like no recorders. You can talk with my attorney if that's what you want. I'll give you his telephone number over in Vidalia."

"Well, I guess we can do without it today." The marshal knew he'd probably just blown the interview.

"So, you've heard talk of what?" James Luke asked. He acted somewhat disinterested, leaning back in his chair a little, away from the table. He rubbed a speck of dirt from a sleeve with his thumb.

"The murder of Sloan Parnell and the rape and beating of Sara Hardin," the lawman said. He sipped his coffee, staring intently at James Luke's face.

"Wasn't no murder of Sloan Parnell. He ran clear off the road as fast as a five-legged gazelle and flipped his little truck. He was as drunk as a coot. Simple as that. And I got no idea about Sara Hardin. Although I do recall the shame of it, but that was way back in the early 1960s, Marshal."

"It was November 9, 1964."

"Why are you here?"

"A person told me you were involved in some kind of sexual relationship with Sara. I have an informant who says there was a love triangle between you, Sara, and Sloan Parnell. The person claimed you committed the assault and rape of Sara out of spite. Then you set him up, and his death was out of revenge. I have sworn testimony, an affidavit." Brownlow lied about the veracity of Charity's words, but police officers weren't compelled to tell the truth when talking to a suspect.

James Luke looked up at the marshal. "It's like this all the time. People lie. Some lie day and night. Surely you've found this yourself in your line of work." He appeared cool, as calm as a poker champion.

Brownlow knew this himself. All men are born liars, and in the practical application, some are more brazen liars than others. He remembered one of his favorite verses from the Bible related to police work, Romans 3:4, which said, "Let God be true, but every man a liar." That verse and one from the Old Testament, Jeremiah 17:9, were his best guidance: "The heart is deceitful above all things, and desperately wicked: who can know it?" Indeed, Charity was a known shoplifter, a writer of hot checks, and a compulsive forger. Had her father, the Pentecostal preacher, not come to advocate for her and paid for a local attorney's defense over the years, she might have gone to the women's prison at St. Gabriel on the Mississippi River. Her father always managed to get her out of whatever mischief she'd caused.

The marshal gazed at James Luke. "Denial is also a big part of human nature." He surprised himself with the statement, the handy retort.

"Look, Sara Hardin was a real fine Methodist woman. She used to bake some mighty fine biscuits in the old days and was a simple housewife and my buddy's old lady. She was well educated for Zion. But pardon me, what damned planet are you on? Have you been hanging out with Timothy Leary and taking hits of acid?" James Luke was mocking the marshal.

Brownlow understood he was wasting his time, the mockery causing him to grit his teeth. James Luke became even more defiant as Brownlow continued to provoke him about his escapades.

"I know your source, Marshal. Your lying-assed witness. I hear Charity LeBlanc has done well for herself, too. I used to be acquainted with her back years ago. I suspect she's come to you with some kind of cock and bullshit vision. Yeah, I had a pleasurable round with her a time or two. I'll admit to that. And I'll tell you it was sweet. But I ain't raped nobody, and the only white man I've ever beat up was in a barroom fight back in 1954. Charity, you know her your own self. I bet she's got herself saved again. Shit, she's as crazy as a pail of fishing worms dumped out into the noon sun."

The marshal wasn't happy that James Luke guessed his informant, and he sat there trying to figure a way out of the box he'd now gotten himself locked into. "I never said a word about Charity, Jim. You don't have a clue about my informant."

"Informant, Marshal Brownlow? I ain't no dumbass like you're used to dealing with down in Baxter Parish. I'd call her a lot of names but informant ain't one of 'em. She came to you talking like she does, stirring the pot, because that's all she knows how to do. She's so damned nutty she'd screw an oak limb if it wore a pair of blue jeans and bought her a cold beer, and the next day she'll get reborn in the spirit, all her sins washed away. Then like magic, she'll want to do right by her sins. She's a religious fanatic that ought to be put in the crazy house over in Mandeville where they sent Governor Earl Long, if you ask my opinion."

"I tend to believe that maybe you and Charity and Sloan and Sara had some kind of extended relationship." He looked into James Luke's face to see if he could read any deceit, but the face had gone cold. His eyes showed nothing.

James Luke waved his hand across the table in a nugatory gesture, and said, "No such luck." Then he crossed his arms in front of his chest.

"I could have you arrested."

"For what? Charge me with what, man? Screwing a whore and later that same whore got to talking nonsense and telling tall tales? My lawyer'll get me out of jail before you can break wind. Hell, go on and charge me with killing somebody, but you know good and well what happened that night. Damn, you'll charge me with beating and raping my old buddy's wife? A judge'll cut me lose, and it'll never go to trial. You'll embarrass yourself. It would make about as much sense if you charged Tom. Such a righteous and upright man ain't been found since Job showed up in the Good Book," James Luke said.

"Rape and assault of a housewife are serious matters to a grand jury," the marshal continued

"Whose word do you have on it? Sara Hardin ain't never made no such accusation. On account it never happened. Not with me anyway. And the word you have is unreliable to the point of an insult to the law."

"Where were you on the day of the rape?"

"That's ten years ago, partner. I don't have much memory no more. But I'll tell you this much, I was sitting at home watching our brand new television set for part of the day, when I wasn't out looking for my few head of evicted hogs, and maybe I was drinking a little beer away from the watching eyes of my nagging wife who was working at the bank. I tell you one thing, Marshall, never marry a deep water Baptist. They'll drive you plumb nuts."

The marshal fought off a grin. "Your second wife says you stole money from her. Her grievance against you has plenty of merit. I called the East Baton Rouge Sheriff, and we're going to meet next week." Brownlow lied. He'd never called the High Sheriff, but he had mentioned to Mrs. Lott to find out what she could about the ex-wife and James Luke's split, and she learned that he'd left her and took most of her assets in the divorce.

"Go see the sheriff in Baton Rouge. Everything was clean as a whistle in our settlement. Now you're grabbing at some short straws."

The waiter brought out the marshal's tuna salad.

"Can I go on back home now?" asked James Luke.

"I reckon. But I'll be in touch. Where do you live?"

"South Pearl Street," James Luke said. "Say, while you're here in Natchez, I hope you take time to visit Miss Nellie Jackson on Rankin

Street, because you're just a little uptight, hoss. It's a white house with bright red shutters. She'll make your stay worthwhile, a time to remember. Tell her I sent you, and I'm certain you'll get a proper discount on the evening. Next time you come to Natchez to see me, go talk to my lawyer or have an arrest warrant in hand, because I'm done talking to you."

The marshal watched James Luke as he left the hotel restaurant. Then he started eating his tuna salad.

CHAPTER TWENTY-SEVEN

T om went to church alone for the Sunday morning service, saying the prayers and singing hymns. It had been a long enough time since Sara and Wesley quit attending services that the parishioners and the pastor had stopped asking where they were on Sundays. The marshal and his wife sat in their pew across the aisle from Tom's regular place, where the Hardin family used to sit. After Sara stopped going to church, Tom began slipping into the very back pew on the right side closest to the door. Sometimes he left before the benediction was finished, just so he could be the first one out of the parking lot. Sara sat at home reading novels and watching television during the services.

He ate lunch alone, leftover mashed potatoes and fried chicken from the refrigerator. He and Sara said nothing that wasn't absolutely necessary since the day of the picnic on campus. Sara slept in Wesley's bed after the blowout when the boy came to get his clothes and ask for the college money.

Tom's Bible lay near the coffee pot. After he finished eating his dinner, he sat at the kitchen table with his old study Bible, a *Thompson Chain-Reference Bible*. He hadn't read it in weeks. He couldn't remember a period of time in his adult life when he hadn't at least dipped into the book on a regular basis. Perhaps not since he was a teenager. He had even read books on theology, often those recommended to him by the minister assigned to Little Zion Methodist Church. He'd read Rudolph Otto's *Idea of the Holy*, Karl Barth's *Dogmatics in Outline*, and some of John Wesley's journals. As he read the Book of Matthew, he could hear another text echoing in his ears, the *Autobiography of John Woolman*, a Quaker author in the 1700s. Tom had read the book at the request of his coworker at the Ponderosa, Harvey Shaffer, a man originally from Pennsylvania who grew up Quaker. The words of Matthew 5:9 lay before him and were underlined: "Blessed are the peacemakers: for they shall be called the children of God." The Quakers may be the only real peacemakers left in the world, Tom thought. The possibility of his wife sleeping with his old friend and faking amnesia chilled him. Normally, he'd say he wanted the whole truth, but he was unsure now if it was worth the risk in seeking it. He wondered if Sara had talked to the marshal yet, and what would come of it.

He shut the Bible and quit reading, but his mind never left the words of Jesus. What did these words of good news and the Lord have to say about today's world, a world filled with unfaithfulness, a world where son is against father? This was one more thing to puzzle over, another roomful of darkness and uncertainty to face. And he wished such a crucible on no one.

CHAPTER TWENTY-EIGHT

On Monday morning, the marshal's secretary Mrs. Lott called Sara Hardin's office at the college library. Brownlow had put off the call as long as possible, but now he felt as though he had no choice but to do the interview about her rape and beating.

Sara was on the other line waiting when Mrs. Lott buzzed him.

"Hello, Mrs. Sara. This is Marshal Brownlow. How are you this morning?" he asked.

There was a long pause, and she took a deep breath, a slight gasp. "I'm fine. Is everything all right?"

"Well, I reckon it will be all right bye and bye, or as good as it'll ever be, Lord willing. I'm calling on account I need to talk to you about something that has come to light about your assault in 1964."

"Why would you need to do that? Did you find out who did it?" Her voice cracked.

"No, but I have a lead. I need to ask you some questions about what all you remember."

"Marshal, I don't have any better memory now than I had back then. In fact, I recall far less today." Her voice cracked again. She sounded truly shaken.

"I need to try and clear the air on some things. I suspect nothing'll ever come of it. But I do need to talk to you if I can," he said.

"You know, I really don't remember anything. I was hurt so bad. It affected my short term memory, and it's been a very long time ago."

"Mrs. Sara, I do need to see you face-to-face if you'd oblige me. Today if possible. Can you come over to my office when you get off work this afternoon?"

"I suppose I can," she said, sounding like she'd been caught off guard but resigned to the invitation.

"Thank you. What time can you be here?"

"I'm off work at four-thirty. I can be there at ten before five, no later than five."

"And I do appreciate your cooperation. If you talk to Tom beforehand, tell him I send my kind regards."

"Yes, Marshal."

He sat deep in his chair after he hung up the phone. Any time in the past forty years, he would have smoked a cigarette, but he reminded himself that he'd quit. He reached into his desk drawer and took out a piece of mint candy and unwrapped the wax paper and placed it into his mouth. The bottle of gin was gone. He threw it out along with a new carton of Winstons during the first morning he got back to work after the heart attack.

Sara arrived at the office a few minutes before five. She drove a little silver AMC Gremlin, which they had bought because it got good gas mileage and was dependable. They paid monthly notes to the Tickfaw State Bank. She was almost quivering as she got out of the vehicle and walked to the door.

As best she could, she tried to recall what she'd said a decade earlier, and she'd been rehearsing every detail since she spoke to the marshal on the telephone. While at the library, she wrote out her story longhand, the whole lie told in 1964, and then studied it and threw it away after she'd cut it up into a thousand pieces with a pair of scissors. To be safe, she placed the little pieces into three different trash cans in different sections of the library. Now she was anxious that the lies she'd told years ago were coming upon her like her worst possible fear.

The little walk from the car to the marshal's building were some of the hardest steps she'd made in her entire life. She opened the office door, and Mrs. Lott welcomed her inside. Rita Lott was a long-time member of Little Zion Methodist, and now Sara worried that the meeting with the marshal would be all over the church, though she had not been attending worship lately.

Mrs. Lott buzzed the marshal and tried to make small talk. He came to the front room and waved Sara inside his office. "Thank you for coming," he said.

"Well, I'm here," Sara said.

He shut the door behind them.

She saw the recorder on the desk and took it in with an element of shock, but she tried not to stare or mention it.

"How's Tom getting along?" the marshal asked.

"He's fine."

"And Wesley?"

She stalled a second to collect her thoughts and glanced at the silent recorder. "He's about to graduate from Baxter State, and he's enrolling at the university in Lafayette."

"That's mighty good to hear, Sara. Mighty good. He's growing up like Priscilla. She's at Centenary College in Shreveport, and she'll be studying in London, England, this fall for a whole semester. I'll have to take a second job to pay for the trip, but she's going." He grinned, an element of pride and self-deprecating humor used as a way to disarm the woman across from his desk.

"Priscilla's such a pretty girl."

"Thanks to her mama, she is. Mary Anne and I have sure missed seeing you at church."

"Well, I've been busy working at the house and taking a class at LSU. Sunday is my only free day to get things done. I've been sick some lately, too." She felt unconvincing in her tall tale.

"I hope everything shapes up for you and you get to feeling better. Now Sara, I should tell you that I drove up to Natchez, Mississippi, in order to speak to James Luke Cate. I've interviewed others as well—"

She interrupted. "Why are you going back to all of this? Do you have a new lead?" Sara moved forward in her chair, her black patent leather purse held tight in her lap. She tried not to appear nervous, and she attempted to look genuinely concerned about the investigation, as if she wanted the marshal to make an arrest and solve the old crime.

"Kind of. A person came forward with some new information. I don't know if anything'll ever come of it, but I have to believe you're the key witness." Brownlow paused, as if trying to let things sink in.

"Oh." Her eyes cut to the recorder. Then back to the marshal without turning her head. She hoped he hadn't seen her look at the machine again with her eyes, but she knew her fear must show like a bright light.

"I'm going to tape our little visit with this machine if I can figure out how to turn it on." He gave a reassuring smile and turned on the recorder with a loud click.

Sara slumped in the chair, her prepared defense lost. She looked worn out with her long gray hair, and she was having trouble breathing. Her right pinkie twitched atop her black purse like a tremor.

"I really do wish you wouldn't tape this," she said, pleading.

But the recorder started rolling when he clicked the button. He acted as though she hadn't said a word. He raised a brow and looked at her. "Well, let's go on and get started. This is Donald Brownlow, Marshal of the Ninth Ward, Baxter Parish, Louisiana, and I'm here in my office at five o'clock on Monday, July 15, 1974, interviewing Mrs. Sara Hardin of Zion."

She placed her left hand over the trembling right finger, but the tremor spread from the pinkie to the whole hand, which she pushed down into her lap, praying the marshal wouldn't see it.

"Sara, I know some of this'll probably be a little unsettling for you, and I'm sorry about it, but I need to rule some things out. I'm really dealing with two events, your attack and the death of Sloan Parnell, and how they might somehow be related together."

"All right," Sara said, still stunned. She wished to God she hadn't shown up in the first place. This was a big mistake, she thought.

"Can you tell me a little about your relationship with Sloan Parnell?"

Again, she couldn't understand how everything turned on her all of a sudden after so many years. She stammered, "I didn't really know him."

"But you did know him."

"Ah, a little. I knew his family, one might say. I know the Parnells. Everyone knows who they are. It was so very long ago. I do seem to recall seeing him around once or twice now that you mention it. I suppose we chatted at the public library in Pickleyville a few times."

"Sara, I need you to take this the right way, and I don't mean no lack of respect by it. As you say, this has been a long time ago, over nine years, but did you ever have relations of an intimate nature with Sloan Parnell? I have an informant that says you did."

At first she made a low grunting noise in her throat, a smoker's hoarse cough. She voiced a strange sound, "waaah-waaah-waaah." The sound came from her lips and mouth, an odd shrieking noise that fell off her tongue like a moan, an ecstatic utterance, as if drawing near to Christ at a frontier camp meeting as Methodist Bishop Francis Asbury preached the gospel. Her next word was "naa-naa-noo," and the denial came out from her face like a dagger, and she almost confessed to shocking things, details of the affair, but she stopped herself cold. It was on the tip of her tongue, and she knew it. She gathered herself. There was very little natural light in the room. The window shade was drawn tight. Sara blinked her eyes, making them look strained in the lamp light. The artificial light did no justice to the dark words on the edges of her lips.

"No, I did not," she said. "I'm a married woman." She recalled having sex with Sloan. She remembered sex with James Luke over the course of a decade, more times than she could count. During the weeks preceding her attack, she'd had sex with James Luke and Sloan on the same day. She brought James Luke into her marriage bed, and she slept with Sloan at the old Parnell place.

James Luke had taken the day off from work and was casing the old Parnell place to burn it when he saw Sara pull into the long driveway. There she was, driving Tom's truck into the belly of the beast.

When she got back to her house in Zion, James Luke was on the front porch waiting for her smoking a cigarette. Jubal was loose in the yard, a link snapped from wear on his chain, and James Luke was petting the dog when she got out of Tom's truck.

Later she undressed in the bed and waited for him to join her. He'd never said a word about seeing her two hours earlier at the Parnell place. Then he confronted her about being at Sloan's house. He beat her unmercifully, almost to the point of death. He raped her. The one thing he made her understand before he finished with her was that he'd murder Wesley if she ever said a word. He'd kill the boy like a sack of kittens thrown into a creek, he told her.

The woman stared blankly, expressionless, caught up in her own suppressed memories.

"Sara," he said, he tapping the edge of the desk with a finger.

She sat dazed.

He tapped louder, and she made eye contact. "Sara. Why don't you go on and tell me the whole truth? You appear mighty shook up. The Lord says 'the truth will set you free'."

"I really can't remember anything, Marshal," she said. She was thinking that she'd saved her son's life. Maybe she'd saved Tom who would have killed James Luke, and maybe her, too, and gone to jail for the rest of his days. By lying, she was the only one hurt. She'd preserved what life she had with Tom and Wesley. She always considered it an act of courage.

"Did James Luke and Tom kill Sloan?"

"I don't believe they did. I wasn't there, but I don't think so. It was clearly an accident."

He raised his voice. "I know for a fact that you've lied to the sheriff's department. You've lied to me today. You could be charged with obstruction. I have a sworn statement from a witness that says you slept with Sloan and James Luke." He was bluffing, which was the key to any good interrogation. He'd been a lawman long enough to use necessary shock to rattle a subject.

"I bet it was that bitch Charity LeBlanc," she said under her breath.

The marshal blew out the air from his lungs and stared at the woman across the desk. He didn't acknowledge her comment. "I reckon I've got just a few more questions if I can figure what's left to ask," he said.

The marshal drove home for the day, but the house was empty. Mary Anne had gone to Shreveport to visit with their only child who was working at First Methodist Church in a children's summer program. Shreveport was the city where her church-related college was based. Soon, Priscilla was going to leave the country for the first time, a major event for the family. Mary Anne had graduated from Centenary College thirty-three years earlier with a degree in French. It was a wonder how she and the marshal had gotten along as well as they did, considering the marshal's lack of formal education. He graduated from high school at seventeen and never looked back. The couple worked well together and made a home out of their differences as much as they did their similarities. Regardless, they had mutual fidelity, and they did not mind spending time alone. After the heart attack, there were times when he desired to sit down in the quiet and reflect on his years, which, he knew, were shortened, fleeting like a flicker of flame in the wind if his luck didn't hold out or providence didn't grant longevity.

So he looked forward to the evening while she was gone as a chance to relax a little and pursue his favorite pastime, his bloodhound dogs. They weren't the fastest or the smartest of dogs, but they did have the keenest nose. Some experts said bloodhounds with their droopy faces had some of the best noses in the animal kingdom, capable of sniffing out a single molecule among millions. Brownlow believed in God, but if he didn't have any faith, he'd often said the existence of a bloodhound would be enough evidence to sway him. Just one search and rescue mission to find a lost child would make him think the animal was a true miracle of creation and proof of divine governance in an often chaotic world.

During the evening, he retreated to his kennel while it was still daylight. The hounds began barking, leaping as he walked back to the concrete slab and hurricane fence. His two bloodhounds were hardy and loud, plenty of loose skin around the jowls and neck. They jumped up on the fence when they saw him coming.

"Dixie and Duke, quiet on down," he hollered over their barking. He took a leather leash from a post. The roof was a few inches above his head, and it kept the sun off the dogs. Heat and sun were bad on bloodhounds, and he was always wary of losing one to stroke in the Louisiana sun. Under harsh conditions, they could die or come close to death in a single afternoon heat wave.

Brownlow opened the gate. "Come here, Duke," he said, as if he needed to say anything with the dogs clamoring for his hand and affection. The big red hound poked his nose out of the door, and he clipped the leash to the collar. He then led the dog through the gate and into the backyard. Duke was the younger of the two dogs and a less experienced tracker. He was a good dog already, but he needed more work. The marshal rubbed the dog's slick coat for a moment as he looked on, hound eyes longing. Brownlow and the dog went toward the house and his Dodge pickup truck. Once he dropped the tailgate, Duke loaded into the bed and entered a large kennel that was bigger than a typical dog box. It appeared jail-like and was the size of the truck bed and tall enough for a man to stand in. The floor was filled with horse hay for comfort. On top, an aluminum roof kept out the sun and rain.

Brownlow drove away from his red brick house and onto the road. Deputy Marshal Freddy Wentworth, a part-timer, awaited him deep in a pasture a half a mile off Upper Louth Road in the Zion community. Wentworth had left a shirt stowed away inside a hollow water oak that Brownlow planned to use for the training exercise. When the marshal arrived, he got the dog out of the kennel and Duke gave a loud "woof," and they went through an open gate to the hay field and to the water oak where the flannel shirt lay. The marshal removed the shirt and gave it to the hound.

The dog took the scent from the shirt and began tugging on the leash and barking wildly, head close to the ground and trying to run. The marshal was not up to this much activity, he thought, yet he felt energized by the rush of the hound on the scent. This marvel of selective breeding and genetics was nearly dragging the big man across the field, ready or not, heart attack victim or not. Brownlow was well into middle age, and he was in poor health overall, but he kept up the pace and tried not to choke back the hound with the leather leash as he dug in with his paws and pulled him along. He felt like an old-timer as he followed behind the dog, the leather leash encircling his right wrist, but the thrill made him try his best to keep up with the hound's kinetic energy.

They passed the edge of a fence line and into a stand of trees, and then to an overgrown bed of a dummy line railroad. After another five minutes into the woods, the "escapee," Wentworth, was found sitting in a fork of a rangy mayhaw tree just above eye-level. The dog treed him, barked madly and jumping in the air as if to pull him down to the ground and maul him.

"Halt," he said to Wentworth in the tree. The dog howled and lunged, bellowing an ear-rattling noise of continuous barks.

"That dog has got plumb good," Wentworth said.

"Thanks. Now get down from that tree, Zacchaeus," Brownlow said. "Let's go eat some dinner in town. I'm already about pooped out."

CHAPTER TWENTY-NINE

S ara was tired of Tom's stringent discipline, his perfectly squared corners, and the constant demand that every angle be right and every wall plumb. His superlative sense of rightness, however, and reliability was what drew her to him in 1950 soon after taking the job in Pickleyville as a library clerk. When he showed up at the library reference desk and asked her for a copy of *Their Eyes Were Watching God*, which the nearly comatose head librarian kept locked in a cabinet, Sara was smitten. The book was authored by a Negro woman, and the head librarian hated Negro authors. The copy of Zora Neale Hurston's novel was a donation, and she kept it locked away. In truth, Sara had purchased the novel herself at Bayou Booksellers in the Vieux Carré and gave it to the library, slipping it into the night book drop at the front door with a typed note saying it was donated by the local NAACP chapter. The reason Tom wanted to read it was because he'd seen an enthusiastic recommendation of the book in a magazine. When he returned the novel a week later, they chatted about it, and he asked Sara out on their first date. What made her accept the offer of a movie and dinner was that Tom seemed solid, honest, a religious man, and certainly the only white person other than herself in Baxter Parish reading Hurston in 1950. She wanted a change in her life. She longed for a stable life with a trustworthy man, and Tom Hardin was that man.

As good as Tom was at his carpentry, Sara was even better at concealing things. She was able to camouflage almost anything. She was, to his right angles and plumb walls, a crooked mystery hidden from view and outside of normal geometric calculations. At first, this didn't diminish their marriage, but over time, it caused a distance and aloofness, something she tried to overcome with other men during intermittent liaisons. Her relations with Sloan Parnell had never been a romance, but only rebellion against Tom and her cloistered life in Zion. The affair with James Luke added excitement, and it ended after he almost killed her in 1964. It was Sara's specialty to hide and conceal everything closest to her true self, and the attack was no exception.

She took the day off from work after meeting with the marshal, calling in sick. She pulled the pack of cigarettes from her purse. Tom didn't even know that she smoked. She could wait two or three days if necessary before she lit one, before the flash of fire and the hot breath of nicotine. The woman could then be satisfied with one draw if that was all she had available. It was half the joy to realize she could smoke and Tom, her husband of so many years, didn't know it. His daily schedule and structure lent to this and other deceptions great and small. She could smoke on the back step or in the yard. And if he smelled something, she'd blame it on a neighbor who'd come over to visit earlier in the day. It was this private world that gave her pleasure, like the pages of a banned novel offering delight through its taboo.

Wesley knew about her cigarettes, but there was an unwritten agreement between them. He was never to speak about her smoking in front of his father, which signified a note of loyalty they had for one another, a bond of loyalty and subversion they held together as one since his birth.

With the marshal's investigation menacing, the series of falsehoods that made up Sara Hardin's life was essentially over and she knew it. Two decades of attending Little Zion Methodist Church had taught her that the only clear pathway to salvation was through heartfelt repentance and holy living, but the hard edges of her life were closing in around her. The attempt at controlling the world was destined to end badly. She put down her cigarette, and the smoke made a half-circle in the ashtray on the window sill in the kitchen. She poured herself two fingers of vodka in a porcelain coffee cup. This was her chosen spirit, a secret drink without any smell and as clear as water. She had loved to drink it with Sloan and James Luke and other men over the years. Sometimes she liked to sip intrigue beyond just dusty old books in the library. Though she was stranded in Zion, Louisiana, she was free to roam elsewhere in her daydreams. For years, she could escape through sex during secret rendezvous with men. Now every swallow of vodka reminded her of the past.

She could see her accuser's face, Charity Claiborne's lurid smile. The woman's eyes, the sun-scorched crow's feet covered up by makeup, the cost of sin and strife, the late night carousing that never ended. Sara had been nominally Baptist before marrying Tom, dunked in the Shipley Creek outside of Blytheville, Arkansas, as a child. The Methodists were rarely negligent in lambasting sin, but who could hold court with the Baptists? Their only joy was in self-denial and self-loathing, putting sin under the blood of the Lamb. Either repent or hide from it, she learned, was the central message, and she chose the latter.

Sara walked out into the yard and took a final drag from the Viceroy cigarette and dropped the butt onto the ground to extinguish it with her heel. She then picked it up and emptied the remaining tobacco from the butt into the grass. She wrapped the filter into a piece of tinfoil and placed it inside her purse until she could find a safe place at work to throw it away. She put a piece of Wrigley's Spearmint Gum into her mouth to cover her breath and conceal the tobacco even more fully, and she cleaned out the ashtray with water from the sink and put it away in the kitchen cabinet where it stayed when she wasn't smoking.

CHAPTER THIRTY

The marshal's visit had persuaded James Luke to act, though he pondered it over the course of three weeks, trying to make a clear and precise plan. James Luke was sure that he had to do something about Charity. She was like a loose wheel on a car, and somebody was going to get hurt sooner rather than later. He decided to return to Pickleyville to take care of the trouble first hand.

A few days after the marshal came to Natchez, he told Heloise about a special fishing trip coming up that he'd been invited to attend with a bunch of Army Corps of Engineers bureaucrats. These men were several steps up the ladder, and he needed to get to know them for his own advancement. He said that he was going to an Army Corps reservoir near Hot Springs called DeGray Lake. They'd spend a few days fishing, drinking, and playing cards at the lake, and he'd use boats brought along by other men. He didn't want to go, but it was all necessary business, Army Corps political games required to get ahead.

He told her about the trip while they were eating dinner at Queen's Tavern in Natchez, the oldest standing building in town, which dated from the 1700s. They ate porterhouse steaks and drank red wine. When they were done with the steaks and waiting for dessert, they continued talking more about the fishing trip to Arkansas.

"James Luke, I fully understand the point behind the trip," Heloise said. "Business is business, even if it's government business. It's all the same. Don't feel guilty about leaving me."

"That's why I married you, honey. You're a woman that understands how the world works," he said.

"That I do," she said.

"Well, take this for your prize for letting me go away for a few days," James Luke said as he reached into his sport coat pocket and retrieved a new necklace, pearls that he'd bought for her in Jackson at Fondren Jewelers. He displayed it to her in the velvet case and then stood and put it around her neck.

"My dear, you're one of a kind," she said.

"I know it," said James Luke as he kissed her cheek and rubbed her shoulders.

On Friday, July 26th, he packed the Suburban. He loaded it with food and camping supplies, his canvas sleeping bag, Coleman lantern, and a propane cooker. He prepared a week's worth of dehydrated vegetables and plenty of water. He could stay longer than a week depending on how he rationed the food and if he caught any fish, or so he told his wife. But it was all a ruse. This was just a precaution. Indeed, he planned to be back not long before midnight on Sunday evening. He hid the Remington Gamemaster deer rifle with a scope in the truck the night before. It was nestled away in a steel storage box with plenty of ammunition. He was going on a journey, but not to catch any fish.

The marshal's visit itself had not bothered him too much, though he wasn't disregarding it in the least. James Luke was used to jostling with lawmen through his rent houses, the clandestine drug activity, and his regular work as a field supervisor on the take with the Army Corps. He had bought and paid for several lawmen on both sides of the river since coming to Mississippi, and he learned that they mostly wanted the pretense of power, and that their loyalty was always offered to the highest bidder or it went to the most aggressive sycophant in their midst. What did bother him, however, was Charity's constant talking. That was the real threat, and he saw no choice but to stop it. She wasn't rational, so he needed to shut her up fast.

Much of James Luke's approach to human affairs was learned in Korea. The military lessons were just as true now as they were in 1951. He faced the same kind of duplicity and human emotions, the exact same hypocrisy. He was usually taking something away from a person and knew the processes for forcing things to go in his direction. He believed stealing wasn't stealing if you got to keep the booty of war free and clear, and it didn't matter what kind of war: personal or international. It didn't matter as long as the winner took all.

He believed the easiest approach to break a person was not to torture him with inhumane cruelty, but to use either pandering or shame. Either exploit their egos or their guilt for a higher purpose, your own purpose. James Luke's understanding of man's natural weaknesses served him well, and he planned to use this knowledge in Baxter Parish.

When the marshal told him about the complaint coming forth all of these years later, he immediately knew who it was. Charity was the only person alive who knew what went on between him and Sara and Sloan—other than Sara herself—and if the marshal had come to see him after Sara's erstwhile confession, it would have been with a warrant, he was sure of it.

He shared a bed with Charity at a camp on Lake Ponchatoula a number of times in 1963 and '64, and he enjoyed her sex. He believed she was scared to death of him. He hit her a few times one night just for good measure, when she was acting like a religious nut, and she stayed away from him afterward. He knew her better than she knew herself, however, and he understood that her mind was scrambled like an egg in an electric blender. She was as crazy as a Christmas hen in a lightning storm. Though she had been granted eternal salvation, he thought it a tragedy that redemption of this sort would fail to make her remember her limits and her place in the world.

The .30-06 rifle and the .45 pistol, his old comrades, were taking the ride in case any trouble came to town. Though he mostly understood Charity's state of nature, he never could be sure what religion might do to her perverted little mind. There was but one way to reason with her, and it was not like a normal person.

He looked down at his truck seat at his leather-covered Bible, the King James Version of 1611, a copy with red edges that reminded him of Jesus Christ bleeding on the cross. He knew what he'd do to talk sense into her: Beat her with the one book she respected until she either died or learned again how to behave herself and quit squawking to the law.

James Luke ordered a second gas tank when he bought the Suburban a year earlier. He had it installed in the undercarriage, a retrofit that cost him extra money at the dealership. This was just the kind of journey he had in mind when he added the tank with its twenty-five gallons of gas in escrow. It might come in handy one day. He wanted to keep a low profile, and the Chevrolet 454 lapped the gasoline at twelve miles per gallon in normal driving, and the high price of gas since the Arab oil embargo made James Luke curse. The four barrel carburetor was practically a sieve if he pressed down on the pedal. He didn't want to gas up anywhere in Louisiana, so he took enough fuel to fulfill his little mission. In case things went awry, he had plenty enough for the trip there and back plus any essential excursions.

He could not remember the exact date of his last trip to Baxter Parish—or even his last time driving through the place. He seemed to think it was in 1967. Today, he drove east toward Meadville and then farther east past I-55 and to old Highway 51.

On the highway south of Summit, he listened to the radio. Fire and brimstone preachers and twangy gospel music always gave him a peculiar comfort for some indescribable reason. He preferred listening to the high drama of the Pentecostals, and their hard singsong voices punctuating the truck cab with the words of death and life.

An evangelist named Leviticus Showers gasped for air and breathed hard, as if the good news included a long marathon up a steep spiritual mountain that left the preacher seeking just enough oxygen to finish his sermon. The preacher on the AM station in McComb proclaimed, "The Lord is ever-following you with his watching eyes—AH-HA. His eye is upon your—AH-HA-LA—sinful ways day and night—AH-HA-SHA—night and day." James Luke smiled as he listened to the preacher, an evangelist at the Full Faith Church in Progress, Missis-sippi. He was pleased to hear the message on his way through this hard and treacherous world. He could visualize the preacher sweating and wiping his forehead in the radio studio, his Bible wide open on a rusty music stand in front of him, the microphone square before his lips, not a single page of prepared notes in front of him.

But this message did not bring James Luke to a sublime religious experience. Instead, it was simply free entertainment, a way to pass the time when he drove. At best, God was a cosmic entertainer. James Luke had a peculiar fascination with the Almighty. He was drawn to any source of power, and he liked to observe devotion to a true master. Fur-thermore, he wanted to elicit fear rather than devotion. Devotion was cheap, but fear was a fine currency. He believed the fear of God was the beginning of power, and power was what James Luke liked most.

He planned for the battle. He was working hard to bring the parts together that had been dropped into his lap by Marshal Brownlow. James Luke would take the trouble to its natural end if necessary. He'd do whatever nature required, and then go back home to Natchez and his profitable work in the slums. "I'll deal with flies by swatting them—AH-HA-SHA. Let the flies die, by God—AH-HA—or let them re-pent—AH-HA-SHA—of their sins against me," he said, mimicking the evangelist on the radio station.

CHAPTER THIRTY-ONE

M arshal Brownlow cared for the citizens of the Ninth Ward with whom he was entrusted, families that he was charged to protect and serve. While he didn't have as much energy as before the heart attack, he hoped he would compensate for the lack of strength with heightened wisdom and experience. He couldn't be sure of this, but he didn't take anything for granted either. Sometimes he wondered if he had learned anything significant in his fifty-four years of living. There was a better focus afforded by age that he understood came from his closeness to death. Yet he doubted his own wisdom now more often than not. Just working in the Marshal's Office for his career was evidence of bad judgment in and of itself, he regularly told people. Any fool should know better than to do such a thing.

Death was coming soon like an old friend or neighbor stopping by for a visit. So he tried to keep watch over important matters. He'd been invited by fate to do what was crucial now and let the trivial fall by the wayside. The grave would soon call and say the hour was right for a final reunion, a call impossible to miss or refuse. During despondent moments, it seemed as if life was failing, going down like a shooting star. The job itself and the heavy responsibilities could cause his death before he could retire.

Regardless, he had been reunited with some old acquaintances, Sloan Parnell, Charity LeBlanc Claiborne, and James Luke Cate. These, along with Tom and Sara Hardin together, now resembled one big unhappy family. More like a circle of hate, the marshal thought.

One of the difficulties in dealing with Charity's story was that he didn't really know what he should do next. He didn't have any new evidence at all. All he really had was the testimony of a crazy woman, a woman who said she was led by the Holy Ghost.

As a Methodist, the marshal believed in the Spirit, but not all spirits could be trusted. Didn't the Bible say in First John to "test the spirits," a verse he learned as a youth? He dared not forward anything to the District Attorney prematurely and create more havoc. And what was there to forward anyway? He had nothing to give the High Sheriff either, a man who cared not a whit about Zion or Lizard Bayou or the dealings down in the lower end of the parish. Sheriff Haltom Roberts had written off Zion and Milltown from his work responsibilities years earlier. The marshal was glad, because Roberts was always more trouble than he was worth, as rotten as a sack of putrid apples, corrupt all the way to the core.

He bet himself that if Charity went crying to Judge Parnell, it would cost him a hundred dollars' worth of hell. So now he had to be sure, completely certain about who beat and raped Sara Hardin. Even the manner of Sloan's death had to be questioned again. He had some suspicions that people were lying all around, everyone but Tom. In fact, he trusted that Tom was telling the truth, and as dangerous as it was to trust another man, he had to believe in Tom Hardin.

Yet the primary question remained. He had to solve the rape and beating that nearly killed Sara Hardin. Why didn't she tell him the truth in 1964 or now in 1974? A secondary question was why were the two men following Sloan Parnell the night he died if not to kill him? Did all of these really loose fitting people fit together somehow like gears in a mechanism? Who was lying about what and why? Worst of all, the marshal began to doubt he still had the ability to follow the questions to accurate conclusions. It all might be too much for him now.

CHAPTER THIRTY-TWO

S ara reached for the small hope chest that her father had given her for her birthday the year before he left Blytheville for good. The chest was made from cedar and was smooth as glass. It was hidden in the top of the hallway closet. The chest was overhead, and she stood on a footstool to get it down. She could barely pull the thing down without dropping it on her head like a big brick.

The chest had a brass lock and matching hardware hinges. The green brass was corroded on its edges. She placed it on the bed and unlocked the box with a key that she kept in the bottom of a small wicker purse stowed away inside the bedroom chifforobe, hidden in a location Tom would never look. He wasn't one to dig through the house anyway, and she was sure he would never try to mess with the locked box.

Inside the chest was her trove of letters, diaries, and handbills from plays, movies, evidence of relationships with men before and after her marriage. Some were erotic letters from the Newcomb College days, personal memoirs of lustful men in different places and times.

Sara grew up hardscrabble in Arkansas. Blytheville was a farm town on the Mississippi River. Her father was a gambler, and he abandoned the family and moved to Louisiana's Crescent City when she was twelve years old. Her childhood was spent from pillar to post, in and out of rent houses in the Arkansas Delta, never knowing which night the family would be forced to move, or under what kind of dire circumstances. Her father's departure only made matters worse. The poverty went from bad to horrible. She spent her teen years wondering about his life in the Big Easy, wondering why he left.

One Christmas she received a card from her father with a return address of Pirate's Alley in the French Quarter, the same block where

William Faulkner had written *Soldiers' Pay*. The card said he was working hard on the docks, and he would send her some money soon. It said she ought to do well in school and listen to her mother and grandmother. Sara was a precocious girl. Throughout her childhood, her only refuge was the county library, and her studious reading made her one of the best pupils to graduate from Blytheville High School despite her rural poverty. She wrote him numerous times, but her father never responded to the letters. This postcard was the last word from him. When she turned seventeen, she applied to Newcomb College and moved south to New Orleans. She attended the school on a full scholarship.

She never found him in the city, nor did she ever locate a grave. Her mother grew deathly ill back in Blytheville, and she died during Sara's second year at Newcomb. But Sara stayed in school until she graduated. Then she took the job as a library clerk in Pickleyville and soon met Tom.

In the box, there were pictures of old boyfriends and lovers. She had keepsakes, a gold necklace James Luke had given her and a bracelet with some small diamonds and rubies that Sloan bought for her in 1964. There were pictures of men, one of herself nude and taken by her boyfriend, a photographer and film developer at the *Times-Picayune* newspaper. The photographs made her wish for her younger days before she met Tom, a time years before James Luke beat her and left her for dead.

She had spent this formative time as a woman living a hidden sexual life in the Crescent City, and the hiddenness continued intermittently until the attack. Afterward, she never had another liaison, now almost ten years, as if she had learned her lesson.

The diaries recalled trysts, several with strangers in the library book stacks on St. Charles Avenue in New Orleans, where she had worked while in college. Her sex with James Luke started soon after he married Nelda, not long after the Korean War, and her fling with Sloan began in 1964 when Sloan came to the house to apologize to Tom after the fight at the feed store. Sara was at home alone. She knew him from back when she worked at the public library in Pickleyville. They used to flirt a lot when she worked, and he was just a high school kid. On the day he showed up at the front door to see Tom, she invited him inside for coffee and was soon on her knees and in his lap at the kitchen table, his blue jeans pulled down to his boots. This is how their sex got started— just as fast as a fire burning in the woods.

After she married Tom, the writing in her diary was done in code. Going out for ice cream was sex in a public place like the library, falling ill was sex in her marriage bed with another man, and buying a new robe was nearly getting caught. She wrote of these occasions to document her infidelity for her own recollection, never to be read by anyone else. A level of power was involved in these events. But times had changed now. Sara had aged over the past ten years, and the former decadence was little more than a ghost. The woman, now forty-six years old, had saved the secret history in the hope chest, "hope" being a peculiar name for what she kept in it. Everything in the box came from the past, not unlike the beleaguered and forlorn contents of a coffin. Hope seemed to mean a bright future, but this was a time of unending darkness.

She made a plan to sell the jewelry to a pawn broker in Baton Rouge on Highway 190 and to burn everything else. She believed she needed money to leave Tom, now that the marshal was snooping around, not to mention the rift between her husband and Wesley, which was about all she could take. It was time to offer these worthless mementos to the flame as if sacrificed in some religious rite, but the valuables she'd redeem for cash money.

Sara took a burlap feed sack from Tom's shop, the old livestock barn now remodeled for carpentry work. She half-filled the sack with all she kept from her hidden life, layers upon layers of it, and packed it all into the sack, which made the cedar box as hollow as a cave echo. She took a black diary from the burlap sack and skimmed over it one last time. These words could cause a man to kill his wife or lover or give the law reason to put me in jail for obstruction of justice, she thought. The past needed to be burned now.

She put the much lighter hope chest back into its place at the top of the closet where it had reposed for over two decades. She stuffed the jewelry into her purse and walked outside with the burlap sack. She lit a cigarette when she reached the back steps and smoked. After a quick break sitting on the steps looking at the sack full of ghosts, she walked to the steel burn barrel in the backyard near Tom's workshop and dumped the sack, lighting some letters with a match. She took the last pull from her cigarette and dropped it into the barrel. There was little wind, not enough to even make the pine needles move on the trees. The paper made good kindling. The letters were dry as dust and the fire took off quickly. She could see the contents of the sack uniting with the flames, diaries and letters, even some small sketches from college art classes. The fire made her little historical record escape from public scrutiny for all time, the diminutive library archive burning.

Sara stood and watched the pyre go upward like a rising obelisk. She was repelled by the glowing heat. She smoked a Viceroy and watched the fire die down slightly. Then she went over to the workshop and took a long mimosa tree limb that Tom used to stoke the fire in the oil drum. Jabbing it, she made the fire grow again, the paper circling and cycling into carbon. It was a consuming fire, erasing the only hard evidence of years gone by.

The woman watched it burn for a while, and then took the cigarette pack from her front pants pocket and lit a new one. She stared at the fire. She smoked. She talked quietly to herself. "That LeBlanc woman is pure evil. She always was the worst. A jealous woman. Truly the worst I've ever known. A sorry godforsaken woman, wide-eyed and always talking," she said aloud. Sara took another deep drag. "The Parnells will be involved before it's over with, just watch."

She thought about hitting Charity with a wooden club. She spoke to the pyre. "What a fraud, a commoner just like me living in a rich man's house. A man and woman living in a big house. And why is she doing this now? Just because my husband wouldn't build some shitty shelves for her. Because I slept with Sloan so long ago. Did she think he was going to marry her or something? And Sloan is dead. I was the only other person who got hurt because of this, nearly killed. I swallowed it all and kept the peace, just tried to protect my son and family. For what? I should find her and kill her."

She stared at the oil drum. Everything burned as she smoked the cigarette. She held the soot-darkened mimosa limb in her hand and stirred the dying fire. She recalled Ray Bradbury's *Fahrenheit 451*. Paper burns at 451 degrees. She could tell the diaries were gone now, nothing left but the book boards. Just a little flame and smoke. She didn't want anything left, not a single readable page in the barrel or floating in the air. "Where will it all end and who will live to stop it?" Sara asked the smoke.

After a time, she peered into the drum and saw that it was gone. She believed it was good. She gave the ashes a final stir with the limb and walked back to the house. She was dry-eyed, not a tear on her face. She was doing what needed to be done, and she needed to do even more.

That afternoon, Sara drove to Baton Rouge for an evening class at the LSU Library School. Each semester and summer for more than two years she had driven to Baton Rouge for a night course at LSU, slowly working her way through a master's degree in library service.

On the drive over, she stopped just past the East Baton Rouge Parish border. It took nearly an hour to make the drive in her little Gremlin. She stopped past the Amite River and brought the jewelry to a pawnbroker for cash and few questions.

The pawnbroker was a tall, thinly built man with hair slicked back on his head and laced with Pomade. He wore a dark leather vest and looked like a gospel preacher with his hair and attentive manner. For the jewelry, he counted two hundred and thirteen dollars into her hand. She was shocked by how much the items brought.

The woman had always kept a little money back from Tom in a maternal stash, money stowed away in a desk drawer at the junior college library, funds if she ever needed it. Now was the time when she needed it. She was sure it was time to leave him, and she believed he would know about the affairs with Sloan and James Luke before it was said and done, the marshal slipping around asking questions, Charity talking. Perhaps Tom already had his suspicions.

Sara had a vision of Charity singing like a witch in the woods, calling down curses upon her head and the heads of her family members. Lightning cracked, the devil beat his wife as the rain fell to the ground, a tale like she'd heard as a child in Arkansas. And if Tom Hardin ever finds out who raped me, it won't be because I told him, she thought.

As the pawnbroker thanked her for the business, Sara glimpsed a glass case with pistols in it. She stepped over to it and bent at the waist and stared at a snub-nosed .38 Special, a Rossi. It was a small revolver, and it had a stenciled sign in front: PERFECT FOR LADIES. Her right hand passed over the top of the glass.

"Are you in the market for a handgun, ma'am?" the pawnbroker asked. "This old world sure ain't getting no safer."

"No," she said as she slipped the bills into her pocketbook. But she looked again at the weapon and then at the pawnbroker, and she thought about Charity and the current troubles, how the woman was causing a train wreck that needed to be stopped.

"Ma'am, that sure would be a fine pistol for a lady such as yourself. It's just the proper size. My lovely wife has one exactly like it. She keeps it in her purse at all times." He reached into the case and took the pistol from the velvet shelf, and he placed it in front of her on the top of the glass, laying it directly before her.

Sara could see the paper tag on a string that read "$94.95." She felt the wood grips, held the pistol in her palm, pointed the revolver to the floor, sighting the concrete. Then she stared at the slim man and asked, "Would you take eighty?"

"Since you've done business here today, I can let you have it for that amount plus tax."

"I'll take it. And a box of bullets."

"God bless you, ma'am. I hope it protects you and yours from this profoundly wicked and fallen world."

When the university class was done that evening and Sara had driven back to Baxter Parish, she went to the campus library and put the remaining jewelry money with her other cash in the manila folder in her desk drawer. The folder was marked S. HARDIN'S PERSONAL PROPERTY.

She went inside the Periodicals Room and searched the Pickleyville *Star-Register* for a cheap rental, maybe a garage apartment downtown. She wasn't ready to leave yet, but she was getting close, and she worried about waiting until the fall when the junior college students took over most of the open apartments. She was far too old to rent a room in anyone's house, and she wanted a place of her own. Wesley might need a couch to sleep on when he came home on the weekends, and the apartment needed to be a price she could afford on her little clerk's salary, half of what Tom made as a carpenter. A man working at the college always made more money than a woman. With his side carpentry business, Tom brought home three times as much as she did after taxes. No matter what, she had to come up with a way to live on her own.

On the way home from stowing the money at Doolittle Library, she thought about Wesley and his troubles with Tom. But Tom wasn't the ultimate problem. It was Charity LeBlanc and James Luke Cate. She wondered if using the loaded pistol in her purse to get Charity and James Luke off her back and out of her life would take care of it. She didn't know what she wanted to do, or if she had the courage to do anything, but she decided to be ready for the worst kind of hell coming on the horizon, something even worse than being beaten, raped, and left for dead. Sara decided to be the world's punching bag no longer.

CHAPTER THIRTY-THREE

I t was dusk when James Luke took a room at the Sweet Camellia Motel in Pickleyville. The place was a no-tell motel with a seedy little history as early as the 1960s when he'd last lived in the area, and the establishment had gone downhill ever since. The motel was made famous locally by Dolly Parton and Porter Wagoner who stayed there when they played the Louisiana Hayride, and folks said Dolly had the time of her life at the Camellia. At the front desk, James Luke said he wanted two nights, and he wrote, "Solomon Burstein, Houston, Texas," on the room ticket, no address, and no identification offered.

The night clerk took notice of the extra twenty-dollar bill placed on the Formica desk. "Three nights, right?" the clerk asked James Luke. His hand touched the extra twenty.

"Like I just said, two nights, and no phone calls. I'm not here. A man needs a little peace and quiet away from the old lady sometimes, you see. Two nights if nothing changes."

"And the extra bill?"

"Oh, it's Hanukkah in July, my brother, a little tip to help out on life's little journey."

"Yes, sir, Mr. Burstein. And I don't know nothing about anything."

"Right again."

"Cool. Merry Christmas or Happy Hanukkah, whichever you'd prefer, Mr. Burstein."

Once inside the bleakly lit motel room, James Luke took the city directory from beneath the Gideon Bible where it lay in the nightstand drawer, and he found the number listed for Howell Claiborne. Then he drove across town to Cowart's Meat Market where he used a payphone outside. When he called the phone number, it was the current residence of the college president. Dr. Myles Polk's wife answered. She said Dr. Claiborne was no longer living there, and that he'd retired. He now lived at his family home on Thomas Jefferson Avenue. James Luke told her he had found a purse belonging to Dr. Claiborne's wife with some money in it, and Feliciana Polk quickly passed on the telephone number to the house, as well as the street address downtown. He wrote on a slip of paper he took from his shirt pocket.

Good God, this is easy, James Luke thought. He called the house but got no answer. He immediately drove back to the motel. He stretched out on the hard bed with his black cowboy boots still on his feet and took a long and restful nap, the sweet sleep of success.

When he awoke, he decided to go drive past the place to see what lay ahead at the Claiborne House. James Luke took a fifth of Old Crow from his suitcase, poured himself a Dixie cup full and drank it down in three strong swallows. He figured it had to be a mansion by the address on Pickleyville's wealthiest street. After taking a shower, he got dressed in some fresh clothes. He lit a Camel. Best to go over to the house and take a look around. It being Friday night, maybe Charity and her old man are out for a night on the town. Shit, maybe she's got somebody else, fast as she is to move from one to another.

He found the big house. He passed it twice in the Suburban. It was eleven o'clock at night, and he saw a Mercedes parked under the carport. Lights were on inside the house, first and second floors, and he wondered why they'd be up so late. He scoped out a safe place to access the house from the back, and a spot to park the vehicle two blocks away. He settled on the street beside the Federated Presbyterian Church. It was near the private alley that led behind the big houses on Thomas Jefferson Avenue. This will do, he thought,

So he drove out to Cowart's Meat Market again and called the house. Charity answered, and James Luke immediately knew the voice. He asked for her husband, and she said he was gone to Washington, and before she could say another word, he hung up the phone and howled into the night, a holler that no one heard as he stood on the empty road-side at the payphone in front of the aging butcher shop. Then he drove back to the Sweet Camellia.

CHAPTER THIRTY-FOUR

D r. Howell Claiborne spent his summer doing research for a book on the Southern Agrarians, a group of Nashville poets from the 1920 and '30s who argued for conservative approaches to nearly every social endeavor, all of them Anglo-Saxon bigots, reactionaries, intellectuals and writers that came from old money. The research time was funded by his severance package at the junior college, money to keep him quiet about where the bodies were buried over the years, cash to make him fade quietly and loyally into the shadows. For travel expenses, he was supplemented by the National Endowment for the Humanities. He was gone so much it made Wesley wonder if the old man had another woman on the side. In fact, he had seen Dr. Claiborne only twice during the nearly two months he'd stayed at the house.

On Friday morning, Dr. Claiborne returned to the Library of Congress. He'd only spent a few days in town. While he was home, Wesley slept in the pool house. After Dr. Claiborne's departure, however, Wesley spent the night in Charity's queen-sized bed just like always. Sometimes he felt a little ashamed of himself, embarrassed by his role at the Claiborne place.

He eased awake on Saturday morning and saw Charity sitting in a wing-backed chair smoking a marijuana cigarette and reading a copy of *Cosmopolitan*, her wet hair wrapped in a towel. She'd just gotten out of the bathtub. He saw her legs tan and shining in the morning light that came from the second floor window, the terrycloth robe covering her upper thighs. He felt happily exhausted from the sex and the strain of the night, the two of them out late before coming home to their bedroom play. They'd attended a musical at the Saenger Theater on Canal Street in New Orleans after driving the old man to the airport for his trip to D.C.

"I bet that was the best sex you've ever had," she said.

"Every time we make love it's better than the time before," he said, and he sat up on his elbows in bed.

She stood and walked over and pinched his right cheek. "You've been with the best and you're a real pro already." She extinguished the joint in the ashtray on the nightstand beside the bed.

He blushed, almost high from the smoke.

"You'd better go to your apartment before Cornelius comes here to do yard work this morning. You know how the coloreds talk."

"Okay."

"Wesley, you need my help on the project today?"

"No, I'll be all right. I'm almost done."

"Good, I'm going to drive back to New Orleans and look at some clothes I saw in a window on Canal yesterday."

That evening, Wesley was tired from working on the shelving at the junior college Industrial Arts Shop. His car wouldn't start, and he realized the starter was out. He had to walk all the way back to Thomas Jefferson Avenue.

Despite the car trouble, he'd planned to get almost everything finished by the time he brought it to the house, a prefabricated job. He would simply screw the pieces into place in the room with Nate's help. This was his goal. He was almost done with everything, and could do touch up work on the stain at the house if needed. Dr. Claiborne had ordered a fancy wooden ladder with a brass rail from an advertisement in *The New Yorker*, a magazine the old man bragged that he'd read since his undergraduate days at Ole Miss. Wesley took the ladder out of the cardboard packing and saw that it would be easy to attach once he got the slide installed. The shelves were adjustable with setting holes and wood pegs to raise the track that held individual shelving in place.

His mind was hardly on his work, however. Images of Charity's naked body in the bedroom, her long hair invaded his mind like the aroma
of a swamp after a storm. But as soon as his daydream and lust became
particularly titillating, he'd remember the verse from the Bible: "Be not
deceived; God is not mocked: for whatsoever a man soweth, that shall
he also reap." The memory disturbed him, and he tried to push it out of
his head.

Wesley spent time planning the details of the installation so that he'd
only need to make one trip with Mr. Kirby's truck and the trailer from
the shop to the house. Keep it simple, he thought. He'd grown so accus-
tomed to Charity's bed and the love-making that he hated to finish the
job and move to Lafayette, and at times he even plotted ways to remain
in town, maybe commute to the architecture program at LSU. He'd even
slowed down finishing the work to make it last the whole summer. He
knew better than to ask Charity if he could stay. Deep down, he understood his role in her life. The rejection would have been too much for
him. Had she wanted him to stay during the fall, she'd be the first to tell
him not to leave, and he knew it. The lack of invitation bothered him.

Charity bought a new pair of black go-go boots, a short skirt, and a
red blouse at Reed's on Canal in New Orleans. She had her nails done
and her long hair styled in a feathered flip. She was going to model the
new outfit for Wesley, she said before she left to shop, and take him to
dinner at Clay's Restaurant downtown. She liked controlling him, and
she acted as though she had him on a tether like a little lapdog.

On Saturday evening, Wesley drove Charity to Clay's in the Mercedes, and they ate filet mignon. She ordered an Old Fashioned with
double shots of bourbon. She relished the stares from townspeople
when the pair went out in public. The few who spoke to her gave her an
opportunity to introduce him, which she did—as her personal assistant,
an artist friend. After the dinner, they watched a pornographic movie at
the Joy Drive Inn. Hers was the only Mercedes in the dark lot, and they

put the top up after a while, fondling each other in the backseat like a pair of high school students during prom night.

Wesley sat at the table in the little pool house Sunday morning. He was finished with the work on the shelving project in the Claiborne study. One day during the upcoming week, he planned to ask Nate to help him start the installation, assuming he didn't push it ahead yet another week to stall his departure from Charity's bed. He was finished with his summer independent study at Baxter State, and with C.J. Kirby's final "A" grade, Wesley's associate's degree coursework was complete, except for attending the December commencement ceremonies. Kirby had given Wesley an "A" for the course, and he said he would be posting the official grade at the Registrar's Office in a few days.

Now that he was basically done working on the shelving, he could return to his art. Some months before, he'd started painting a scene from the Big Natalbany River, the green color almost black over the brown water full of silt, the depiction of a creek after a spring rain. At Baxter State, he'd won the second-year student art award in December, a juried show judged by an Alabama artist with only one name: Beeson. He had some paints and oils, a palette that fit his hand, and he wanted to offer the finished product to Charity as a parting gift when he left for architecture school in a couple of weeks. There was added excitement because she said her husband had called President Van Broussard at Lafayette, and they were committed to a Presidential Scholarship, though he didn't know the amount. He was thankful for how well everything was going, especially after the hard rift with his father. Wesley believed he needed to make his own way in the world, and he now had a real peace about his decision to move into the Claiborne House.

Regardless of the assurance of a right decision, he missed his mother. Wesley often visited with her at the campus library. He decided to call her at home with the telephone in the little pool house. He planned to hang up if his father answered, because he didn't want to deal with the man.

Sara answered the phone. She said she was by herself. "Oh, Wesley, you haven't called me in over a week. I was worried."

"I've been busy with the job at the Claibornes' place. And the Maverick broke down yesterday. It's parked at the shop on campus. It won't crank. The starter's out. I'm going to have it rebuilt over at the machine shop on Cherry Street. It'll only cost twenty dollars to fix it, but the old guy says it'll take a few days. I almost called you for a ride, but I didn't want to deal with Pops, and—"

She interrupted him. "Why didn't you tell me your car was broke? Are you able to fix it yourself?"

"Nate and I can do it. But Pops has gone crazy. I don't want to talk to him. It's not worth it."

"Like I've said before, you had nothing to do with the dispute between him and Charity. And I've had about all I can take of him. He is completely rigid and won't give a damned inch. We're done talking. Tom is set in his ways, and I think I'm going to leave him."

"You're not serious."

"Yes, I am serious. I don't like how he's treated you. It's never going to get any better between us. It's just not right. I've had enough of his self-righteousness. If there's an innocent person in all of this, it's you." Her voice cracked, and he thought she might start crying.

His eyes began to well up with tears. "Mother, I don't know what to think."

"Let's get some lunch tomorrow and talk. We can go to the Hard-Row Barbeque. He never eats there, and I'll pack his lunch for a change. I haven't fixed him lunch in almost two months."

"Okay. What time should I get there?"

"Quarter after noon. How are you doing with the carpentry project?"

"I'm about done with it. Just the last details left."

"Good. And I have some money I'm going to give you. I can pay to fix the starter. If you need a ride, call me."

"Thanks, Mother."

"I love you."

"I love you, too. Bye."

Charity attended the morning service at Federated Presbyterian Church two blocks away from the house. She kept the normal routine while Dr. Claiborne currently absconded in Washington. The old man couldn't abide the holy rollers, so she went with her husband or alone to the Federated Presbyterian Church on Sunday mornings and to Reverend Hussert's congregation by herself on Sunday nights. Even when he was out of town, she followed the usual split service routine to keep up appearances. She hadn't seen Wesley all day.

At Federated Presbyterian Church, she mouthed the traditional prayer of confession with the other Reformed congregants, but her mind was as blank as an empty tablet when she said the words. She took lunch at the country club, and she played a round of tennis with a young man she was trying to seduce, a love interest she'd cultivated as Wesley's replacement to live at the pool house and to sleep in her bed once he left for Lafayette. After the country club, she went to the evening service at Reverend Thad Hussert's Flaming Sword Church at five-thirty, where she had been baptized and born again for the seventh time a few months earlier. On stage, she fronted the band with a tambourine as she danced in a long dress covering her go-go boots, her good looks and flamboyance making her the center of attention of every man in the sanctuary.

The amplified band played hard driving gospel songs with drums and electric guitars with riffs like rock anthems sung by the Rolling Stones. Church members played instruments on stage behind and beside the pulpit. She'd seen the Stones in 1972 with Sloan Parnell in Houston, and she had not been as excited by any music until she started attending the Flaming Sword. The major difference between the church band and the Stones was the lyrics to the tunes that they played but not the sensual allure of the rhythms and beat. The raw sex in the music was exactly the same.

Later in the evening, Wesley heard a knock at the pool house door, a steady but feminine sounding knock-knock-knock. He figured Charity had come back home from the Flaming Sword. He quickly covered the painting on the easel with a cotton cloth. The young man walked over to the apartment door and opened it. Charity smiled. She wore a long dress with her hair pulled up like a Pentecostal church lady, but the top three buttons on her blouse were splayed open. "Hi babe. You're looking mighty good," she said, sounding upbeat. She walked over and kissed him, and they embraced. She was three inches taller than Wesley in her new boots.

"I'm fine."

"Good." She looked at the painting on the easel stand, his oil tubes spread out. "I didn't know you were working on any art."

"I'm trying to finish a piece. I worked on it a while back."

"What are you painting?"

"A scene from the river near where I grew up, the Big Natalbany River."

"Can I look at it?" Without waiting for an answer, she removed the cloth covering.

"Yes," he said, a little perturbed.

She stood staring at the work. "The Big Natalbany sure is small, ain't it? But it's beautiful. The painting is almost done, right?"

"Nearly. Maybe in a week, maybe less. Now that I'll be finished with the study soon, I can devote more time to the painting."

"I want it, and we'll buy it. It's simply stunning."

"Well, my plan was to give it to you."

She squeezed his upper arm and held it. "I've got an idea. Have you ever drawn a nude before?" she stared into his face. He could feel her breath.

"Sure, for the art department last year. It had to be done on the QT at a gallery in New Orleans. My professor said it would have been a complete scandal at the junior college."

"Did you do a good job on it?"

"I think it came out all right. Here, I have it in my portfolio." He reached into his portfolio and pulled out a piece done in charcoal on canvas, and he took it out of a slip to cover. It was a nude woman with short hair, a bob cut, sitting in a straight back chair.

"You've got a great eye. My husband collects art, as you know, and I bet he'd pay well for some of your pictures if you have more. And the great thing is that his friends will get jealous, and they'll want to buy some stuff, too. They'll bid your price up out of pure jealousy. Greed and jealousy make the world go around."

"Like I said, I was going to give you the river painting when I leave for Lafayette—as a present."

"Please, you need the money, and Dr. C. has plenty of money, believe me. He inherited property and Wall Street stocks galore, and it'll be just as special of a gift. He'll pay at least two hundred dollars, and you should take nothing less from him," she said.

Wesley thought about the money for a second. "That would go a long way. It would pay to fix my bum starter and loud muffler, and buy a new set of tires, too."

"Would you draw me nude? That's what I'd really like," she asked.

He hesitated, his conscience gnawing at him. It was a risk. He would leave behind a record of sex. He wanted no evidence of their tryst, their ongoing sexual relationship. She always supplied him with a condom to wear, and she was on the pill. But the picture could get him busted for sure.

She gazed at him, touched his chest. "I'll let you keep it for me as a little memento."

"Okay, I'll do it."

* * *

Wesley set up his charcoal pencils and easel in the informal den of the big house. After they finished eating burgers and fried onion rings in the kitchen that she'd picked up from the diner a block away, he began to draw her as she sat unrobed in a chair in the den. Her legs were crossed, just like the model for the class in New Orleans. He sat with his easel and pencils. He began to square her from the rough edges, and he saw that she was even more beautiful nude inside the living room than in the darkened bedroom where they made love, even more striking than her body at poolside in the warm sun. Her legs crossed like scissors and cut into his heart. He couldn't understand how he had wandered into such a magical place.

Wesley listened to her chatter, going on and on about her trip to Paris and Rome with Dr. C. last April. Her talk was constant. She said she was planning to attend school for art history, though she had not taken a single class since she graduated from high school.

Sometimes he thought she was lying out of habit. She didn't mean anything by it, just routine deception as a means to keep the conversation lively. He tried to stay focused on his work, trying not to be aroused by her naked sex. Her breasts were unblemished and firm, round, and her thighs full of lust, her proportions almost perfect, unlike the nude model in New Orleans who was plain and slim with an average face, a kind of gangly woman. Charity looked like Miss America plus ten pounds at thirty-one years old, the sunlight's effects on her cheeks and near her eyes. She'd won the Milltown Strawberry Queen title and had kept the tiara and sash, she said. He didn't want to think about the love they'd make after the painting, after he was done, because he'd fail to concentrate on the depiction.

Twice, unsolicited, she assured him that Dr. Claiborne wouldn't return for another week, and she would personally go pick him up at the airport in New Orleans. Dr. C.'s schedule never included any surprises, she promised. But for some reason, she looked a little nervous to Wesley.

Wesley was good at doing portraits. He had been drawing and paint-ing them for years, sketching horses and animals, drawing members of the family and his classmates. He'd even tried his hand at drawing dead birds like John James Audubon when the naturalist was marooned at the Oakley Plantation House in St. Francisville during in the summer of 1821. The Hardin home was full of portraits and drawings that Wesley had completed over the years.

As he concentrated on his pencil and tried to keep his mind from wandering, he acknowledged her with nods and whispers of "hum," "huh," and "that's so funny," as she kept talking endlessly. He drew her curves and tried to stay focused on the shapes. There had been little sexual interest with the model at the gallery, but Charity was different, and the eroticism poured into his eyes with a sharp light.

He had watched The Graduate, and sometimes Charity reminded him of Anne Bancroft as Mrs. Robinson. Charity was as cynical deep down, he knew, just as jaded as Mrs. Robinson. But he loved her and wanted to stay in her bed forever despite the danger and the obvious finitude of their relationship. He lusted over her, and he tried to draw her perfectly with every stroke from his charcoal pencil. And like many men his age and many far older, he had mistaken good sex for love. This was the great weakness of men the world over.

CHAPTER THIRTY-FIVE

Other than two quick trips out of the motel, one for a phone call and the other to look around Thomas Jefferson Avenue and to call the Claiborne House, James Luke never strayed from his room. He ate the food he'd carried with him, heating and cooking some of it on his Coleman stove inside the room. He went to the payphone in the motel lobby on Saturday morning and called the Honey Tree Lounge in Trebor Heights, and he arranged for a prostitute to come to his room later, a little entertainment he looked forward to during the whole ride down from Mississippi. And the Honey Tree Lounge did not disappoint in the least.

At dark on Sunday night, he drove back to the Heller-Reid neighborhood and parked on the street beside the red brick Presbyterian sanctuary. It was three minutes before eight o'clock. He sat with an open Bible on the seat beside him. Dressed in church clothes, a long sleeve white shirt, black trousers, but no tie, he looked like he had been next door to the service. His matching suit coat was hanging in the backseat window.

The Presbyterians met at seven o'clock. If the police or anyone else stopped him, he'd say he was going to or from the worship service, depending on who was doing the asking, and what time it was. The reason he hadn't left his vehicle was because he fell ill, too sick to drive.

He looked in his open Bible at an underlined verse in Isaiah 53. He read it aloud, "All we like sheep have gone astray; we have turned every one to his own way; and the Lord hath laid on him the iniquity of us all." It was the book Tom had given him fifteen years earlier when he'd voiced some fleeting interest in God and religion. Tom had read the verse aloud to him and flagged it with a pencil mark and a red ribbon in the spine. James Luke sat in the truck sweating. Beneath the seat was his .45 pistol with the pearl handles. The high-powered rifle was secure and waiting in a long steel storage box behind the backseat.

Now the man watched a couple of dozen souls leave the front doors of the church. He was thankful that it was cooling a little as the sun fell. James Luke witnessed the last car leave the empty parking area and drive away. The area was poorly lit. Nearby was the alley behind the big houses, a strip of pavement that allowed the residents access to their homes from the rear. He got out of the Suburban, put on his dress coat, the Bible in one hand, his pistol in his waistband, and two bullet clips like blocks in his pocket. He crossed the sidewalk and into the alleyway. The night was now the hue of coal, no sun at all, the back alley as opaque as a tomb.

He could see the lights on when he arrived earlier, see the Mercedes parked outside. He'd driven past the house again. He didn't want to kill anyone unless the course of events forced it, but he wanted to deal with Charity. His plan was to teach her a lesson just like he taught Sara Hardin years ago. And he wasn't driving back to Natchez without coming to a personal understanding with the nutty woman. She needed to shut the hell up or recant what she had said to the marshal and to everyone else. At the back steps, he hesitated, and then grabbed the doorknob. This could go south quickly, he thought. He turned the knob, and he could tell in an instant the door was locked. The unbuttoned dress coat covered his big pistol. He stood with his hand on the knob. He pushed against the door hard and it rattled in the frame but felt solid.

"Hell," James Luke whispered, "I'll go to the front door just like regular white people." He left the backdoor and picked up the Good Book. He didn't want to make noise breaking down the door.

"Did you hear something?" Charity asked. She fidgeted in her nakedness.

"No." Wesley held the pencil in his fingers. He looked thoughtful, wise, a curious enough guise on his face. He resembled a street artist in the French Quarter making portraits of tourists.

"Can I have a quick break? I need a cigarette."

"Sure," he said, looking up from the sketch in progress.

She stood. There was a slight line of goose bumps on her arms.

The doorbell rang. James Luke stood at the front door with the Bible under one arm like a preacher or perhaps a summertime book salesman, dressed in all black except for the white shirt. In many ways, he resembled the Apostle Thad Hussert at the Flaming Sword Church.

"Damn it," Charity said, "probably a neighbor lady wanting something, trying to invite me to another bridge tournament. They're relentless and all twice my age." Her pubic hair was visible when she stood. She put on the robe that she had placed across the arm of the couch, and she reached for her pack of Kools and lighter on the end table. "Wesley, answer the door, and tell the old woman I'll be right down. But don't dare let her in. We'll never get rid of the old bat." She climbed the stairs in a rush.

"Okay," he said, standing up, a little rattled. He put his pencil on the easel ledge and walked over to the door.

The bell rang again before he could reach it. Wesley opened the heavy front door and stared at the man dressed in the suit with the Bible. James Luke held the book in one hand and the other hand was at his waist, not far from the pistol. They eyed one another for a couple of seconds.

Wesley was perplexed at first, then sure. "Uncle Jimmy," he said. He was shocked, as if he'd just seen an angel or something from another world.

"Yeah. I'm James Luke Cate, but who the hell are you?" He glanced away to the street and then back to the young man's face.

"I'm Wesley Hardin. Tom and Sara's boy."

James Luke shook his head. He turned a dark shade of reddish purple and ground his teeth. "I guess you are. I need to talk to Charity. I know she's in there."

At first, Wesley wanted to hug the man just like when he was a boy, but he could sense a strange distance that was alarming. James Luke Cate was not his real uncle, but he'd been like a brother to his father ten years before he left the region. Wesley had never seen him again until now.

"Come in. She'll be down in a minute." He walked James Luke through the living room into the den. The odd visitation made no sense to Wesley. Why would he come here? He still wanted to shake the man's hand or hug his neck, but James Luke seemed to be agitated and tense by the way he gripped the Bible tight, his face hard. There was some kind of a sneer wired across his mouth that never eased.

"You just leave church?" Wesley stared at the book. He rubbed his pants legs aimlessly with the palms, fidgeting.

"I guess you could say that," James Luke said, looking down at the Bible in his hand as if he hadn't realized it was there.

Wesley offered him a seat on the couch. They both sat down. Then Wesley realized he needed to go tell Charity about the visitor. He stood to go upstairs.

"By God, you've grown a lot, way bigger than Tom and every bit as tall as me. How is Tom doing?" James Luke's voice and manner softened slightly.

"He's all right. He works as a carpenter at the junior college."

"You live here?"

"I stay at the pool house out back."

James Luke gazed at the painting, the rough sketch of Charity nude. He looked back at Wesley and grinned. "Yeah, I'm sure you stay up in that pool house. I bet stolen water is real sweet."

Wesley knew he was being mocked. He quickly covered the easel with a cloth. "In two weeks, I'm going to go to Southwestern in Lafayette, the School of Architecture, and I've been staying out back at the pool house this summer while I'm working on a carpentry project here. It's some shelving and cabinetry to go into the study. I need to go tell Mrs. Charity you're here."

"You do that."

Wesley walked up the stairs and down the hall into the master bedroom where Charity stood at the bathroom doorway in her robe. He could see that her face was contorted. He moved toward her. She had the telephone receiver in her hand, her fingers tight around it. She put the phone to her ear and gave the address, saying she needed the police to come immediately to her home on Thomas Jefferson Avenue. A man was breaking into the house.

She threw the phone down on the bed and snatched open the nightstand drawer, pulling out a little black pistol that Wesley hadn't seen before. A burning cigarette smoldered on the edge of the nightstand and fell to the floor. She was standing by the bed where they'd made love last night and many times before. She cocked the black pistol with a click.

"Charity, what are you doing with the pistol? James Luke Cate is here. I know him from when I was a boy in Zion. This seems strange," Wesley said.

"Oh my God, Wesley," she said, "you get in that bathroom and lock the door. Get in the bathroom right now, dammit." She had the little Beretta pistol in her hand, her finger on the trigger.

"I don't understand," he said.

She grabbed his arm with her left hand and tried to push him into the bathroom. The phone was lying on the bed, the receiver making noise.

"He's a dangerous man. I've called the police. You go hide. Open the window and jump out and run away." She pushed him into the bathroom. Her face was ashen, and the look was nothing less than terror.

Before Charity could shut the door and hide Wesley in the bathroom, he saw James Luke raise the big Colt pistol from the hallway just past the bedroom door. He'd seen the pistol when he was a child, and James

Luke had let him fire it once. It was pointed toward them. Wesley hollered, "No!"

James Luke trained the pistol on Wesley, and he was hit with a round to the skull. Blood and brain sailed across the vanity mirror six feet away and splattered the wall like John F. Kennedy's cranial matter across the trunk of the Lincoln Continental in Dallas.

"I'll kill you, you loudmouth bitch," James Luke sneered as he pointed the Colt at Charity.

She got off a quick shot with the .25 automatic, and plaster split from the wall beside James Luke's head. He moved beside the doorframe, but she fired at him again, missing a second time. He stepped out from the hallway long enough to squeeze off a round at her, and simultaneously she at him. Her bare chest became a massive butterfly as the heavy bullet entered above her left nipple. She, too, scored a hit unwittingly, a round piercing high on his shoulder, lacerating his right trapezoid. It stung him like fire, and he began to curse the pain.

Charity fell to the floor. James Luke stepped over to her body and shot her again in the face for good measure, her blood spattering on the side of the bed sheet.

She lay dead. He began to kick her with his black cowboy boots. He smelled gunpowder in the air and the burnt flesh of death that reminded him of Heartbreak Ridge in Korea.

After James Luke quit kicking her, he saw that Wesley looked dead, too. He stopped cold and sized things up. He gazed at Wesley's mangled forehead. He spoke to the young man on the floor in the bathroom. "What a damned waste." He stared at his head and scowled, feeling sad for a brief moment until the pain wiped his conscience clear, and he focused his attention back on himself. He dropped his Bible on the bed and surveyed the damage.

He put Charity's little pistol in his back pants pocket, took a towel from the rack in the bathroom, and pressed it against his right shoulder. He could tell the wound was more of a glancing blow than a direct hit, the meat cut with a deep indention on his shoulder through the dress coat, and it hurt with pulsing pains in his neck. His shoulder burned, bleeding down his arm on the towel.

"What a batshit whore!" he said. The pain was intense, almost breathtaking. He turned to go downstairs, and said, "Woman, everything you touch turns to shit."

James Luke stuck the big Colt pistol in his waistband and fled the room. Blood filled the white towel he had pressed to his shoulder which he held tight. The crimson dripped onto his boots, and his stomach immediately started to feel swollen with pain.

This was the law of unintended consequences, bad luck, or perhaps bad karma, he thought. He almost tried to feel guilty over it all, but he could not. He was suffering a considerable amount of pain, and he felt fortunate to be alive when he left into the night as fast as he could, out the back door and down the steps and through the yard and into the alley. He was not going to expend any of his strength dwelling on the lost boy and the lost world he'd just made.

CHAPTER THIRTY-SIX

A police officer arrived in less than ten minutes. The officer on duty had been working a wreck over at Dead Man's Curve in the middle of town. James Luke had passed the fender bender and the officer on his way to Old 51, where he made the turn north toward Mississippi. The officer left the accident and headed back downtown, now going in the direction where James Luke had just left, the patrol car lights flashing.

Less than a half an hour later, all of the old bridge ladies were out on their front lawns, and plenty of the town and gown learned of the gruesome murder at the Claiborne House. A reporter from the *Star-Register* who lived in a garage apartment up the street was onsite writing notes for a story in his little steno pad, gathering the facts for the Monday, July 29, 1974, afternoon paper. He was almost jolly because he knew it would make front page news above the fold. "If it bleeds, it leads," and this story was drenched in blood.

Later in the night, Marshal Brownlow drove over with his bloodhounds. He had been called because he was the brother-law to the Pickleyville chief of police, Bruce Nesom, and because he had tracking dogs. It took less than ten seconds standing in the bedroom for him to recognize both Wesley and Charity, and to see that they were as dead as stones.

Coroner L.B. Wallace, a veterinarian in Ruthberry, said they'd died within minutes of the phone call to the police station. There was enormous blood loss, and the two beautiful people were pretty no longer.

He said this was the worst murder scene he'd witnessed since the stabbing of a Negro boy in 1957 for whistling at a white woman in Liberty City.

The marshal had never seen anything quite like it either. And it was not just the gore in the bedroom and the bathroom. It was the unmitigated waste of it all, the loss of human life, the potential for good lives lost. Or at least one good life, Wesley's, whereas Charity's ship had long sailed, gone to sea ever since she was a girl and into a dark water forever.

Chief Nesom and the marshal spoke to the Presbyterian minister in the front yard of the big house. He was the Claiborne family's long-time pastor. An erudite man who had graduated from Princeton, he said he would call Dr. Claiborne in Washington, D.C., just as soon as he got the number from the man's sister who lived in town and was also a member of the church.

"You know," the Reverend Hannibal Knox said, "there was a gentleman sitting in a panel truck parked on the street. It was a blue Chevrolet, I believe. I saw him when I was preparing to leave for the manse after the service. He got out of his truck, and he was dressed for worship, well dressed. I think he carried a book, a copy of the Holy Scriptures, but I did not recognize him at all. He was headed west toward the little lane behind the houses. This was peculiar, because as I said, he was not present at our evening worship service, and the automobile is now gone. We had perhaps thirty people in attendance tonight, and I would have noticed any visitors. I almost went over to speak to him before I walked to the manse."

"Can you tell me what he looked like?" asked the marshal.

"Average-looking, a Caucasian gentleman with black hair. The darkness was hardly overcome by the street light," said the minister. "This probably will not help you. I wish I could offer more details."

"It helps a little," Nesom said.

* * *

The marshal and the chief were standing outside on the front steps of the Claiborne place. The chief smoked a Tampa Nugget cigar, and the marshal chewed a piece of gum.

"This Bible was on the bed," a detective said. "It had a little blood on it and looked out of place. It seemed odd, the woman being naked under her robe and all, and the kid not far away from her, all of that with the Bible laying on the bed. Plus she was drawn on a big poster board on the first floor like the kid was drawing her naked or something."

The detective held the book carefully with a handkerchief. Brownlow and Nesom inspected it. The detective avoided the blood stains on the cover with his bare fingers. They could read a note written in black ink on the front flap. "From Tom to James Luke. Seek and ye shall find. God bless. December 24, 1961, Thomas E. Hardin."

"Our man is James Luke Cate," the marshal said. "And this is a disaster right out of hell," Brownlow told the chief.

"Somebody might ought to go see that old boy," the chief said.

"If he ain't blood loss dead already. He left here with a blood trail, drips and drops," Brownlow said.

"We couldn't be lucky enough to find him dead," the chief replied.

The marshal took his dogs from the kennel on the back of his truck. He aided the Pickleyville police with tracking a blood trail that left the house heading out of the back door. He'd brought both of his hounds, Dixie and Duke, and they picked up the trail and were soon making a beeline through backyard and the alleyway toward the Federated Presbyterian Church. Once at North Spruce, they stopped. The marshal and the city detective watched the dogs go cold on the trail. The hounds had lost the scent and sniffed the air above the street.

"Drove off, huh?" Chief Nesom said, stating the obvious.

"I'd say so," the marshal answered. "Did y'all find any weapons?" he asked.

"No, but there was an open box of .25 autos on the nightstand and there were three spent .25 casings and three .45s on the floor," the chief said.

Two hours passed. Tom and Sara Hardin were met at the front door of their house in Zion by Marshal Brownlow and Reverend Poole. The marshal said, "We are sorry, but we've come here to tell you that Wesley has been killed at the home of Howell Claiborne. Both Wesley and Mrs. Charity Claiborne were shot to death in the house, and the best I can tell it was murder. The shooter has not been positively identified yet. I am deeply sorry to carry the news to you." He was withholding information until he could locate James Luke or get a little closer to doing so.

Tom said, "When I find out who did this, I'm going to kill him."

Marshal Harington nodded. He didn't want to say anything to the contrary. He was angry enough to kill someone himself. Still, he didn't want to chase two men instead of one.

In the living room of the house on Lower Louth Road, the old Hardin home place, Tom held Sara for the first time in many weeks as they both wept the uncontrolled tears that accompany the death of an only child, a grief so inconsolable that not holding one another up, each would have fallen down to the wood floor.

Marshal Brownlow stayed at the house for a while with Poole. They stood on the front porch in the night air and talked. Corrine Travis, Tom's faithful cousin, arrived. Brownlow said he wanted to escort Tom to the city morgue to claim the body as soon as he was able to go. Wesley's driver's license was in his wallet, and the marshal knew exactly who the boy was despite the disfigured head.

Corrine and Reverend Poole said they would stay as long as necessary. The marshal left this house of mourning and went to put the dogs in the pen. He asked Reverend Poole not to let Tom or Sara leave. He would return shortly or try to figure out the best way to persuade Tom to go to the morgue.

CHAPTER THIRTY-SEVEN

The marshal called the police station in Natchez and alerted the officer on duty about the murders in Pickleyville, Louisiana. He said he had a warrant issued by the police in Pickleyville. Then he asked for permission to interview James Luke and his wife, depending on who could be located. The officer said he'd call the chief at home and get back to him.

Brownlow needed to meet again with Tom and take him to claim the body. So he called the house and spoke to Reverend Poole, who said Sara was in bed and two female co-workers from Doolittle Library were there holding a vigil, as was Corrine. One of the women had given her enough valium to sleep a standing horse.

The marshal asked the minister to drive Tom over to City Hall to claim the body. He said he'd do it.

Soon, the marshal met Reverend Poole and Tom at the Pickleyville City Hall, where the police station, jail, and makeshift coroner's office were housed. The minister had driven Tom in his Oldsmobile. Inside City Hall, they sat on a recycled church pew in the hallway when the marshal arrived. The place smelled like Pine-Sol, ammonia, and death.

"I'm sorry," the marshal said as he walked in.

"I thank you," Tom said.

Reverend Poole stood and shook the marshal's hand absently.

"Are you up to seeing the body?" the marshal asked.

"Not really, but I don't guess it's right not to," Tom said.

"No," Brownlow said. "I don't guess it's much of an option."

Tom claimed the body. The head trauma had swelled, and the face only half resembled his son. He could recognize the left side of the face, which was unharmed. The big bullet had hit the right side of the forehead with explosive force and disfigured it beyond natural recognition.

He did not linger long while Coroner Wallace pulled the cover back over the body. The veterinarian casually noted that Charity was in the cooler, too.

"The loss of a son is the greatest of all losses," Tom remembered reading in his world literature class at the junior college. It could have been the words of Professor John Coumes or the writings of Heraclitus, though he could not recall which one. But now the words belonged to Tom Hardin, and they were purchased like an oath.

Reverend Poole went home. Just the marshal and Tom sat in a City Hall interview room drinking coffee. The building was empty except for a night dispatcher. The marshal had said he'd take Tom back to his house. He updated Tom on how the dogs closed in on the trail, losing the track and the scent two blocks over on North Spruce. He told Tom about finding the bloody Bible with James Luke's name written on it. He mentioned the Presbyterian preacher said he saw a vehicle.

"Are there any fingerprints?" Tom asked. It was as if he'd been crushed by a giant weight, his body drawn into itself like a turtle in a shell as he sat in the chair.

"I don't know," the marshal said. "You'll have to ask the chief. But your name was written in front of the book."

"That's the Bible I gave James Luke, that no-good bastard. You know he did it. I guess what Charity said about my wife must have been true," Tom said.

"Is there any chance that Wesley'd have the Bible you gave James Luke in '62?" Brownlow asked.

"None, no chance," Tom said.

"Well, I'll have to get a warrant, and Bruce Nesom is working in it. Cate's surely wounded, shot by either Charity or Wesley. I don't know which at this point."

"Did my boy suffer?"

"No, Tom, not from the looks of things." The marshal took off his cowboy hat and wiped sweat from his forehead. He sipped the coffee trying to stay awake.

"We need to find him," Tom said. "Or I need to find him. I'll damn well find him."

"Best to let the law handle this."

Tom made a fist. "I've got a dead son here. Where was the law for him when he needed it?"

The marshal was worried the time was short before there would be vengeance. He decided to take Tom home immediately and get Freddy Wentworth to watch the house to be sure Tom didn't leave. When he got back to the office after dropping Tom off at home, Mrs. Lott was waiting for him, where she'd kept her post since he called earlier in the night. She had phoned every hospital between Pickleyville and Vicksburg, and no patient fitting James Luke's description or name had staggered in needing treatment. This fact did not make finding the man any easier.

He called James Luke's house in Natchez and woke his wife, who said he was on a fishing trip to Arkansas. The marshal asked about the make and model of the truck. She said he owned a blue Chevrolet Suburban and that he'd been gone for a couple of days now. No, she didn't have the license plate number on the truck off hand, nor did she expect him to be home until Monday. She said there was no way to reach him. The marshal asked her to call him the minute he arrived.

"Is he in some kind of trouble?" she asked.

"I just need to talk to him as soon as possible," he answered.

Brownlow was caught up in the case because of the hounds, or so he had told himself, even though the primary reason was that he was deeply involved in the Zion community and everyone who lived there. He was able to assist in the investigation with Chief Nesom's permission, and the bloodhounds had raised his status. He'd gotten to be a major player in the region's law enforcement activities because of his dogs and his decades-long connections to area lawmen. Some local folks wanted him to run for the state legislature in Baton Rouge, but the heart attack was slowing his ambitions, not that he'd ever had much ambition to begin with. His dogs were the only trained tracking blood-hounds east of Angola Penitentiary in Louisiana, and recently he'd been called out to a county on the Mississippi Gulf Coast to help find a lost child.

Brownlow felt responsible for this disaster in many ways. By talking to James Luke Cate in the first place, he had allowed the man to connect the dots back to Charity, and this led directly to the deaths of two people. But even if it was inevitable, Charity was the one digging up trouble like a dog after a long-buried bone, causing anguish for others and even herself. The first level of culpability was attached to her.

He was worn down by the long day that had spread into the night. The only time he had any real energy was when he was with his hounds, and having them in the truck box buoyed his strength. After the long night, his wits were not slowed, even if his body was anything but spry. He had succeeded in getting Tom sequestered for a couple of more hours, at least until he could figure out a plan to do something with him.

Deputy Marshal Freddy Wentworth waited at the Hardin family's driveway with instructions not to let Tom leave until the marshal arrived. Brownlow was worried about Tom going off the reservation, taking justice the old way, and he did not want another murder to deal with inside his district or anywhere else if it could be prevented.

At eight-thirty on Monday morning, Marshal Brownlow awoke from a few hours of sleep. He had a solid plan worked out in his mind. He placed an all-points bulletin on the Suburban after getting the license number from the Adams County Sheriff's Office. He spoke to the Natchez chief by phone.

He then called Chief Bruce Nesom at his house at nine o'clock. "How are you?" he asked.

"Donald, must you harass me? I just fell asleep a couple of hours ago, and I'm not going to work till noon. Lest you forget, I was up all night."

"Brother-in-law, I needed to wake you," Brownlow said. "I have a plan to deal with Tom Hardin. I've got a reasonable feeling he might try to go after Jim Cate, and that would mean more trouble by far."

"He'd be mostly justified. No jury'd ever convict him in Louisiana. Mississippi maybe, because Cate lives up yonder and not here. How's Tom doing now?"

"I don't know. He was pretty shook up. Freddy is at Tom's house parked in his driveway making sure he doesn't leave—assuming Freddy ain't asleep on the job."

"At least somebody'd be getting a little sleep. I'm for that. You can't keep him boxed in forever," Nesom said.

"I have a plan to handle it. I want to take Tom with me to find Jim Cate, keep him close to the breast. Otherwise, like I said, I'll be chasing two people, and one is plenty hard enough to deal with."

"So, why'd you call me? To ask my permission? I ain't your boss. Besides, you're overstretched plenty with the heart trouble, Donald. It's not even your jurisdiction. It's nine in the morning, and I'm trying to sleep. You see how important it is to me, don't you?"

"Well, I'm looking for sound advice from a friend and fellow peace officer. And yes, it's your jurisdiction, not mine."

"They say Cate's old lady's daddy's got big money. I asked one of my officers who just come here from working up at the Natchez P.D., and he said James Luke Cate married into the Tartt family, and his wife's daddy's the president of the biggest bank in Natchez. You'll be up against some old money in Mississippi. Liable to get your ass in a hard pinch, and you well know the man has left the parish."

"But I can't rest till I lock him in jail. Then they'll lawyer the hell out of us. That's okay, I guess. We always have to deal with that. I need to help old Tom out."

"Can Hardin be trusted? Because it's a pure-d risk having him along. The fellow's a common citizen with no law enforcement background at all as far as I know."

"Yes, he can be trusted. He's a good man."

"Can anybody really be trusted?"

"You've been in politics too long, Bruce."

"Damn, you're the one that got me into politics, and you've been elected even longer than me."

"I know, I know. To hell with it. Glad you answered the phone. Go on back to bed."

"I will, Donald."

CHAPTER THIRTY-EIGHT

Tom went outside and talked to the deputy marshal at the end of the driveway. Wentworth radioed and relayed to Brownlow that the cat had climbed out of the sack. Brownlow drove over immediately in his pickup truck.

The marshal and Tom sat on the front porch.

"Look, Tom, this is just a real heartbreaking thing that's happened to your family. And I'd understand if you were not agreeable, but I have a plan on how to go after Jim Cate. I want to make you my deputy marshal, unpaid, of course, so we can apprehend the man together. I really need your help."

Tom was surprised. He was silent, unsure what to say. His wife was in shock where she lay inside the old farm house. He had his son's services to plan, and his own grief to bear.

The marshal stared at Tom. "I hate to be direct, but I need your answer now and not later. Yes or no? If you want to help me, I need you to follow my lead. Categorically, I don't want no mavericks going off the reservation. We'll need to go hunt him down today. Hell, I need you to help me find him."

"I'll do it," Tom said.

The marshal drove Tom to get a late breakfast at Pete's Café in Milltown. He went inside and brought back two bags of egg, bacon, and sausage biscuits, and two paper cups of coffee. They ate the meals in the truck.

By the time they returned to Zion and finished loading the truck for the trip to Mississippi, it was already noon. The marshal put the hounds in the cage-like dog kennel in the truck bed. He warned Tom about Dixie. "Tom, the gyp'll bite. Be careful around her," he said.

They returned to Tom's house a mile away. The truck had a siren, lights, and NINTH WARD MARSHAL stenciled on both doors. Brownlow sat in the cab and waited for Tom to gather his things.

Tom put his Savage 99 lever action rifle in the gun rack in the marshal's truck glass, and he carried his Smith and Wesson .38 pistol strapped to his side in a leather holster. This was his old hog hunting sidearm, and it was loaded with copper jackets.

Inside the Hardin home, Sara was on tranquilizers. She had been visited by Dr. Carl Roswell, the only doctor left in the parish who still made house calls.

Tom walked into the bedroom. He was restless, barely coherent. He gazed at his wife for a few moments. She sat in a chair and either couldn't or wouldn't speak to him, so he left the room.

He talked to Corrine in the living room. "I'm going to go with the marshal to help find James Luke. He's the main suspect, and when I get back, I'll plan the funeral," Tom said.

She clenched her teeth, shook her head. "Tom, you couldn't have stopped it."

"You might be right, but I could have tried a little harder than I did."

"Wesley was completely sold on staying at that house with that damned woman. That's what Sara said to me. She says she doesn't blame you. It's not your fault."

"I don't know."

"You believe James Luke is the one that did this, Tom?"

"Yeah, he's the killer. And a lot of things make sense now that haven't made any sense to me for twenty years or longer."

"He was more or less family."

"Yeah, that's the worst of it."

* * *

Out at the truck, the marshal made Tom raise his right hand. He said he was a duly commissioned deputy marshal of the Ninth Ward. He gave Tom a tin badge, and he told him to clip it to his shirt.

"Look, if you have to shoot Jim, be sure he has a gun on him somewhere," Brownlow said.

"Okay," Tom said.

"If not, I've got a throw down weapon in the truck, but you've got to be careful with such things."

Outside of the Ninth Ward of Baxter Parish, they were both on thin legal grounds, especially in Mississippi, where they'd be foreigners at best and would have no rights to arrest James Luke. The marshal explained to Tom that three-fourths of their job consisted of trying to get the local authorities interested and involved, motivated to arrest Jim Cate, just to help locate him. The other part was finding him. However, he wasn't particularly confident they'd even find the man anyway.

They left out from Zion in the marshal's pickup truck and headed north toward Natchez. The hounds were riding in the big cage behind the cab, occasionally letting out a stray howl. It was warm and sunny, a beautiful day.

Tom was feeling an acute sense of grief that grew worse with each mile he traveled north away from Baxter Parish. He kept pushing it down into his gut. His regret overwhelmed him like a growing cancer, and he wondered what he had done to deserve this pain. He could not find an answer in the short time he had to contemplate it, and he doubted he'd ever have enough time in this life to understand why the events came to pass. The catastrophe of the past twenty-four hours had left the most important person in his life dead and gone in his youth.

They checked into a room on the sixth floor of the Rosalie Hotel overlooking the Mississippi River, which was higher than normal with Midwestern floodwaters coming down like an avalanche of wasted history. The room had two double beds and was charged to the marshal's office. The two men ate an early supper downstairs in the hotel restaurant. They had not eaten since breakfast. Tom was having trouble talking. He didn't care to say much, and he was choking up, trying hard to get his words out. He could hear the dogs barking outside where the truck was parked on a side street underneath a shady oak.

Marshal Brownlow and Tom met with the Natchez chief at his office on D'Evereaux Drive. Brownlow was careful not to stir the hornet's nest with local Mississippi politicians, so he asked up front to assist the Mississippi officials in finding Cate. He said repeatedly that they were there only to assist, especially since he had the dogs, if tracking dogs were ever needed, and he'd be there any time in the future for manhunts that came up in the environs around Adams County. He carried with him a warrant for James Luke's arrest for capital murder.

At the Slocum Cottage on South Pearl Street, they met with James Luke's wife, Heloise. She said little other than to deny any knowledge of his exact whereabouts or what he might be doing. As far as she knew, he was fishing near Hot Springs, Arkansas, with a bunch of Army Corps managers. Her father's attorney, Theodore Barnett, a respectable ambulance chaser, sat with Heloise at the dining room table. He wore a pinstriped seersucker suit, and the edges of his bowtie were as sharp as glass. The lawyer drank milk from a coffee cup and interjected from time to time to reinforce the denial. James Luke had given no phone number due to the remoteness of the lake, she said. Her husband was staying at a park owned by the Corps of Engineers somewhere near a reservoir, he'd told her. He had some new business associates to get to know in the upper echelons of the agency.

"It's just a bunch of good old boys doing what good ol' boys always do," Heloise said. "That's all James Luke is about anyhow. He's just a fun-loving good ol' boy."

The Natchez chief had said earlier that his office would telephone the Corps and the Hot Springs sheriff.

"Ma'am, does Jim have some place he might try to stay here in Mississippi?" asked the marshal.

"My husband has more than thirty properties, most of them in North Natchez, but they're all occupied, as far as I know. You're quite welcome to check any place if you like, but we'll have to go to the business office to get a list of rentals and addresses," she said.

Lawyer Barnett agreed with the offer though he said it was pointless.

"Does he have a hunting or fishing camp?" Brownlow asked.

"No," she said.

"He doesn't hunt anymore?" asked Tom, speaking for the first time.

"He hunts. He either hunts in the swamps up in the Delta near Greenville, or he hunts at my daddy's old camp in the Homochitto National Forest. But Daddy never hunts anymore. All he does is play golf, but James Luke uses it every deer season," she said.

"Where is the place in the Homochitto?" Brownlow asked.

"It's on Union Church Road near Meadville," she said.

"You ever been there?" the marshal wanted to know.

"A number of times, but not in years. It is, shall we say, 'primitive,' with no electricity and an outhouse. I don't desire to spend much time in such a place," she said, her nose turned up slightly.

"Can you give us directions on how to get there?" the marshal said.

"I believe so," she said.

The marshal had a hunch, a burning in his gut when he heard about the camp. At the hotel, the marshal phoned the Franklin County Sheriff's Office and spoke to the first deputy, the only person on duty for the entire county, and also the dispatcher on duty at the moment. His name was Chesterton Lewis, and he said he would go see if anyone was out at the property. The marshal warned Deputy Lewis how dangerous the man was. The deputy said he'd meet them over at the national forest in an hour. Brownlow gave him directions, sending him there from what Heloise Cate had offered as the easiest route to the camp.

Brownlow had already paid for their room at the Rosalie, a room they'd never sleep in. It was almost six o'clock when they drove southeast toward Franklin County through the piney woods. "I've barely heard of a faster room check at a hot-pillow joint," the marshal said, smiling.

Tom didn't laugh.

The national forest was an expanse of land owned by the federal government. It covered parts of several counties and was known as the notorious place where two young black men were murdered by the Klan in 1964. Some locals suspected they were civil rights activists, radicals planning an armed uprising, which was false. But to venture into the Homochitto's dismal labyrinth was to court danger in and of itself, 189,000 acres of backwoods mystery, and the risk weighed heavily on the men as they traveled in the marshal's truck.

CHAPTER THIRTY-NINE

James Luke had a large first-aid kit in the back of the Suburban. He'd bought it stolen from an ambulance driver in Vicksburg for five dollars cash. He sat at the camp table. The remote place was surrounded by forestland. He worked a pair of small tweezers through the proud flesh of his shoulder, pulling out nasty woolen fiber and festering flesh that had gone into the muscle from the little .25 pistol round. He had already done this the night before, but more of the cloth seemed to be working toward the surface now. He poured hydrogen peroxide into the crevasse of his shoulder, the hole ripped open by the bullet. After he got fatigued from doctoring it, he taped down the gauze on his shoulder. The muscle felt like a burning mound of meat, and the pain hardly eased.

He wondered how he'd made the two-hour drive in such pain the night before. A few more inches, and I'd probably be dead or crippled, he thought. That crazy bitch was a better shot than I'd've ever bet good money on.

Charity's automatic lay on the kitchen table. He gazed at it, a Beretta with black plastic handles and a pop-up barrel. "That little piece of shit liked to have got me," he said.

James Luke was sick to his stomach with no appetite. He had plenty of food, and though the camp had no electricity or telephone, it had kerosene lamps and a propane stove and refrigerator. The silver tank behind the camp was full of propane. The well was outside near the front porch, and water came from a hand pump. James Luke tried to eat, but he had vomited up his breakfast. When he finished the vomiting spell, all of the food was gone from his stomach. He just sat drinking Old Crow, smoking, and thinking.

He hadn't wanted to involve anyone but Charity. It compounded the risk of getting caught. Now he thought it was stupid to go to the house instead of catching her alone in her car someplace. One of the last people in the world he would have wanted to shoot was Wesley Hardin, but he told himself it was an accident, that he was aiming at Charity who had the gun. Moreover, he reasoned that it was all self-defense in a roundabout way. He'd planned to scare her, beat her with the only thing she respected, the Holy Word. Knock her senseless, pound her with the Good Book until she quit confessing her misdeeds and the sins of others. He never realized he'd dropped the Bible until he was north of the Mississippi line, and he almost turned around to go back for it, but he quickly and wisely decided not to return to Pickleyville. He was worried now, very worried. That Bible could get him executed. At the minimum, the shoulder injury would take some time to heal, and this was evidence enough to make him mortally fearful. He needed to keep out of sight.

The plan was to leave the camp by the next evening and report to his attorney in Vidalia. But he also needed to conceal the truck someplace safe until his lawyer could offer counsel. Surely they had out an alert for his vehicle.

At least the hunting camp enjoyed the advantage of a clear view across the patch of forest on all sides. It sat atop a ridge that was surrounded by thick hardwoods and pines that were almost impassable at the edges of the property. It was clear around the house and out front to the road. He could see in all directions. Most importantly, the lane in front went straight to the gravel Forest Service road. Unknown to anyone but the best-schooled locals, there was an old logging road at the back of the property that led to Sarepta Baptist Church. It was so obscure that he wasn't concerned about being flanked from the rear. This was where his Suburban was parked just below the ridge, out of view from the front of the camp at the Forest Service road, and no one but a bona fide local woodsman would be aware of the route away from the pasture behind Sarepta to the camp.

Last winter, he took the Suburban on the logging road to go and get a spike buck that he'd shot too far away to drag on foot. The strip was overgrown with grass and had twists and turns, an almost undetectable escape route.

On the kitchen table, he rigged a C.B. radio left at the camp with an extra battery retrieved from his truck, planning to listen to the emergency channel, but the radio was broken. He couldn't fix it. He wished he could call his lawyer, but he was far too worried to wander around Meadville looking for a payphone under such circumstances, a gunshot wound in the shoulder making him look like an escapee from Parchman Farm. His best hope was waiting until the dark of night and driving directly to his attorney's house in Vidalia where he had done business before. Besides, it might be better to let the dust settle and see if he was actually going to be accused of a crime before getting his lawyer involved. He needed to get some tabs on the investigation, see if there were any fingers pointing toward him. His luck, until recently, was the stuff of legend. The wound in his shoulder, however, made him think that perhaps all of the good luck had run dry, and the nausea in his stomach confirmed it.

He kept trying to work up a reasonable alibi if he got stopped. He'd say he was lying to his wife about the Arkansas destination. He'd say that instead of going to Lake DeGray, he traveled to meet a prostitute in Pickleyville at the Camellia Motel. Indeed, he'd done that very thing. They got high on some cocaine she'd brought with her, first time he'd ever used dope. He felt bad for the prostitute and gave her his Bible because he thought she needed it worse than he did. Beyond that, he didn't know anything. So what about the wound on his shoulder? They must have gotten so high on dope that he might have been rolled by the prostitute's pimp. When he woke up, his wallet was missing, stolen when he passed out cold. He didn't go to the police for obvious reasons. Regardless of the tale, he'd have to figure it all out before talking to the authorities, assuming they came for him. In the end, far better to admit infidelity than murder. Heloise's sympathy was more lenient than the law. If called before the authorities, he'd let his lawyer talk for him no matter what.

Not having much sleep the night before, he lay wary and fatigued on a makeshift couch built from pine two-by-fours and plywood, an almost useless homemade cotton cushion placed on top of it. During the night, he took whiskey and aspirins as painkillers for his shoulder. He was at least pleased the bleeding had stopped. In the steel barbeque pit out back, he'd burned his bloody dress pants, jacket, and shirt. He ran his finger through the bullet hole in the jacket and almost laughed as he tossed the clothes into the fire. He wished he'd actually brought some cocaine with him or some painkillers. This was by far his biggest regret.

CHAPTER FORTY

Deputy Chesterton Lewis had written down the directions over the telephone as best he could. He lived in the Bunkley community ten miles away from this section of the national forest north of Meadville, and he was not as familiar with this particular area as he was with other places in the county. The phone was filled with static when the deputy and Marshal Brownlow spoke earlier, and he was coming from the south and the directions were given to him from the north. The region was riddled with nondescript logging roads and Forest Service roads, as well as private driveways, many of which looked exactly the same. He was searching for a Forest Service road sign south of Sarepta Baptist Church.

What Deputy Lewis did not know was that James Luke had driven his Suburban over the wooden sign marking the road, retrieved it, and tossed it into a thicket as he drove in the night before. There was nothing to mark the roadway, nothing at all but trees in one giant landscape of loblolly pines and hardwoods.

Motoring along slowly in his worn-out patrol car, the deputy drove a few miles up and down Union Church Road looking. Along the way, he saw a familiar sight, a man walking north, his thumb out. It was Sonny Boy Cupid, who wandered the byways throughout southern Mississippi hitchhiking, doing odd jobs, just hanging around and talking to folks he met during his daily travels. Deputy Lewis slowed the car. "Sonny Boy, you see a blue Chevrolet Suburban truck yesterday or to-day?"

Cupid tugged his ear, closing his eyes for a second. "Nope," he said. "No version of it at-tall. Say, can you give me a ride home, Mr. Lewis? It's mighty hot out here."

"Not now, I'm trying to find somebody in a blue automobile, and I'm going back toward Meadville anyhow."

"Well, may the Lord bless you on your journey."

The deputy turned around at a logging road up ahead and went back south. He passed Cupid again and both of them waved.

Lewis pulled into a driveway, went a half mile into the woods, and he saw what looked like a derelict hunting camp, which was a sagging trailer with some crude additions built onto it. The place was inhabited by a woman and her stair-step children, the littlest one in a burlap diaper directly out of Erskine Caldwell's *Tobacco Road*, a short book the deputy had read during a nightshift once. The house was nothing more than a silver aluminum trailer with a rusted roof and a front porch, and an outhouse near the side made of tin.

A pack of mutts circled the car as Deputy Lewis pulled up. They came in all shapes and sizes, some with hair, some hairless with red mange and skin showing, two dogs with nipples dragging the ground, one gyp with three skinny pups, heads raised following their mother in a life and death pursuit of milk. From his experience, these mutts were the worst kind of animals to bite a law officer.

He spoke out of his open car window to the woman. "Y'all know anything about a man by the name of James Luke Cate? Does he live here?" the deputy asked.

The woman said, "No, sir." Her dress was a flower sack that could have been made in the 1930s. Her cheeks were sunken, her hair thin and long.

Franklin County was not wealthy or prosperous by most standards, but a sight such as this was out of the usual range of experience for the deputy, even in the black quarters of Roxie. He took note of it. Perhaps he could bring a turkey at Christmas, a gift from the Sheriff's Benevolence Fund. The woman looked like she could boast the poorest family in southwest Mississippi.

"What's your name?" he asked.

"I'm Lyndale McKeever. We is McKeevers out here. I'm a McKeever and these young'uns, well, they got different daddies, but I don't know no Cate nowhere. You need to have these kids' back names?" The children were lined up in the yard close to their mother. They were quiet, as if they knew an unsolicited word could get them hauled off in the patrol car.

"I don't suppose I do." The deputy gazed at the brood for a moment, and then he backed the car away slowly from the dirt yard and turned around, the pack of dogs chasing the vehicle, biting at the tires and hubcaps.

Thank God I didn't have to deal with her, he thought and continued to search for the road to the camp in the national forest. After a half hour of driving around aimlessly, he decided to give up the search. He could not find the right road, much less the hunting camp in the maze better known as the Homochitto National Forest. He decided to head back to Meadville. Perhaps he could figure it all out when he got back to the station.

CHAPTER FORTY-ONE

The marshal and Tom were on the blacktop highway east of Natchez. It was blistering hot in the truck despite the windows being rolled down and the side vents open.

"Donald, you saw this coming, didn't you?" Tom asked. The badge was on his shirt and the pistol on his side. He almost resembled a real law man, though he didn't feel like one.

"In a manner of speaking, I guess I did. But I had no idea Wesley'd be hurt. I take some responsibility for all of this. I do feel responsible and can't shake it. I reopened the investigation and came to believe Jim Cate was the one that attacked your wife, but the fire was set ablaze by that woman Charity. The LeBlancs are a bad seed. Her old daddy, Penrose, might have been a preacher, but he was a genuine pervert, too. They say he'd get in the pulpit and preach down heaven on earth, and when he got out of that bull pen, he wasn't worth a rotten egg. He was tapping half the congregation at the Church of God in Kilgore, all the women past thirteen years old and even some of the boys. It's a true wonder why some man in his church ain't killed his sorry ass. Charity was always bad to shoplift in Pickleyville and Milltown. I had to go pick her up on account of warrants a number of times. She wrote hot checks and was a general menace. You might know that her daddy managed to get her out of trouble coming and going. The preacher was always tight with Judge Parnell come election time. Damn, she was malignant all the way to the root," the marshal said.

"What could we have done to stop it?" Tom asked.

"Nothing. I tried. I even went to see Jim in Natchez, and I interviewed your wife at my office. I'd started to try to get other law enforcement involved with Jim, because he might have defrauded his second wife out of property. He took a bunch of money with him when they divorced. I had the heart attack the day Charity came to see me stirring up trouble, and I partly blame her for it. It might have slowed me down, being flat on my back for a month's time. I don't know. Within the confines of the law, I was about out of options."

"I tried to stop my boy from following her like she was the Pied Piper. I begged him. He moved in over there, and he wouldn't listen to reason."

"He wouldn't hear a word of it, would he?"

"Could not or would not hear a single word of it."

"It's a true blue tragedy, Tom. If I lost my girl, I just don't know. There were plenty of times that I wished your boy and Priscilla had got themselves together, but I was always hesitant to mention it. She went off to that Methodist college up in Shreveport like her mama did and says she wants to be a French teacher, which is all right, I guess. Now she's got a little boyfriend from East Texas, a little ministerial student. I call him 'Whistle Britches.' You can't hardly tell about preachers, especially ministerial students from East Texas. Real hard to say whether they'll be worth a shit or turn into the devil incarnate. But I kind of coveted Wesley. I do hate to say that now. It's the evil in the world, rank evil. I don't know how to discern it anymore, much less how to slow it down." The marshal felt a twinge of pain in his upper chest. The doctor said his chest pain was angina pectoris. He drove on and almost took a nitroglycerin tablet from a tiny pill box in his shirt pocket to slip one under his tongue, but he kept driving.

Tom sat silently, looking out of the dirty windshield in the truck.

The gun rack behind their heads held the marshal's Winchester Model 12 pump, a shotgun made with a special barrel that was shortened by a gunsmith with a modified choke. The pump was a prison shotgun, a gift from the warden at Angola Penitentiary after Brownlow used his dogs to successfully find an escapee. It was loaded with buckshot and was a deadly weapon. Below it was Tom's old Savage 99 deer rifle with open sights.

"My Lord," the marshal continued, "it's been over three decades of me trying to stop evil, and I ain't never stopped the first shadow of it. Pure devilment is as rampant in the Ninth Ward today as the hour I got started as Marshal Slim Rayburn's assistant right after a two-year hitch in the army. I was twenty-one years old. Funny thing that they call us peace officers. We're in no such way peace officers. We haul folks off to jail after the fact, but we never keep the peace. I ain't never prevented nothing from happening myself. Just call me after the shooting stops. Before such an event, we got no role whatsoever. It would be a violation of somebody's constitutional rights. We're practically just reporters showing up after the chaos is over. It gets a man discouraged before too long, and then he either wears out or quits. And some of us turn bad."

"Uh-huh. I'm sure it gets bad."

"Did you see it in James Luke back when he was in Zion? Y'all was big buddies. I mean, did you see the outright betrayal in him?"

"After he married my cousin Nelda, we got to be real close friends. We were all more or less newlyweds living on Lower Louth Road. Both of us hunted, raised hogs and a few cows in the woods. James Luke and Nelda were married a dozen years before he left her. They never had any kids."

"But did you see it in him? The outright devil in him. I don't use the word 'devil' carelessly either. Did you think he had this kind of rank violence in him?"

"It's like this, Donald. You get to be friends with somebody, and you learn what they're made of a little at a time as far as their character goes. And if you become close enough friends, there's no telling what you'll overlook and let slide unless it's some kind of brazen personal attack on you or your family. You'll give them a free pass on almost anything, even some things that could be a threat. By the time James Luke left Nelda, I'd seen enough of him to realize that I was glad he was leaving town. I figured he was being unfaithful to Nelda, and I figured he was one of the arsonists burning half the parish. I've never said this before to anybody, but I was a little glad that he left when he did for everybody's sake. There was a meanness in him that was a central part of his nature, and I was getting wary of being around him sometimes." Tom tensed his shoulders, gripped his right thigh and released.

"I hate to bring this up, but did you have the notion he was involved with Sara, which now grows more apparent by the day?"

"Only after you told me at the hospital in Baton Rouge did it begin to make sense. Of course, I never had any idea that he was the one that went after my wife. It boggles the mind. Maybe there were signs that you just don't want to acknowledge and voices that you just don't want to hear." Tom looked down, staring at the Mississippi highway map. He never saw deception like this coming, the double cross. He was a fool and knew it.

Soon, they found the old Union Church, a picturesque little chapel with a cupola and green shutters, a building that once quartered Union soldiers during the siege of Vicksburg in 1863. The road in front of it led deep into the national forest. It was gravel, a substandard county road that covered twenty-five miles all the way to the hospital in Meadville. Heloise Cate's directions appeared clear enough, but it would have been better had they talked to her father, because she seemed fuzzy in her directions once she got to church. She said Sarepta Baptist would be on the right side of the road, and they were looking for the sign for Forest Service Road 179. She said it was several roads below Sarepta. The camp was near the end of the road on the right side, somewhere before it dead-ended. Heloise recalled a defunct cistern out beside the house that hadn't been used since her father had a well drilled shortly after buying the land. The camp had a front porch. All other details were sketchy.

The marshal drove south for ten miles. "This is the longest gravel road I've been on in a years. Wonder if that woman sent us on some kind of goose chase," he said. "Hell, Jim Cate is probably laying up in her four-poster bed in Natchez."

"No, I believe she was telling the truth," Tom said, rubbing his jaw with his palm. He was now thinking of Wesley and the marshal's daughter, and the happy future missed. He wished that Brownlow hadn't said this about the two of them, about coveting his son for marriage. Then almost in tears, he studied the useless map, looking at nothing on it, trying to pull himself together.

"You all right, Tom?"

"I'll get better."

The sky was eclipsed at times because of the trees as they rode in silence a few more minutes, an uneasy mist in the air. It was seven-thirty, and it would be pitch dark by eight-thirty. After a couple of miles, they saw a steeple off to the west side of the road. There was a steel sign out front: SAREPTA BAPTIST CHURCH, FOUNDED 1810. The house of worship was nestled under a canopy of oak trees and was as empty as a hog trough in the middle of the day.

The hilly road had the occasional curve. It was seemingly built atop a natural ridge or some land formation above the surrounding terrain. Marshal Brownlow slowed down, and they studied the road past the church. A couple of times they stopped to inspect side roads. The men looked for the Number 179 sign but never found it. One roadway appeared promising because of some fresh motor grader marks as it came to Union Church Road.

"That little side lane here is better than this main gravel we're driving on now, so it's probably managed by the federal government," the marshal said.

"That sounds right to me," Tom replied.

Brownlow stopped the truck at the roadway. He stared across the truck cab to the opening in the timberland that ran west. "It's supposed to be at least a mile in that direction. Then a good ways off the gravel road. This might be it, sign or no sign. My experience is the feds generally maintain their roads, while the local governments can't afford to do maintenance hardly at all. This could be the one." The dogs barked loudly as if awakened for feeding time.

"Okay," Tom said.

The marshal continued, "The dogs'll be barking whenever we slow down or stop, so I reckon we ought to drive a half a mile and then just get out and walk."

"You think the deputy sheriff is there now waiting for us?" Tom put down the Mississippi map, folding it away and placing it on the truck seat.

"For some reason, I doubt it. But we ought to see his car tracks along the way if he's waiting. I definitely don't want Jim Cate to run off or kill us, either of us, so we need to be careful. We're dealing with a true serpent," the marshal said.

"You up for a long walk?"

"Sure. I've got to where I walk about two miles in the evenings for my health. I'll make it." The marshal's chest pain had eased. "This sure is a finely kept gravel road, federal work. You can still see the motor grader tracks. It's been here within a day or two, and there ain't many tire tracks from regular automobiles, but maybe a pickup with some mud grips." He had pulled the nose of the truck to the inlet of the side road and was looking out the window to the ground.

"I think you're right. I see some grip tires." Tom pointed to the dirt road.

Then they started idling down the road at no more than five miles an hour. There were grassed-over byways and logging roads but no signs of houses. No mailboxes, just big woods on both sides of the lane.

Dogs were cutting up in the back of the truck. The marshal decided to stop the pickup. He said it was time to walk a while, and that they ought to remove the shotgun and rifle from the rear window. So the men got them down and chambered both weapons with buckshot and bullets respectively. The dogs barked even louder in the big cage, and the marshal threw them a couple of links of venison sausage from his ice chest to keep them quiet for a while.

The men walked the gravel road near the ditch and could see that the sides fell steeply into gullies sixty-five feet or more down, and the gullies were thick with trees and underbrush.

After a few minutes, Tom saw the glint of a tin roof off in the distance. It was some kind of house on a ridge. He pointed to it and stopped. The marshal was walking alongside him, and he strained his eyes to make out the roofline himself.

"Let's keep on walking," the marshal said. "When we get almost square of it, we'll take its measure and decide how to proceed. Be ready to find cover in the trees and get down low." They walked on.

At the driveway, which was nothing but a rusted metal culvert in the dirt, there was no sign of the deputy's car on the road near the house itself, no sign of the blue Suburban either. However, they did see a set of tire tracks turning into the driveway itself, but only one set. Nothing showed any life but the tracks in the freshly graded Forest Service road.

"The deputy hasn't made it out here. There's no evidence of car tracks in this sandy gravel, just a truck with some grips. I'm not a bad tracker." Tom studied the dusty gravel road. "He's not been through here yet with the car. Should we wait on him?" Tom asked.

"I don't know. Maybe he never came this way. But this ain't a clear situation. No way to tell. If Jim's in that house, I don't want him to slip off on us. I ain't waiting no longer on the deputy. I'll lead. If I take off my hat, get down. If I whistle, shoot something. Let's move to the trees," Brownlow said.

"All right," said Tom. He gripped his Savage rifle in his hands.

The men eased over into the tree line and took refuge briefly behind a couple of giant blackjack oaks.

James Luke stood at the camp doorway scanning the front of the property. There was only so much pain the liquor and aspirin could conquer. He could hardly rest or sit still. His shoulder was aching even with new gauze and black salve on it. He needed a doctor or at least a good nurse. His lawyer bought and paid for doctors who did work for his clients, dirty work for prostitutes and shady people in slip and fall cases, even injured hit men. He wanted to see the lawyer's paid doctor soon, but he couldn't travel until it was dark. The camp was hot inside with no electricity and no fan. He'd raised the windows the night before, which mercifully had bug screens on them, but the camp was a veritable sauna.

He stood at the screen door and looked toward the road, and he took a hit of whiskey. He drank from a tall glass of bourbon. The camp had an adequate stash of hard liquor, plenty of canned food, too. He could stay there through half of the fall and summer if the festering wound didn't kill him. His rifle, a Remington pump, lay on the kitchen table. The clip and chamber were loaded with soft point .30-06 cartridges. He looked across the front of the property through the screen door, the whiskey glass at his lips, took a swallow and lowered the glass. Then he saw a gray cowboy hat. He couldn't make out a face or body, just the crown of the felt hat amongst some trees. Alarmed, he ran to the table, put down the glass, and grabbed the deer rifle.

Back at the screen door, he opened it and dialed the Redfield telescopic sight to six power. He looked through it aiming at the hat, but it went out of view. He kept the rifle and the scope ready and scanned the tree line. Then the hat as well as the face came back into view. "That dumb-assed Donald Brownlow," he said.

James Luke shot so quickly it surprised him. He immediately realized that he'd probably missed. He pumped the gun and leaned against the door jam, bracing the rifle forearm against it. His shoulder throbbed. This time he tried to find the marshal in the optical sight, put him in the crosshairs and take a decent aim, make it slam home. But the marshal was no longer there. He couldn't see anymore. James Luke searched back and forth. Maybe the stupid bastard slipped off, he thought. Maybe I hit him after all. Maybe he's dead.

But before James Luke could find the marshal again, his right hand exploded in blood, the pinky finger a mangling of flesh that flowered before him. He screamed and howled in pain and got back into the house, slamming the screen door and bolting the solid door shut. The twice-wounded man dropped the gun on the table and wrapped his hand in a dishtowel, holding it above his head. He paced a few agonizing steps. Then he removed the towel and looked at it. It wasn't as bad as he'd thought, but a chunk of flesh was gone from his hand, and his little finger was now baptized in blood. He writhed in pain, grabbing another towel from the cooking area and then ran to the truck out back with his deer rifle hanging over his shoulder on a leather strap. He cranked the Suburban and looked at his hand under the towel again, unsure how he wasn't hit in the chest with the bullet. He barreled down the logging road wide open and cursing. It snaked behind the camp as it came near a hay pasture at the rear of Sarepta Baptist Church.

"Oh my God," the marshal hollered. He lay flat on the ground like a big hound dog flopped out for a rest. "I thought we were pinned down, but I hear a truck."

Tom crouched behind a beech tree. He'd leaned over and used a low limb to steady his rifle for a second shot. He saw a glimpse of the blue vehicle as it fled from behind the camp into the thick woods. Much of Tom's life had been spent trying to avoid violence, attempting to live in a manner different from his fighting uncles, and now he was just like his father wading into the fray to stop the conflict. Yet now he wanted to kill James Luke and wished he had. "I just saw James Luke's blue Chevy. There must be a way out the back of the place. But you okay?" Tom asked.

"Yeah, but I heard a bullet hit a limb above me. Did you do any good?" The marshal sat on his butt.

"I believe I hit him, but I don't know how bad. Not bad enough to stop him from driving the truck."

"His wife didn't say nothing about a road into the woods. Look, you're in better shape than me. Go get the truck and come on back for me. I'll wait here in case he doubles around. But Tom, I didn't whistle."

"No and you're mighty lucky I didn't wait."

"Thank you. Give me your rifle in case he comes back through. I might need some range."

Tom helped the man to his feet. They swapped guns and a cardboard box of ammo apiece. Tom took the truck keys. He left jogging in his cowboy boots, pounding the dirt and grass to get to the road, the short-barreled 12 gauge in his hand.

The marshal's heart was throbbing, beating dangerously fast. He checked the rifle chamber in the Savage lever action for a live .308 round and tried to get into a better position to see the driveway and the front of the house, but he heard the truck winding out in the woods covering a distance, leaving north of the camp at a demonic pace.

James Luke's countenance fell when he saw a new bright yellow gate ahead on the pathway to the pasture. It was a steel gate made of sturdy oilfield drilling pipe painted canary yellow. It was at the end of the easement through the woods and on land owned by the church. He had driven this route many times since he started coming to hunt in Meadville. There had never been any talk of a new gate, and this yellow monster must have been built by the church after hunting season ended. He could see a heavy brass padlock on it, and at first he thought about taking the rifle to it, shooting it clear through. He was half a mile from the camp and knew better than to try to back out on the trail. Bleeding badly from his hand, he had no time to waste. Instead of using the rifle bullet in place of a locksmith, he backed up the Suburban about fifty feet. He strapped himself in with the seatbelt, the first time he'd ever put it on, and he had trouble doing this because of his wounds. Then he floored the accelerator on the big block engine and was at the gate in seconds, feeling the concussion run through his bones like lightning, causing his shoulder and hand to throb even worse than before, the towel falling off his bleeding left hand. He barreled past the gate and into the open pasture and heard steam spraying out of the radiator, but he slammed down the pedal again and headed across the pasture toward the rear of Sarepta Baptist Church.

Hot steam began to cover the windshield, and he could tell the truck was favoring the right side. The rifle had fallen to the floorboard and lodged itself halfway under the seat. He hoped it wasn't broken. James Luke was trying to drive as fast as the motor could turn by the time he hit the main road, but he knew he'd blown a front right tire, and all he could do was curse like a demon.

Tom drove the marshal's pickup all the way to the camp. Brownlow met him near the front steps of the place and stood at the passenger side door, the dogs barking madly when they saw their master at the front of the camp.

The marshal said, "It sounded like a genuine collision, but the truck kept on a-going. Let's try to follow him. But Tom, I'm about whipped. Crawling on the ground took my strength."

"All right, get in," Tom said, staying put in the driver's seat.

The hounds barked in the truck bed. They made a commotion as soon as the marshal got into the passenger's seat. Tom drove around to the back of the house and followed the tracks in the tall grass where the old logging road was located, and they followed James Luke's route through last year's orange sage grass and over some young saplings.

Marshal Brownlow sat with the shotgun barrel out of the window, having swapped weapons again. The rifle lay propped up on the seat beside Tom, the steel barrel pointing to the floor. Tom drove down the logging road at a reasonable speed. He was cautious. The worst thing that could happen was an ambush, Tom thought. I could get myself killed in a hurry just like my son. He grimaced.

They came to the tangled yellow gate and saw the skids in the dirt and the tracks where the tire had gone flat, but the vehicle tracks kept on heading across the field.

The chrome bumper lay on the ground. "Son of a bitch. He 'bout tore his truck to pieces," Brownlow said. He got on the radio and began to attempt to call any law enforcement in radio range. After a time, the marshal found a volunteer fireman listening, and he said he'd telephone the sheriff's office in Meadville to ask for help. When they passed Sarepta Baptist, they could see a line of ruts going north toward the old Union Church.

They followed the tracks cautiously, unsure of what might await them. The men didn't even know if James Luke was alone. It appeared that two tires were flat, the front tires. The vehicle couldn't go very far. They slowed, listening for the truck, but he could no longer hear the revving Chevrolet engine. It wasn't long before dark.

"He can't be no piece from here. Let's hold out a while," Brownlow said.

"We'd better wait on that deputy. At least we have the dogs if we need to hunt him up," Tom said.

A Volkswagen Beetle with two teenaged boys careened toward them on the gravel road. The marshal waved his arms to get them to pull over, and they skidded the tires to a stop near his police truck.

"Howdy, officer," the young driver said to the marshal.

"Did you see a blue panel truck on the way over here?" Brownlow asked

"Yes, sir. It turned toward Aldersgate Chapel back yonder, and the front tires were on the steel rims. We about met him head on. I saw that he made the right turn onto the chapel road. I watched him in my rearview mirror. Looked kind of funky, officer."

"Boys, y'all stay away from here. There's a killer on the loose, and you just passed him on his way to hell," the marshal said.

Brownlow thanked the boys, and the Volkswagen traveled south toward Meadville.

Tom and the marshal discussed the danger, their guns held tight in their hands. The Franklin County deputy sheriff soon pulled in behind the marshal's truck where they'd been waiting ten minutes on the road.

"What happened to you?" the marshal asked.

"I never could find the camp or the right road," Deputy Lewis said. "I drove all around here but gave up. I never found the right Forest Service road. Ain't no Number 179 sign nowhere."

"We tried to radio you but never got anybody," said the marshal.

"My radio is dead broke," the deputy said, a frown on his face.

"Y'all can't buy a new one?"

"No, the county's broker than I am, and that's awful damned broke."

The marshal gave him a summation of events. "Can't we assist you in discharging the warrant?" The marshal tried to be deferential.

"Yeah, don't mind if I see it, do y'all?" Lewis said.

"Be glad to show you." The marshal gave the deputy the warrant. "You got any backup?" asked Brownlow.

"No, I'm it. The sheriff's in Osyka at a funeral. At least you got them tracking dogs." The deputy handed the warrant papers back to the marshal.

"Yeah, I've got two good bloodhounds. And Tom here's a marksman." Marshal Brownlow gestured to Tom.

"Is the Aldersgate Chapel Lane a dead end?" Tom asked.

"I reckon. I don't recall ever going down that lane, but I suspect it's like most of these little side roads that go nowhere," said Deputy Lewis.

They drove a couple hundred yards to the chapel road, and the tracks clearly made an easterly turn into it. Deputy Lewis established a roadblock with his patrol car to keep anyone in or out, and the marshal parked his truck near Aldersgate Chapel Lane, but not in the middle of the road in order to provide a safe place to hide if necessary.

Up ahead was an opening where they could see the front corner of the white clapboard building with its tin-topped steeple as sharp as a bayonet. The Suburban was stopped on the side of the road, and steam spewed out of the radiator at the front of the vehicle. The driver's side door was open. The men studied the situation but were cautious. They stood behind the patrol car.

"He's either inside or behind that church," the deputy said. "I guarantee it."

"Yeah, I believe he is," said the marshal. "If I can keep from getting shot, I'll turn my dogs on him, but I've got to be careful when I let 'em go. I don't want to lose a dog or have one take a bullet. Dixie's bad to bite, and she might get on him. I don't want her shot today. Don't try to catch her neither."

They discussed the situation, night falling on them fast. They decided to flank the church by going through the woods, the deputy and Tom, taking three coordinate positions. Let the marshal go straight in from up the road following the dogs.

The marshal took the pair of dogs out of the cage and put them on the leather leash with a two-way coupler on the end, and they followed the ruts in the dirt road with Tom and the deputy behind, the dogs pulling and tugging Brownlow, the hounds happy to be out of the big cage in the back of the truck and doing what they were bred to do.

Tom and the deputy followed the marshal as he led with his dogs up to the Suburban and saw it still steaming from the busted radiator. They realized the engine was probably burned up. It must have seized by the smell of it, the front tires flat on the rims. The Chevy was empty. James Luke had fled, which was obvious when they first saw the broke down truck as empty as a pauper's cupboard.

The evening gloam was all around, sounds of crickets in the air. Deputy Lewis and Tom took to the woods at the right to flank the chapel.

Marshal Brownlow saw a bloody rag on the seat and gave it to the two bloodhounds, and this got them excited. Howling with canine joy, they immediately took the scent. He stood behind the truck door, hoping to use it as a shield if shooting started. He waited to give Tom and the deputy ample time to move into place. He braced the shotgun against his hip. Then he let the dogs go, and they made a beeline howling and barking toward the church house. He pointed the 12 gauge at the building like a gun bull at a penitentiary, though he knew it was out of buckshot range.

From the place where Tom stood taking his position, he could see the deputy and the little church. He hid behind a magnolia tree and waited with the Savage deer rifle trained on the front steps. There was an uncertain haze out, a light fog all of a sudden, and the cross on top of the steeple gave off a strange glow.

Both dogs went up to the front door of the church and stopped. They sniffed around and then came down and trailed beside the chapel, tails wagging, followed by barking with their deep bass tones. Afterward, there was a commotion coming from underneath the building, a gunshot and a loud yelp.

Tom could see and hear from his post. He began to run toward the chapel as fast as he could. He held the rifle in his right hand as he dashed forward. When he got near the building, he saw James Luke beginning to emerge from beside a concrete pier under the church and into the evening dusk. The Remington barrel came into view first and then his head. James Luke had pushed the gun forward from under the church and pulled himself out. The man lay flat on his stomach, his rifle in his hand, as he struggled to get to his feet, a bloodhound fighting him and biting his legs. He was hollering as he fought, trying to get loose. He attempted to stand and tried to aim the rifle at the snarling animal attacking his leg, but he was off balance, unable to shoot.

Tom slowed to a stop and pointed the rifle at James Luke, and he hollered, "No!" He was twenty yards away and could have split James Luke's skull like a dropped melon with one shot from the .308, just like James Luke did his boy. The front sight took in the man like a deer in the swamp. But Tom began to run faster now than he'd run in years. Tom saw James Luke trying to fight off the dog, trying to point the scoped rifle, but he was upon him, and he hit James Luke in the jaw with the steel butt of the gun, a blow as hard as a mule's kick.

James Luke fell backward, several teeth shooting out of his lips, and Dixie grabbed at his legs as he fell to the ground. Then the second dog, Duke, scrambled out from underneath the church bleeding, and both set upon him like bulldogs, the man crying for mercy when Tom hit him another blow with the butt of the rifle. James Luke's jaw went crooked in his head, and his lights shut cold and dark.

CHAPTER FORTY-TWO

S ara wanted to die. She wanted to take her newly purchased .38
Special from her purse and kill herself. There was nothing left
to do now, she thought, but suicide. She'd dreamed of shooting
Charity with the pistol, but now she wanted to shoot herself. Killing
Charity Claiborne was on her mind when she bought the gun at the
pawnshop in Baton Rouge. She was ashamed now. She had thoughts of
shooting James Luke Cate, and she regretted not taking action. For
years after her rape, she pondered shooting him. He was the cause of
every curse to come upon her family, which now evolved into an even
greater catastrophe. It was too late now, her anger and despair just
wasted emotions. Today, only shooting herself made sense. The irony
of it all was not lost on her, the circle of events like a grand mockery of
her intentions.

The main reason she'd been silent over the past decade was because
Wesley belonged to James Luke, and he'd threatened the boy's life the
day he tried to kill her for sleeping with Sloan Parnell, sleeping with his
enemy. He swore to her that he'd kill the boy if she ever said a word.
This was the supreme irony. It was as if she'd received yet another assault on top of the previous damage James Luke had caused.

Despite the opaqueness and melancholy, the Hardin home in Zion
was buzzing with people. Corrine, Martina, Sara's sister and brother-
in-law from over in Fairhope, Alabama, and several ladies from the library were at the house. The kitchen was full of casseroles and cakes, a
good portion received quietly at the front door by Corrine, most of it
brought over by members of Little Zion Methodist.

It was all Sara could do to stand up, trying to wake herself from the
near-comatose state brought on by prescription tranquilizers and guilt.

She fantasized about Tom returning from his journey with the marshal, waiting for some news report that said Wesley was not dead after all, but alive, the resurrection of the body, which never seemed to occur in this earthly life.

When she finally became semi-lucid, Sara told Corrine about the pistol, asking her to keep it indefinitely. She knew better than to go get her purse and retrieve the loaded gun. She said committing suicide would be an easy way out, and she didn't deserve such a painless escape. Corrine took the purse from the bedroom to her car. She emptied the rounds from the Rossi cylinder and locked the now unloaded pistol into the trunk of her Monte Carlo.

It was dark out when Tom arrived at the old farm in Zion, well past midnight. The Hardin home was quiet except for the low hum of the television in the living room where Corrine sat crocheting a baby blanket for a young child in the Little Zion Methodist congregation.

In the bedroom, Tom hovered over Sara where she lay. There was the dim light of the lampshade's forty watt bulb. She lay on the bed with a towel over her eyes. "Do you want to know what happened to James Luke?" he asked.

"No, I don't. Rita Lott called and said he's in jail. That's enough. I wish they'd give him the electric chair." She removed her towel, gazed at Tom. He was now at the dresser taking off his shirt. "I want to die," she said.

"I could have killed him. I didn't. He was in my rifle sights not fifty feet away. But I choked," he said.

"You should have done it," she said, making a fist.

"Sara, are you going to be able to make our son's funeral?"

"What did you say, Tommy?" she asked, staring at him. There was a familiar sound in his voice that she despised, an unmistakably self-righteous tone.

"Are you planning to go? You don't appear capable of leaving the house. I hope you can drum up the strength out of respect. I have to make plans with the mortician in the morning and figure out how long to hold the body."

She hated herself and hated Tom Hardin, this man she'd made a life with for twenty-three years. And more than anything else, she loathed his sense of moral superiority, his solid footing on every issue. She shouted, "He was my son. My damned son! My son and James Luke's son, you damned fool. You are such a blind-assed fool. You're a hopeless fool who can't see anything. Wesley was James Luke's son. He was the father, you stupid bastard. Can't you see it? It's right in front of your eyes."

Tom looked at her. He was stung. And though he was stung by the words, he didn't shout back. "No, that's where you're wrong. Wesley was my son. I raised him, and no matter what you say or whatever happened, I was his father. I was the one that loved him and lived for him. He was more my son and I was as much his father as any that ever lived."

CHAPTER FORTY-THREE

F our days after the double homicide, the late afternoon wake was held at Little Zion Methodist Church. Dr. Myles Polk, the new college president attended. He told Tom and Sara that Wesley would be awarded his degree posthumously at the fall commencement ceremonies held at the Cow Palace on campus. Teary-eyed young people lined the inside of the church and filled the churchyard making a long line to pass by the closed casket, which was placed in the front of the church atop the dark oak communion table that Tom's father had built in 1955. No one had ever seen the likes of the funeral service at Little Zion since Leander Brownlow died, the marshal's father. The windows of the church had to be opened for people to witness the event from the outside because so many crowded the sanctuary when Reverend Poole led a prayer service and visitation. Tom and Sara received the mourners as if no rupture had ever occurred between them, standing side by side and bracing one another in their inconsolable grief.

The next morning, Wesley was laid to rest in Little Zion Cemetery, and Poole eulogized him as a fine Christian youth slain by a cruel and violent world, snatched away from them in the prime of his life. Only God could bear such a burden, the death of a son, and so Tom and Sara would need to lean on the Lord to walk through this heartbreaking valley of death. Such compassion was seen in Jesus Christ hanging on the cross, man's burdens placed upon His only begotten son, the suffering Savior of all mankind.

Charity, too, was interred the same morning, her burial at the Melrose Memorial Cemetery near the junior college. Both the Presbyterian minister and the fire-breathing Pentecostal preacher delivered sermons at the cemetery and placed her in a costly stainless steel casket in a marble crypt.

James Luke was treated for the gunshot wounds and a broken jaw. He was held without bail in Mississippi for the attempted murder of a peace officer, and then extradited to Louisiana and to the Baxter Parish Jail in Ruthberry for double murder in the first degree.

Tom and Sara never reconciled, even though they appeared as husband and wife during Wesley's funeral services. But they could not fake it afterward. She moved out of the house and into a little duplex apartment by the railroad tracks on North General Pershing Street three blocks south of the college. By mid-November 1974, she had transferred to a job at the State Library of Louisiana in Baton Rouge, and she took an apartment nearby in Spanish Town. Tom filed for divorce.

The days of mourning took the edge off of Tom. He no longer needed to square every angle and plumb every line. A plumb line was only a vain illusion in this life, the appearances of having everything correct, unblemished, and perfect. He could square a wooden angle but not life itself. Over the months following Wesley's murder, Tom learned that his standards of decorum were more of a fantasy than anything attainable. He just tried to do the best he could, to form a hedge against the cruel world he faced.

One Sunday in the early winter, Tom attended a special singing service at Little Zion Methodist Church, a late afternoon event with potluck food and music, but no sermon. "His eye is on the sparrow, and I know he watches me," sang Priscilla Brownlow in a solo. She'd just returned from France, and even sang a verse in French. The Brownlow family had invited Tom to join them on their pew for the first time. He sat on the end of the pew near the window, the far end away from where Donald, Mary Anne, and Priscilla always sat close to the center aisle in the church. Tom listened and enjoyed the gospel song, but he now had his doubts about the whole proposition.

The congregation sang their favorite song, "Marching to Zion." Tom had sung it at least three hundred times before in his five decades attending the church. As the piano played the fourth stanza, it caught his attention for the first time:

> Then let our songs abound, and every tear be dry;
> we're marching through Immanuel's ground,
> we're marching through Immanuel's ground,
> to fairer worlds on high, to fairer worlds on high.

Yes, Tom thought, perhaps only on Immanuel's ground will my tears be dried. Maybe then I'll see and understand, but not now. Not today or tomorrow. Not on this ground.

CHAPTER FORTY-FOUR

After Wesley's death, Tom Hardin and Donald Brownlow became close friends. Brownlow retired as the Ninth Ward Marshal in January of 1975. He had plenty of time on his hands, and the two men visited each other often. Brownlow sometimes worked with wood and used Tom's tools at his shop. Because he was retired, Brownlow used the shop more than Tom did.

In exchange for using the tools, Brownlow paid a year's membership for Tom in the Zion-Lizard Bayou Hunting Club. Brownlow bought a young bluetick hound to use for hunting raccoons. Blue was a started dog in his second season, and the hound was capable of treeing raccoons by himself. It was dead winter, and Brownlow had persuaded Tom to go hunting with him. Tom went to the Land of Sports in downtown Pickleyville to buy a hunting license, the first he'd purchased since 1964.

Tom was beset by grief, but he was determined to go along with his life. He kept working at the junior college, reading a couple of books a week, mostly history books, and he kept up his household chores, cooking for himself, keeping a tidy house, piddling around in the shop out back, and doing the occasional small carpentry project. He missed his wife and son, and though the divorce was not yet final, they were each one dead to him now, each in their own particular way gone from his world.

He rode with Brownlow to the hunting grounds one Saturday night. The club was in an area he often traipsed during the open range years prior to January 1, 1965. Brownlow had a new pickup truck, his own personal vehicle with the big dog kennel cage on the back, which looked like a rolling jail for hounds, but there were no police lights on this truck, no marshal's office signs on the doors. No siren. The tall hound stood in the bed of the truck. Tom could hear the bluetick howl as they drove south of Zion.

They pulled off the blacktop onto Turnpike Road. Tom unlatched the gate, and they entered the hunting club. A long straight road slipped into the timberland, property generally considered low and too prone to flooding for building subdivisions. The hunting lease went almost as far as the north edge of Lake Tickfaw.

When they stopped the truck deep in the woods, Brownlow let the bluetick hound loose from the cage, and he jumped down from the tail-gate. The dog cocked his leg on a bush beside the truck in the darkness, the only illumination coming from a full moon and the battery-powered lamp that was wired to the top of the cage. When the hound quit urinat-ing, he kicked his back legs as if to throw turf, almost like a bull about to charge, and then he bolted for the forest.

"He might make a good coon dog eventually," Brownlow said. He offered Tom a plastic cup. "Coffee?" he asked.

"Sure, I might drink some," Tom said. He pulled out his father's watch from his blue jeans pocket. It was hanging from a leather fob. He popped open the hunting-case and shined his flashlight on it. The watch read half past eight. He placed it back in the little pocket in his jeans. "Thank you," Tom said, taking a sip from the steaming cup in the cold night.

Brownlow poured himself a cup of coffee from the green thermos. "Reverend Poole's been preaching out of Lamentations for the prayer service on Wednesday nights. I don't believe I've ever read the book before now, nor heard a sermon from it. There are things in that book that'll give you reason to wonder about it all. I guess he's been preach-ing through Lamentations for a month or more, verse by verse at the service. He says it's poetry. Now the first thing, it don't seem like no poetry I've ever read, not that I've read a lot of it since high school, or even much back then. Poole says that it's Hebrew poetry. What a thing to write poetry about, losing an entire city and no comfort in it. Your friends turn to enemies. Nothing but tears and affliction through the whole damn book. That Lamentations'll send you to the crazy house, it's so hopeless and dark. But I kind of enjoy it. It seems appropriate to our days here in Zion. I know you don't normally come to the service on Wednesdays, but there are many times when I have sat there listening and thinking about you and all that you've gone through, and at times in prayer I remember you and Sara and all of the hell you've faced. I just wanted to tell you that." He took a swallow of coffee.

"I appreciate the prayer," Tom said.

"You know, Jim Cate will be prosecuted one way or the other the rest of his life. With trials in Mississippi and Louisiana. His wife's money won't help him on account she's already filed for divorce against him, come to find out. They'll take Jim to trial next year. Fact of business, Dr. Claiborne is the reason the judge in Ruthberry has kept him in jail without bond. The real shame is the moratorium on executions put in by that crazy-assed Supreme Court. He might never get the chair. Don't seem like there's a lot of justice in this old world. It don't seem the way it ought to be to me, that's for sure."

Tom said, "Well, he'll get justice either here or later. I don't worry about it. None of it comes close to what I've lost and nothing can bring back my boy. I might not even go to the trial unless I'm forced to. Nothing can bring him back, and I've left it to the Lord. I don't understand much of it, but it's in the Lord's own hands, as far as I'm concerned. It's out of mine completely."

Brownlow shook his head. "You could have killed him that day at the church house. Nothing would have ever come of it, him trying to shoot me down earlier with a high-powered rifle."

"Yes, I could have and almost did. My finger was on the trigger."

"You regret it?"

"At times. I think about it daily, and sometimes I wish I would have done it, other times not. Today, I'm glad I didn't kill him. But like I said, it's in God's hands now, and I'm thankful for that. Everything else I think I can control falls short somehow."

"You reckon there's any good that'll ever come from what happened?"

"No. Some people try to tell me this good or that good will come from it, the Lord having a plan and all. I haven't ever seen it as something that good will ever come from. I see my son's death as a catastrophe and an affront to the love of God in the world. The only thing I hope is that James Luke'll never get out of jail and never hurt anyone else. Hopefully he'll spend the rest of his days in Angola. And if Sara and I can just live the remainder of our natural lives in our right minds, it'll be a witness against him."

"You hear that?" Brownlow put down the coffee on the tailgate and stared into the darkness, his chin high in the air. He cupped his hand around his right ear.

Tom was quiet, listening.

"Blue's done treed already. Must have run up on a coon slipping around on the ground and put him up a tree. Let's go," Brownlow said. He strapped a miner's hard hat and light on his head, and Tom followed him with a flashlight in one hand and his Winchester .22 magnum rifle in the other.

It was dry out for February, almost parched, and they moved through the forest. It was surprisingly free of underbrush, the winter cold killing the thickets clear enough to walk through, and it reminded Tom of an era long ago when the cows ran free and grazed in the woods.

When they found Blue, the hound was jumping in the air and circling the base of a hardwood tree, and he barked a constant barrage of bellowing. The hound grew more intense when he saw the men and their lights coming.

"Speak to him, Blue. Speak. Speak to that old coon. Speak at him," Brownlow hollered to the hound. The dog kept jumping up the side of the tree as if he would climb it. "Call to him. Talk to him," Brownlow continued to holler.

Their lights shined into the treetops. The animal's silver eyes were forty feet up. The raccoon turned away from the light beam, and Tom made the sound of a raccoon calling to another, a squalling noise deep in his throat, and the animal looked back down at him again.

"Do you want me to shoot him down?" Tom asked. He pointed the rifle at the glowing eyes.

"Might as well go ahead. It'll be something I can take to the Widow Lazarus tomorrow. Trade it for one of her good pies."

Tom took aim. He had a clear shot. He held the rifle a half-dozen seconds while the dog treed. He hesitated, dropping the barrel down. "Donald, why don't you shoot? I don't feel like killing a coon tonight."

"Okay."

Tom passed Brownlow the rifle. And he shot.

Twenty Questions for Group Discussion & Reflection

1. Is *Zion* a mystery, a thriller, or a literary novel?

2. Does "Zion," the novel and the place, live up to the meaning of the term?

3. Which characters do you like or identify with the most? Why?

4. Is Tom a good man?

5. Are Tom's standards of perfection responsible for the problems in the family?

6. In which way is Tom partly responsible for Sara's secrets?

7. Is Tom simply nostalgic about the past or is he delusional about the past?

8. Did Sara ever love Tom?

9. How does Sara defy the stereotypes of a housewife and later a librarian?

10. Does the loss of Sara's father influence her life?

11. Why does Wesley feel justified in rebelling against his father? Is he right?

12. Is James Luke evil or just an economic pragmatist?

13. How is Charity a victim? Is she a bad person or simply misguided?

14. Were the farmers and hunters justified in rebelling against the timber companies?

15. Was Marshal Brownlow corrupt in the 1960s? Did he change?

16. Flannery O'Connor said the South was "Christ-haunted" but not "Christ-centered." Is that the case in Baxter Parish?

17. Why was the Methodist church used as a backdrop for the book?

18. Is the story told in *Zion* more Old Testament or New Testament?

19. What is the most tragic aspect of *Zion*?

20. How could the disasters in the story have been avoided?

AUTHOR Q & A WITH DAYNE SHERMAN

QUESTION: Why did you write Zion?

DAYNE SHERMAN: One day my fourth cousin once removed—we keep track of things like this in Southeast Louisiana—told me about an old dispute over the killing of hardwoods. In an area well known for arson, the locals had a slogan, "For Every Oak a Pine!" The timber companies were killing hardwoods to plant pines. But folks in the parish didn't want to lose the good hunting lands where hardwoods dominated. So they burned perhaps a thousand pines for every oak killed. Within a few days of hearing about the pine tree war, I'd finished a third of the novel. It took several years to complete the rest, but I was on a clear path.

I wrote the novel to unburden myself from the image my cousin gave me. I married the burning timber to some local folk tales and the end of open range. The open range ended in my native Tangipahoa Parish, Louisiana, in the 1960s. In nearby Livingston Parish, however, the open range wasn't banned until the early 1990s, and I experienced life in the woods to a limited degree. I'm thankful I saw firsthand the last of the Old West in Louisiana.

Q: It's surprising that you decided to self-publish *Zion* and republish *Welcome to the Fallen Paradise* on your own.

DS: Well, I never intended to start a publishing company. For years I tried to get my rights back from MacAdam/Cage, the now defunct publisher that released my first novel. It was both a battle and a disappointment. Finally, MacAdam/Cage went bankrupt, and I was able to secure all of my rights. I decided it was best to go it alone and never fight over my book rights again. The publishing world has changed, and I wanted to take advantage of new opportunities.

Q: Why did you start Accendo Books, L.L.C.?

DS: I wanted to do something radical, a real challenge. I wanted to start a "micro press" or "nano press." My plan is to publish my own work but also to edit anthologies. My goal for 2015 is to publish a great collection of Louisiana short fiction, works by living authors. Then do one collection per year state-by-state. I may never get to all 50 states, but I hope to finish the South. I also want to publish interviews with artists and writers, and I plan to collect these through Accendo Books. All of my books will be released in print, ebook, and downloadable audio formats.

Q: Where does the name "Accendo Books" come from?

DS: *Accendo* is Latin for ignite, spark, or kindle. It has connotations of creating an idea that starts a fire. I like what the word means, and it explains what I'm trying to publish: "Fine Books. Inspiring Ideas."

Q: What books most influenced the writing of *Zion*?

DS: There's no question that I am a product of my reading habits. After I wrote *Welcome to the Fallen Paradise*, I was upended as a writer by Marilynne Robinson's *Gilead*, which was such a big influence. It's hard to say how much her work changed what I believed about writing fiction. I read the book in late 2004 or very early 2005. The next book that gave me whiplash was *No Country for Old Men*. Unlike Robinson, I had been reading Cormac McCarthy for years. I read *No Country* soon after it was published. Those two books can be seen in every page of *Zion*.

Q: What are you working on now?

DS: I have a large backlog of completed works and works in progress. I have a "finished" novel titled *Louisiana Public Integrity* that I would like to see published near the 2015 Louisiana governor's race. Plus I have published about twenty short stories in little magazines that need to be collected into a book. I have a comic novel mostly done, and a memoir titled *Confessions of a Redneck Genius* that I want to finish. Now that I have control of my artistic work post-MacAdam/Cage and with a future of Indie publishing ahead, my goal is to release two new books a year as long as I want to write. Deciding to go Indie was an incredibly exhilarating feeling. I'm no longer waiting on or trying to please some unknown force in New York. I can go directly to readers. That's the ticket.

Q: Do you have any advice for writers struggling to get their works published?

DS: First, focus on the craft. That's the big pay-off, spending adequate time with the writing process. It may take the proverbial 10,000 hours of practice to master the art. Second, get the work on paper or at least digitally on the computer. You have nothing as long as the writing is in your head. It has to be on the page. Third, join a writing group of some kind. You can do this through a college class or the local public library or even online. Last, decide whether or not you want to go with legacy-traditional publishing, the old agent-editor publishing route. Since 2009, it has made little sense for authors earning less than six figures per book to give away their rights for a pittance. I understand why Stephen King publishes through the Big Five publishers but not mid-list authors. Not any longer. "The Times They Are A-Changin'," as Bob Dylan sang. Two final words of advice: Go Indie.

ACKNOWLEDGEMENTS

First and foremost, I would like to thank my wife Kristy for reading this manuscript at least ten times. Thanks for the love and care. I wish to thank our son for enduring this book since shortly after his birth. It's done: let's go fishing.

Perhaps all books are written in collaboration. I hate to leave out significant people, but I will do my best to acknowledge my co-conspirators below:

My cousin Dr. Ronald Traylor ("For Every Oak a Pine!") and my late Uncle Harry Sherman ("The End of Open Range") provided inspiration that sent me down the winding road to write this novel. I spent a year working as a carpenter's helper at Southeastern Louisiana University from 1988 to '89, and some of the story was informed by day-to-day work doing maintenance.

David Campbell and Davy Brooks have been great readers and friends. Thanks for the heavy lifting.

I'd like to thank many of my friends and relatives for helping in so many ways: Mama, Nikki Barranger, Wilford Wade Cowart, Judy and Haywood Loyde, Elizabeth Lafarge, Dr. Bill Thompson, Pat and Tina St. Clair, Dr. Tim Wise, Carl and Carolyn Higginbotham, Karen Taylor, Dr. William Hamilton, Jason and Staci Parrie, Lamar Wascom, Jesse and Ashley Brown, Monique Soudelier, Dr. Kathy Kolb, Charlotte Hill, Stephen Winham, Burleigh and Pat Soape, Dr. Randy and Barbara Davis, Dorcas Perrin, Dr. Lee Rozelle, David Campbell, Paul and Betty White, Fr. Steve Petrica, Charley Vance, Vivian Solar, Rev. Roger Dunlap, Jamie Fitch, Don Barker, Mike Tournillon, and Duncan Kemp IV.

Five writers were instrumental in helping me decide to go Indie: Officer O'Neil De Noux, Katie Wainwright, Brenna Barzenick, J.A. Konrath, Barry Eisler, and Hugh Howey. Inspiration met perspiration. I hope they like the book. Two thinkers helped me better understand how to sell a book, Seth Godin and Tim Grahl. I appreciate the tools.

The writers with the Southeastern Louisiana Writing Project, an affiliate of the National Writing Project, were always encouraging to me. Dr. Kim Stafford was the great, and I hope I can marathon with all of the writers again soon. Through Kim I discovered the late Dr. William Stafford, my favorite poet and a constant literary guide.

Stephanie Kaye Smith, Joel Friedlander, Jose Canales, Staci Parrie, Sigrid and Paul Kelsey, Karen Taylor, Dr. Karen Williams, Laura Brooks, Barry Dunlap, Dr. Tim Gautreaux, Dr. Richard Louth, Dr. Jack Bedell, David Campbell, Dr. Mackie Blanton, Alan Marsh, Will Johnson, Lori Smith, and Ben Bell saved me from bad art at various times. Thanks.

Dr. James Kirylo, Tim Parrish, Bev Marshall, David Armand, Jonathan Chandler all gave early endorsements of *Zion*. More will come later, but y'all were great. Drs. Norman German, Martie Fellom, and Richard Louth helped make me a full professor of library science. It's all your fault! But thank you.

Two authors and two novels influenced the writing of *Zion*: *No Country for Old Men* by Cormac McCarthy and *Gilead* by Marilynne Robinson. Both authors deserve the Nobel Prize.

My supervisors at the library have been supportive over the past seven years that it took to write this novel: Eric Johnson, Dr. Lynette Ralph, and Beth Stahr. Most writers need a day job for bread and sanity. Thanks for both. For the postal workers in Ponchatoula, Hammond, and on campus: I appreciate the patience. Kenny Ribbeck and the Louisiana Department of Wildlife and Fisheries were helpful in determining hunting regulations for 1964.

I have been treated well by libraries and bookstores. Anthony Loum at Brooklyn Public Library, Livingston Parish Library, Tangipahoa Parish Library, the State Library of Louisiana, John Evans at Lemuria Books, Square Books, That Bookstore in Blytheville, Burke's Book Store, Reed's Gum Tree Bookstore, Pass Christian Books, Maple Street Books, Faulkner House Books, and Bayou Booksellers, all champions of my work. Thank you.

Several editors have been helpful getting the word out about my writing: Lil Mirando of *The Daily Star* and James Fox-Smith of *Country Roads*, as well as Chad Rogers of *TheDeadPelican.com*. *Action News 17*, *The Courier* and *The Comet*, and *The Shreveport Times* have been very supportive, too.

Several political writers keep me informed about the underbelly of Louisiana: Tom Aswell, Robert Mann, C.B. Forgotston, and Elliot Stonecipher. Thanks for the material.

Thanks, Coffee Culture in Ponchatoula, for good chicory. PJ's Coffee on Thomas and University in Hammond: You should dedicate a chair to *Zion*. I paid for several chairs while writing this book.

Perhaps no teacher in school did more to make a reader out of me than Norma Webb. Every word I write can be traced back to English II at Albany High School in 1987. God bless you.

ABOUT THE AUTHOR

Dayne Sherman is a high school dropout. He has worked a variety of jobs as a grocery store clerk, carpenter's helper, door-to-door rat poison distributor, watermelon salesman, itinerant Baptist preacher, English as a second language teacher in Russia, paid fitness instructor, and most recently as a reference librarian. At 18 years old, he took the GED and went to the university in his hometown. A member of Phi Kappa Phi, Sherman earned master's degrees from LSU and Southeastern Louisiana University.

Sherman's first novel, *Welcome to the Fallen Paradise*, was published by MacAdam/Cage in 2004. It was named a Best Debut of the Year by *The Times-Picayune* and a Notable Book by Book Sense. Recently, *Welcome to the Fallen Paradise* was the sole "Louisiana" pick for *Booklist's* "Hard-Boiled Gazetteer to Country Noir."

His writing has appeared in many literary magazines, and one of his short stories was nominated for a Pushcart Prize. Sherman lives in Ponchatoula, Louisiana, with his wife and son. His website is daynesherman.com. *Zion* is his second novel.

ABOUT THE BOOK

From the critically-acclaimed author of *Welcome to the Fallen Paradise* comes a gothic treatment of the American South: a hard-charging depiction of religion, family, friendship, deception, and evil.

Zion is a literary mystery set in the rural South, the story of a war fought over the killing of hardwoods in Baxter Parish, Louisiana. The tale begins in 1964 and ends a decade later, but the Hardin family, faithful members of Little Zion Methodist Church, will carry the scars for life.

ABOUT ACCENDO BOOKS

Founded in 2014, Accendo Books is a small press located in Hammond, Louisiana. Taken from the Latin, *Accendo* means to inspire, ignite or kindle. Both fiction and non-fiction will be published in print, electronic, and audio formats. Accendo is a micro-press with a focus on publishing the best books available in print, one book at a time, one author at a time. Our goal is simple: Fine Books. Inspiring Ideas.

Accendo Books
Fine Books. Inspiring Ideas.